BOOKS BY CLAIRE COOK

Must Love Dogs: New Leash on Life

Must Love Dogs

Time Flies

Wallflower in Bloom

Best Staged Plans

Seven Year Switch

The Wildwater Walking Club

Summer Blowout

Life's a Beach

Multiple Choice

Ready to Fall

and coming soon . . .

Must Love Dogs: Book 3

"Eternally hopeful book reviewer seeks wildly witty novel on singles scene/personal ads. Stylish prose and sense of humor preferred. Looking for fun, not longterm entanglement. Must love readers. Respondents to such an ad might include Claire Cook, whose new novel, *Must Love Dogs*, tells the story of a down-to-earth divorcee seeking companionship through the personals."—*USA Today*

"Cook employs just enough glibness and smarty-pants humor to make this tart slice-of-the-single-life worth reading."—*Publishers Weekly*

"[A] laugh-out-loud novel . . . a light and lively read for anyone who has ever tried to re-enter the dating scene or tried to 'fix up' somebody else."—*Boston Herald*

"Claire Cook's *Must Love Dogs*, a book that's got more giggles than soda bread has raisins."
—*Hartford Courant*

"This utterly charming novel by Cook is a fun read, perfect for whiling away an afternoon on the beach."
—*Library Journal*

"A hilariously original tale about dating and its place in a modern woman's life."—*BookPage*

Must Love Dogs
New Leash on Life

Claire Cook

Marshbury Beach Books

Publisher's Note: This is a work of fiction. Names, characters, places, and incidents are a product of the author's imagination. Locales and public names are sometimes used for atmospheric purposes. Any resemblance to actual people, living or dead, or to businesses, companies, events, institutions, or locales is completely coincidental.

Marshbury Beach Books
Book Layout: TheBookDesigner
Author Photo: Diane Dillon

Must Love Dogs: New Leash on Life/ Claire Cook
ISBN 978-0-9899210-2-2

For Gary David Goldberg
Rest in peace, my friend

My brother Michael was staying with me until his marriage got back on track.

"Don't you molly coddle him, Sarah," my father said. "Just give him three squares a day and make sure he has a starched white shirt to wear to the office."

"If he so much as looks at a beer bottle, hide his cell phone," my sister Carol said. "Do not, under any circumstances, let him drunk dial Phoebe. She was a witch with a capital B when he married her, and she'll be a witch with a capital B when we find her replacement."

"Why does Michael have to stay at your house?" my sister Christine said. "We have plenty of room, and no offense, but it's so not fair the way you *always* have to hog him."

After months, maybe years, of trying to hold his marriage together while he lived at home, Michael hoped that absence would, in fact, make Phoebe's heart grow fonder. So he moved out and now he drove his daughters, Annie and Lainie, to Irish step dancing on Wednesdays after school and took them out to dinner afterward. They also spent every weekend with him.

With us.

At my house.

"How much longer do you think it will be?" John Anderson finally asked. This seemed a reasonable question from the man who had become my significant other.

"Does *until hell freezes over* seem too pessimistic?" I answered.

After a bumpy start to our relationship, John and I had shared six months of dating bliss. We were now basically on hold. I wondered sometimes in the middle of the night if we'd accrued enough bliss points to get through this. And did bliss have a shelf life? Would it expire of neglect before we could fan the flames again on a regular basis?

Tonight, my brother Michael and I were kicked back on my couch. A week's worth of starched white shirts in dry cleaning bags were draped over my treadmill. Two empty Sam Adams beer bottles flanked a half-eaten cheese pizza on the coffee table. I was a good sister.

I burped.

"Nice," Michael said.

"Thanks," I said.

Over the weekend, Michael and Annie and Lainie and I had pulled down my rickety old attic stairs and gone on a hunt for toys. My nieces weren't overly impressed with the relics of my childhood and were back downstairs and lost in cell phone games in no time. Apparently my brother felt otherwise, because right now he was playing with my Growing Up Skipper doll.

"She's two dolls in one, for twice as much fun!" I recited in my peppiest imitation of the 1970s commercial.

Skipper was Barbie's little sister. Like the Doublemint of our childhood that had been touted as *two, two, two mints in one*, this version of Skipper really was two dolls in one. When you first saw her, she appeared to be a sweet little blond elementary school student. But if you rotated her left arm back, she actually grew breasts right before your very eyes.

As if Barbie's impossible body hadn't screwed me up enough in my formative years. Thanks to Growing Up Skipper, I'd spent at least a year of my prepubescent life circling my left arm backward like a one-armed backstroker while I knelt beside my bed saying my nightly prayers. After asking God to bless Mom and Dad and my three brothers and two sisters and all the starving children in China, I prayed for boobs, bigger than my sister Carol's, who was two years older and, *please God*, arriving before my seventeen-months younger sister Christine's showed up.

"We must, we must, we must increase our bust," Michael said beside me all these years later as he pumped Growing Up Skipper's left arm up and down. Her breasts appeared and disappeared in perfect time to his chant.

"Knock it off," I said. I reached for my old doll.

Michael yanked her away. "Who's gonna make me?"

"Give her to me," I yelled as I lunged for Skipper. Old habits die hard and all that, but it was truly amazing the way my brothers and sisters and I could revert to our childhood selves in a nanosecond.

A loud bark made me jump. Mother Teresa, Michael's humongous St. Bernard, who was also staying with me until Phoebe missed her or until hell froze over, grabbed Growing Up Skipper.

I screamed.

Michael jumped to his feet. "Mother Teresa, drop it."

Mother Teresa held Skipper's left arm between her teeth as she shook her head in some ancient prey-killing ritual she hadn't quite evolved beyond. The doll's breasts appeared and disappeared with each shake.

I ran to the kitchen and grabbed the doggie treat jar. I held out a bone-shaped biscuit.

Mother Teresa appeared to raise one eyebrow.

I put the first treat on the floor and took a second one from the jar.

She gave Growing Up Skipper another shake.

"Fine," I said. "But fair warning, I'm drawing the line at three."

Mother Teresa placed Growing Up Skipper gently on the floor and collected her three treats.

"Good girl," Michael said.

"That's debatable," I said. I picked up my drool-covered doll and started wiping her on my jeans. I reconsidered and grabbed a pizza napkin.

"Here, I'll get that," Michael said.

I handed over Growing Up Skipper and the napkin and plopped down on the couch.

Michael finished grooming Growing Up Skipper and was back to rhythmically pumping her left arm.

I knew it was a cry for help. I recognized my sisterly duty. I'd get his mind off Growing up Skipper, then I'd get his mind off Phoebe. I'd help him realize his marriage was over and assist him in navigating his divorce while striving to keep the negative impact on Annie and Lainie to a bare minimum. And then I'd find him a more suitable match. As soon as I got that all squared away, John Anderson and I would ride off into the blissful sunset together.

"I think I'll pack it in," Michael said. "Do you want me to take Mother Teresa out one more time, or can you get her before you head off to bed?"

Mother Teresa leaned over and lapped my cheek. I sighed. "I'll take her."

Michael gave a sad half-wave. "G'night, Sarah. Night, Mother Teresa."

He took an unhappy step toward the guestroom.

"Michael," I said.

He turned around. Growing Up Skipper was cradled in his arms.

I held out my hand. "Give me the doll, Michael."

I sat there for a while, scratching Mother Teresa in her new favorite place, right behind her left ear. Then I got up and tiptoed to my former master bedroom, which I'd turned into an office and where I worked on projects and stored extra things for my classroom.

I rummaged through a pile of scrapbooks on the bottom shelf. I pulled out my wedding album, dusted it off with one hand, held it for a moment. I closed my eyes and tried to picture Kevin, my former husband. All I could conjure was a vague image of a man sitting on a toilet seat, his head hidden behind the newspaper, his pants around his ankles, the bathroom door open. I wondered if Kevin read his morning news on an iPad now.

Finally, I found the notebook I'd kept while I was navigating the dating scene. A page for each of my dates, rated with hand-drawn stars and flags. So many red flags billowed across the tops of the pages that it looked like a sale at a car dealership. George from Hanover, who was looking for a relationship one day a month, no strings, no commitments. Ben, who grew his own alfalfa sprouts. The guy looking for a plus-sized Woman, whom I'd briefly considered partly because I liked the way he capitalized Woman, but mostly because I could eat a lot. Ray Santia, the former almost hockey star I'd almost slept with. Bob Connor, a student's father I shouldn't have slept with.

It was a jungle out there. Poor Michael. But if I didn't get him out of my house and on his merry way, before I knew it I might be back out there myself.

I took a moment to shudder at the thought. Then I found the personal ad my sister Carol had placed for me, taped into the center of a page.

Voluptuous, sensuous, alluring and fun. Barely 40 DWF seeks special man to share starlit nights. Must love dogs.

I carried my dating notebook out to the living room, along with my favorite red pencil. I turned to a fresh college-lined page and tapped the eraser against my teeth while I tweaked the ad to suit my brother.

Buff, brilliant, broken but not beyond repair. Handsome soon to be DWM with all his hair seeks special woman who meets his daughters' high standards. Must love big slobbery dogs.

Two

"No, no, no," my sister Carol said. "He's not even close to being ready to date. He's not over his ball buster of a wife yet."

"Plus, if it got out there he could get totally screwed in the alimony department," my brother Johnny said.

I turned to Carol. "Just curious, but can you explain why you have to say witch with a capital B instead of bitch, but you can say ball buster?"

She gave me the look she'd been giving me since we were kids, the one that said *What is your problem?* "Obviously because one's a swear and one isn't."

"Screwed is okay," Johnny said.

"Of course it is," I said. "I think it's even on the kids' spelling list at my preschool."

My father adjusted his cap over his mane of white hair. "'In all the world, 'tis nothing better for a broken man's soul than a rebound relationship," he said as he slid on his driving gloves. Even with a breeze off the water, it had to be at least seventy degrees out already.

"Maybe we can find him a female lawyer who's single and kill two birds with one stone," my sister Christine said.

"Hel-*lo*," my brother, Michael, said. "I'm right here."

My father flung an arm around his shoulder and gave him a leather-cloaked pat with one hand. "That you are, Mikey boy, that you are. And we're right here for you, too, wrapping you in the warm embrace of your ever-lovin' family." He tilted his head to rest it against Michael's. "Let me check my Rolodex when I get home, son. It could be I've got a spare number or two."

Michael opened his eyes wide. "That's okay, Dad. I'm good." Mother Teresa barked her agreement from the other end of the leash.

"Sailor's Bonnet" filled the air and we turned our attention to the bandstand. Annie and Lainie had finished lacing up their ghillies and were standing with the rest of the Irish step dancers, ready to perform.

Michael and I had worked hard on their banana curls last night, winding long brown hair around soft pink foam rollers, but I had to admit Phoebe did a better job of it. I glanced over my shoulder to see if I could spot her. Michael and Phoebe had yet to master the dance of attending the girls' activities as separated parents. Whichever parent Annie and Lainie were staying with at the time took them, while the other lurked at a safe distance.

Relief that Kevin and I hadn't had even a single child to drag through a divorce washed over me for the umpteenth time. And once again that relief was followed by a wave of sadness so powerful that it almost bowled me over. How had my life conspired to leave me, of all people, childless? And Kevin, who for the ten years we'd been married had never been quite ready, was now pushing a double stroller, courtesy of a much younger woman named Nikki, on the other side of town.

Even as my very last eggs were reaching their expiration date. Fast.

"Hey, sorry I'm late." John Anderson kissed me on the cheek and I breathed in the scent of him. "Horatio wanted to come with me, so it took a while to get him settled in at puppy play care."

Horatio was John's puppy, a cross between a Yorkie mom and a greyhound dad who somehow managed to look oddly like a scruffy dachshund. In the first blush of love Horatio was supposed to be our shared puppy, maybe even our practice child, or at least a stand-in.

But, my life being my life, Horatio hated my guts. With a passion.

"Jack, my boy, a top o' the morning to you," my father said as he reached for a handshake.

"Dad," I said. "His name is John."

My father glanced skyward, as if summoning the patience of a saint, and shook his head. "We've been through all that rigmarole, Sarry girl. This family already has one John and, truth be told, our Johnny boy got there first."

My brother Johnny shrugged. He grinned and extended his hand to John.

"I think I can work with that," John said. "Jack's a great name. I might even prefer it."

"Done," my father said. "Now on to the dog. What kind of an Eye-talian name is Horatio? Seamus has a far better ring to it."

"Bonnie Isle O'whalsay" segued seamlessly into an Irish fiddle reel and we all turned our attention to the bandstand. Annie and Lainie danced their way out on the stage along with the other girls, all long legs and knobby knees and big smiles, arms pressed to their sides, upper bodies stiff, hands neat. They did their rocks and clicks, kicks and leaps, and it brought me back, as it always did, to my own step dancing days.

"They're really getting good," my sister Carol said beside me. "Even better than Siobhan was, I think."

"Where is she today anyway?" I asked. Carol's husband, Dennis, was holding their youngest daughter, Maeve, in his arms, and their middle two, Ian and Trevor, were leaning up against the railing that surrounded the inner harbor, pretending to watch the boats while they took turns spitting into the water.

Carol pointed. Siobhan and three friends were sitting in beach chairs on the parking lot. Their chairs were positioned off to the side of the bandstand, a careful distance from the sun-blocking crowd, and they were wearing ear buds and bathing suits. Siobhan's belly button ring glittered as they all worked on their tans.

Through my T-shirt, I touched my own pierced navel, a souvenir from my most memorable outing with my niece, which now displayed a tasteful ring decorated with a single diamond, a gift from John. I flashed back to my long ago sunbathing days—an opened double album cover wrapped in aluminum foil, angled beneath my chin just so to send the rays directly to my face, a slick coat of baby oil covering every inch of me. Not that I ever once tanned. My siblings and I went immediately from Irish white to lobster red, and spent the evening dabbing vinegar on one another's shoulders to ease the pain, and then peeling long strips of skin from the same shoulders a few days later.

I glanced over at John. He was watching a little boy sitting cross-legged on the ground in front of us, playing a plastic pinball game. When we first met, John was winding down a financially unproductive stint as a vintage pinball machine restorer. "It seems," he said on one of our early dates, "that I have the soul of a pinball wizard but the brain of an accountant. Essentially, it's the existential struggle of my life." Even though I already had it memorized, I wrote that down in my college-lined dating notebook when I got home. I wondered if part of what was wrong with me was that I didn't know what the existential struggle of my own life was.

I still didn't know. But John was now head of the accounting department for a big Boston technology and gaming company. He'd held on to two beautiful vintage pinball machines. A framed Peace, Love and Pinball poster graced the space over his fireplace. When he was bored, he played Retro Pinball on his cell phone.

The first time I went home with John, we stood in front of a pinball machine in his dining room-turned-game room. "This," John said, "is an authentic Addams Family model, the most popular pinball machine of all time."

It was clearly made to look like the haunted mansion, with all the spooky stairways, Uncle Fester's electric chair, and even the box Thing slept in.

"These are the flipper buttons." John stood behind me and put one of my hands on each button, placed his hands over mine. It was sexy, in a geeky kind of way.

He pushed a button and lights flashed. John explained plunger lanes and ramps and tubes and nudging and trapping and how points were earned. He released a ball and we went through a practice run. I did pretty well as long as his hands were on mine. Then I tried alone and lost the ball down the drain almost immediately.

"So, this is fun," I said, trying to convince myself. "You know, I appreciate that it's a piece of history and it means a lot to you, but I'm not sure I quite understand the whole pinball attraction. I mean, why pinball and not, say, ping pong?"

"You never know what you're going to get with a pinball game," John said. "It's a lot like life. You can't control it, so you have to just roll with it and do the best you can. And if you do well enough, sometimes you get a bonus play."

"You mean like a do-over?" I said.

"Exactly," he said.

I still didn't quite get pinball, but the lure of a do-over was something I could completely comprehend.

My nieces' step dance ended and we all clapped and hooted as loudly as we could.

My father took off one leather glove, put two fingers in his mouth, and let out a long whistle as the dancers took their final bow.

"That would be my cue," he said. He slid his glove back on and turned to the boyfriend he'd just renamed. "Did my darlin' daughter tell you I've been appointed this year's one and only Grand Marshall of the Marshbury Blessing of the Fleet?"

"Yeah," my brother Johnny said. "And he only bribed three priests to get it."

"No," my sister Carol said. "One of them was a monsignor."

I felt John/Jack's hand on the small of my back and imagined us back at my house. Or his condo. Or anywhere with a bed.

I leaned into him. "Did I tell you my father is the Grand Marshall this year?"

He cleared his throat. "Congratulations, Mr. Hurlihy. And what an interesting tradition. I just finished reading up on it this morning. Apparently it was started by the Portuguese—"

"Bite your tongue," my father said as he walked away.

"Was it something I said?" John asked when he was out of earshot.

"Basically," I said, "in front of my father, if the Irish didn't discover it, invent it—"

"Or do it first," Carol said.

"Or do it better," Christine said.

"Then," Michael said, "your best bet is to talk about something else."

We watched my father join a priest wearing long black robes over short L. L. Bean rubber boots. The town's sole bagpiper, who, along with the step dancers and the barbershop sextet, could be counted on to make an appearance at pretty much every town event, followed them. Priest, Grand Marshall, and bagpiper stopped at my father's shiny new sea green Mini Cooper, parked just to the side of the bandstand, while the bagpiper played his last mournful notes. Then the priest, who in my lapsed Catholic state I couldn't reliably identify, though I was fairly sure he was either Father McDermott or Father O'Callaghan, sprinkled some holy water on the hood while he mumbled a blessing to our father's car.

"Wait," John said. "Isn't this supposed to be for boats?"

"We used to have a boat," Christine said.

Michael sighed. "God, I loved that boat."

"Every time he'd hit another boat, our mother would paint a notch on it," my brother Johnny said. "She started on the port side, worked her way around the bow, and—"

"And when she finally ran out of room," Carol said, "when the entire boat was covered with notches, she said, 'That's it, Billy. Your boating days are officially over.'"

"Aww," I said. "You sound just like her."

There was a moment of silence as we all felt our mother's presence. Even though she'd been gone now for more years than I wanted to count, she was still the force that held us together. Maeve whimpered and reached out her arms to Carol, and Dennis handed her over.

His Mini Cooper fully blessed, my father and the priest walked ceremoniously toward the water, serenaded by the bagpiper as he followed. The crowd fell into step behind them. The rest of my family and John and I took a shortcut and squeezed in behind Ian and Trevor at the railing overlooking the inner harbor.

My father and the priest walked down the rickety wooden ramp, steep with low tide, and climbed into an old lobster boat at the far edge of the floating dock.

"Don't let him get behind the wheel!" my brother Johnny yelled. The crowd burst into laughter. My father shook his fist up at us. The crowd laughed harder.

Fortunately, the lobster boat stayed tied to the dock. My father and the priest moved to the port side, the starboard side rocking upward from their weight. A long line of boats, a parade in every shape and size and condition—cabin cruisers and sailboats and Boston Whalers and rowboats and old Irish mossing boats—

inched its way forward. And one by one, the priest
sprinkled holy water on each boat and mouthed a prayer while my father touched the brim of his white and
gold Coast Guard Auxiliary cap and saluted.

"Way to go, Grandpa," Ian, or maybe it was Trevor,
yelled. The crowd laughed again.

I leaned into John Anderson.

"So, this is fun," he said. "I should have borrowed a
boat. It's a long row from Boston to Marshbury, but
probably only a day or two. If I started training—"

"Let's get out of here," I whispered. "If we hurry, we
can make it to my place, hide the cars in the garage and
barricade the doors before anybody misses us."

John's arm tightened around my waist. "What about
Michael?" he whispered.

"He drove. What about Horatio?"

"He drove, too," John said as I slid one finger behind
the waistband of his jeans.

"Ha," I said.

He pulled me closer. "Horatio has got to be in puppy
heaven playing with all those other dogs at puppy play
care. I'd say I've got a good couple hours. Minimum."

"Okay," I whispered. "On the count of three, we
start walking casually toward your car. Do not make
eye contact. Do not say goodbye. If anybody says anything to us, pretend you don't hear."

He nodded.

"Ready?"

He reached for my hand.

"One . . .two . . . .."

Carol pushed her way between us.

"*What,*" I said.

She jerked her head to the side. "Don't look now."

We looked. On one of the sea glass-studded walkways that edged the parking lot, Phoebe, wearing heels and dressed more for a date than the Blessing of the Fleet, was standing way too close to a guy who looked, well, like a date.

"Oh, shit, " I said.

Christine, holding my niece Sydney, who was two months younger than Maeve, pushed in next to Carol. "Don't look."

We looked again. "Carol already told us," I said.

"Of course she did," Christine said. Christine was the youngest and the thinnest of the three sisters, with a good job, a nice husband, and three perfect kids. But the one thing she aspired to more than anything else was to find out something, just once, before Carol did. "So, what do we do?"

Carol switched Maeve to her other hip. "Okay, I'll grab Lainie and Annie and meet you at Michael's car. Sarah, you grab Michael and the dog and take them the long way around so they don't see you-know-who. And Christine, you make the rounds and let everybody else know that we're all meeting up at Sarah's."

"What about me?" John asked.

Our eyes met and held. Visions of foreplay, and sex, and afterplay—long and leisurely and completely family-less—flashed before me. And disappeared in an instant.

Carol gave John a pat on one cheek. "Just follow the pack, Jack. Just follow the pack."

Three

The sky was baby blue on Bayberry Preschool graduation day, with just a few wisps of cotton candy clouds to keep it from being boring. I took a moment to thank my lucky stars that inclement weather hadn't moved the ceremonies indoors. Outdoor graduations were so much more visually evocative and memorable. Not to mention the fact that there was nothing worse than being squished into a tiny gym where the pungent odor of a younger sibling's poorly timed soiled diaper had nowhere to escape.

I finished putting on my makeup at the final traffic light, then barreled up the hill in my trusty Honda and pulled into the teachers' parking area. I hit the ground running, then slowed it down to a more dignified jog.

Kate Stone, my boss, pushed back the sleeve of her dressiest batik tunic and gave her chunky watch a passive-aggressive check. "It's helpful, Sarah," she said, "when the chair of the graduation committee actually arrives in time for graduation."

I decided it was not in my best interests to point out that graduation didn't start for another thirty-two minutes, so technically I was meeting my responsibility and then some. And furthermore, just wait, because if they gave out Emmys for graduations, this year's would be a real contender.

Instead I smiled and breezed past her and out to the play field, a long, flat expanse of manicured grass tucked behind the school on the highest point of the property. It even had distant views of the ocean if you stood on your tiptoes and jumped. White folding chairs had been set up in perfect rows with a single aisle down the center. The rest of the committee and I had tied white bows on the back of each one before we'd headed out yesterday. I stopped to give a bow a little tweak and move it back to the center of the chair.

Lorna and Gloria, two of my favorite teachers at Bayberry and the other two-thirds of the graduation committee, looked up from putting rolled, ribbon-wrapped programs on the chairs. June, my assistant, paused while arranging baby's breath in a vase on the podium long enough to give me a glittery smile. Even though she was still far too pretty, she'd grown on me during the school year. I'd almost want to hang out with her except that it might get in the way of my ability to boss her around.

"Sorry I'm late," I said as I grabbed a handful of programs from Lorna. "First my brother's dog snored all night and then—"

"Whatever," Lorna said. "Two more hours until another year bites the dust. My beach chair is waiting for me."

Gloria shook her head. "Assuming you survive three days of staff meetings and team building first, honey."

"Jesus," Lorna said, "you don't think she's going to make us do trust falls again, do you? I'd rather hurl myself backward off a cliff than into the arms of a bunch of teachers." Kate Stone was known for making our final student-less days of the year a living hell.

"Doubtful," Gloria said. "I think dropping the art teacher last year wiped that one off the agenda." She walked over to get a better look at June's arrangement. Then she broke off a piece of baby's breath and tucked it behind one of June's ears. June thanked her with an angelic smile.

Lorna stopped to scratch her back with one of the rolled programs. "It was her own damn fault. I mean, come on, you don't fall on three, you count to three and *then* you fall."

I took a moment to fluff my hair and straighten my purple wrap dress, which I'd bought because I thought it might play up my brown eyes and dark hair. And make my skin look more intentionally pale instead of just plain washed out. And double as a date dress once I got Michael squared away. I had to admit it was a lot for a dress to live up to.

The first of the families had begun to arrive, the kids running around like mini maniacs while the parents ignored them, as if just stepping on school property meant they were off duty and the teachers were on.

I caught a cap-and-gown-clad Jenny Browning, mid-leap in an attempt to pull one of the graduation decorations off a tree, by the hand. Wordlessly, I walked her over to her mother, pretending I thought she'd been looking for her. Last week, once the younger half-day students had gone home, the full day graduates-to-be had painted paper plates and drawn faces on them. They'd glued on construction paper curls, and topped each one with a construction paper graduation cap embellished with a tassel of yellow yarn. Lorna, Gloria and I had collected the paper plate graduates from the other classrooms. After getting an all clear from the weather channel yesterday, we'd stapled them to the trees that lined the walkway up to the field.

"Ms. Hurlihy, how do I look?" Austin Connor yelled behind me. I turned just in time to see him trip on his white graduation gown, catch himself, trip again and fall. His dad, Bob Connor, the parent I shouldn't have slept with, scooped him up before I got there. The two of us brushed at Austin's grass stains.

"You look great, Austin," I said.

"Likewise," he said.

"Thank you," I said.

The field filled with families, some taking the day off to celebrate, some clearly dressed to race right back to the office. Big boy dress pants and shoes poked out from underneath the boys' white gowns, and their graduation caps perched on some seriously gelled hair. The girls' hair was curled or braided elaborately, a few caps anchored with a crisscross of bobby pins, shiny patent leather shoes sparkling in the sunlight. Even though I'd been teaching long enough to know the drill by heart, my eyes teared up as I thought of how much they'd all grown.

Bob Connor and I looked at each other over Austin's head and smiled. I didn't feel a single jolt of electricity. Maybe I'd grown, too.

Kate Stone walked up to the podium, tapped the microphone, checked her watch again. Everyone immediately started filing to the little white chairs. I didn't have to like her to see my boss had that magic.

As rehearsed, the rising kindergarteners stood in front of the two rows of empty chairs, facing the audience. They looked like a cross between angels and miniature college students.

A baby screamed.

"No comments from the peanut gallery," Austin Connor yelled.

"Shh," Amanda McAlpine said.

"You're not the boss of him," Jack Kaplan said.

"I'm the boss of all of you," Jenny Browning said.

"Let's get this show on the road," Lorna whispered. Gloria stepped up and blew her pitch pipe. Lorna and I walked down the aisle away from the podium until we were standing behind the seated families. We turned to face the kids. Then we bent our elbows and started circling our arms like The Temptations.

The kids mimicked our moves and sang their first number to the tune of "I've Been Workin' on The Railroad."

I'll be going to Kindergarten
Next year all year long
I'll be going to kindergarten
Because now I'm big and strong
Bayberry Preschool
Was the best
But now I'm ready
For all the rest
I'll be going to kindergarten
Next year all year long

As rehearsed, we each put one hand on our hip and turned the other hand up like a spout. Lorna and I started rocking back and forth and the kids followed. Gloria blew her pitch pipe again and the graduates went into their next number, to the tune of "I'm a Little Teapot."

I'm a Little Graduate
Aren't you proud
I know my numbers
And can yell them out loud
I can tie both my shoes
And know which words to use
(And not to use!)
I'm a little graduate
Aren't you proud

By the time they finished "Hi Ho, Hi Ho, It's Off to Kindergarten We Go," swinging their arms and skipping adorably in place, there wasn't a dry eye in the house. The kids turned around and landed on the empty front row chairs without a hitch. Kate Stone began reading the list of graduates, saying something charming and specific about each one and shaking each little hand. Then Gloria handed out diplomas and high fives to the sound of thunderous applause.

"We're almost there," Lorna whispered. "First round is on me. Nothing says summer like a pomegranate martini."

"We are so going to get a raise for this next part," I whispered back.

Due to carbon footprint and choking seabird issues, Bayberry Preschool no longer allowed its graduates to release a flock of white balloons as the grand finale. So part of the job of the graduation committee was to find a replacement that was both high drama and politically correct. Blowing bubbles and scattering flower petals had achieved only moderate success. Burying a time capsule had turned into a disaster when one of the kids started a rumor that the bad children would be buried along with it.

Lorna and I walked quickly to the butterfly gazebo, which was really a three-foot-tall net cage with an easy access zipper that we'd stashed out of sight in the shade of a grove of pine trees. For weeks, the graduates-to-be had watched the caterpillars spin silken cocoons and waited for them to gradually emerge as butterflies. Once the butterflies appeared, the kids took turns adding sugar water to tiny cups with eyedroppers and soaking flowers in it to feed them. Thanks to my brilliant timing, the butterflies had been fluttering around their gazebo for a while now, locked and loaded and ready to steal the show.

Gloria picked up her ukulele and began playing "Fly Me to the Moon." She was tall and angular, and her frizzy dark hair coupled with the ukulele made her look like a vastly more attractive and feminine Tiny Tim, who'd made the talk show circuit back in the day.

Lorna and I walked down the aisle, carrying the butterfly gazebo between us, doing a pre-rehearsed hesitation step that had been Gloria's idea. Lorna loved it, but with the ukulele as accompaniment, I thought it made us look like bridesmaids in a peppy Hawaiian destination wedding.

We placed the gazebo in front of the podium. Molly Meehan and Austin Connor, chosen by random drawing, came up and unzipped the mesh cover and opened it wide.

Everybody waited. And waited. Somebody sneezed. A cell phone rang. A baby cried.

"Fly, you stupid butterflies," Austin stage whispered.

"Don't call them stupid, stupid," Molly hissed.

We waited some more.

"Balls," Jack Kaplan said loudly.

"Cheese balls, bouncy balls, squishy balls, Daddy's balls," Jenny Browning chanted.

Gloria played her ukulele louder.

Lorna shot me a look. I reached over and gave the butterfly gazebo a casual shake. And then a bigger one.

A single Painted Lady butterfly emerged, its wings a masterpiece of orange and brown and black and white. It soared skyward over the audience.

Everybody oohed and awed.

One by one, the other butterflies followed.

And then they all started dropping like flies.

Four

I knew it was bad when we piled into Lorna's car after graduation and she drove us to a pub two towns away. We hadn't planned on bringing June with us, but she was too traumatized to leave alone. She was still sobbing quietly when we found a dark booth way back in a corner of the bar.

I slid in beside her. "Do you think you can knock it off now? Like I don't feel awful enough already."

"Sorry." June pulled a napkin from the metal container on our booth and blew her nose. She was so blond and blue-eyed and *young* that she even looked beautiful blowing her nose.

She crumpled her napkin and sniffed. "It's just that, even when I close my eyes, I can't stop seeing all the *carnage*."

"Four pomegranate martinis, ASAP," Lorna yelled to our approaching waiter. "Straight up, easy on the pomegranate, please."

Gloria reached across the table and patted June's hand. "Honey, it's not like they were going to last much longer anyway. Painted lady butterflies only have a life span of between two and four weeks."

June's lower lip trembled adorably. "But we *named* them. There was Tinkerbelle and Wings and Flutter and Flopsy and Justin Bieber and and . . . .."

Lorna shivered and reached for a napkin. "Jesus, I am still finding butterfly guts all over me. Two of them dive-bombed right at me as if they were little suicide pilots. And how about that one who hit Molly Meehan's mother's sunglasses and just kept flapping its wings like it was stuck to a mini windshield—"

"Please stop," I said.

We sat in silence until the drinks arrived. Lorna and Gloria held up their glasses. They opened their mouths at the same time to make a toast, then closed them again and simply drank.

"Crap," I said. "The one thing I thought I was good at was teaching." I took a long slug. A rivulet of pomtini escaped and slid down my chin and landed on my new purple dress. "I held my students' hearts in my hands every day and never once took the responsibility lightly. Preschool *matters*. The memories the kids take with them will influence every other rung of their educational ladders. Of their *lives*."

Lorna handed me a napkin. "Sarah, worse things have happened, we all know that. You give it everything you've got, but you can't always protect them."

I dabbed at the dress I'd managed to ruin, too. "And now all they're going to remember are dead butterflies. Did you hear Kate Stone tell the parents that the school psychologist will be available all weekend?"

Gloria shook her head and reached for her glass. "No pun intended, but I think that was overkill."

June wiped another tear from her cheek. "I've got the first appointment."

I put my elbows on the booth and buried my head in my hands. I stayed like that, in time-out mode, letting the conversation swirl around me: Gloria's plans to drag her family to the Grand Canyon before summer camp started and spend a week on Nantucket after it ended. Lorna's plan to spend all non-camp hours at the beach and her determination to get her husband, Mattress Man, to go with her at least once. June sniffling away some more.

I felt a tap on my head. "Honey," Gloria said. "We can't let you have your dessert pomtini until you finish your dinner pomtini."

I sighed and managed to lift up my head and locate my drink. It was tart and strong, just the way I'd like to be. There must have been a design flaw in my glass because another small stream ran down my chin. I caught as much of it as I could with one finger and licked it off. Lorna handed me another napkin.

"Thanks," I said, "and in case you didn't notice, apparently I'm even a failure at drinking."

"Look on the bright side," she said. "Your liver will outlive you." She drained her glass and held up four fingers in the waiter's direction. "And speaking of the bright side, as much as we'll miss you, a break might be just what the doctor ordered. Maybe it's a good thing you're not doing summer camp with us this year."

"Right," I said. "At least with borderline adults somebody has already screwed them up before I got there." I reached past June for one of the straws nestled into the top of the napkin holder and managed to drain the rest of my pomtini.

"Good job, honey," Gloria said. Gloria was one of those preschool teachers who mothered everybody who crossed their paths. The biggest challenge of being around her was that you had to resist the urge to curl up on her lap with your blankie and start sucking your thumb.

"Thank you," I said.

June took another sip of her drink and finally stopped whimpering. "What is it you're doing this summer, Sarah? You've mentioned it a few times, but I still don't really get it."

I switched my straw over to my fresh pomegranate martini. "That's because I don't quite get it yet either. Basically, my boyfriend's boss hired me as a consultant. Some of the younger geeks at the company never leave their computers and he's worried that if they don't develop social skills, there will be no next IT generation because all the internet technology people will stop procreating—"

Lorna leaned forward. "And you're supposed to help them procreate? I must have missed that the first time you said it."

"No," I said. "I'm supposed to run a geek charm school summer session."

"Not to be pessimistic," Gloria said, "but I think there could be an oxymoron in there somewhere."

"Wow, Sarah," June said. "Your life is like just so interesting."

Lorna rolled her eyes. "Yeah, if nothing else, it's got to be a big step up from dead butterflies." She crossed her arms over her chest. "Okay, moving on. So what's the scoop? Are you and the new boyfriend shacking up together yet?"

"Huh?" I said.

Gloria crossed her arms, too. "You know, honey. Cohabitating, living together, sharing a remote?"

My straw made a slurping sound against my martini glass. Apparently I hadn't even fully mastered straws.

I stalled while I took another slurp, then I looked up and smiled brightly. "So, how about that cute new male teacher Kate Stone hired for next year."

"I know," June said. "Totally hot. Did you see his—"

"Not falling for it." Lorna shook her head. "Answer the question."

I sighed. "It's just that things are a little bit convoluted right now. You know, complex. Problematic. Dense. Thorny. Knotty."

"Eww," Gloria said. "His or yours? And by the way, good vocabulary, honey."

"Don't encourage her," Lorna said. "She sounds like a freakin' thesaurus. Come on, Sarah, spill. It's a simple question."

I closed my eyes and tried to come up with a simple answer. "It's just that my house is close to my work and his condo is close to his work. And his puppy needs a lot of attention. And his puppy hates me. And my brother's marriage is breaking up and he's living with me and he needs a lot of attention, too. And his daughters, well, you know how vulnerable kids are when their parents' marriages are falling apart, we see it all the time, so when he has them I feel like I should be there with them to help normalize things, and when they're not with him, he's completely depressed, so I feel like I should be there with *him*. But not as part of a couple, which will only remind my brother that he's no longer part of a couple." I gulped some air. "So, well, everything between John and me is basically on hold until my brother gets a new leash on life."

Somebody let out a bark of laughter.

I opened my eyes. "What?"

They were all staring at me.

I closed my eyes again. "Oh, and my father changed John's name to Jack."

"Wow," June said. "If my parents ever got divorced, I'd call you in a second, Sarah."

Gloria reached across the booth for my hand. "Honey, you're afraid, that's all. Just keep taking one little baby step at a time."

Lorna made a horse-like sound, complete with vibrating lips. "You don't think your brother will drop you like a hot potato as soon as he finds a new wife? You don't think that puppy can hate another girlfriend just as easily? Here's your plan: weekdays at his condo for the summer, and weekends in Marshbury. When school starts up again, you flip it. And if it doesn't work, you put both places on the market and buy something halfway between them. You fit in your brother and his kids between the hot, steamy sex."

"There's that," Gloria said.

Lorna paused for a sip of martini. "Come on, Sarah, get it together. This is your life. Go for it. Seize the diem. Carpe the day. You're not getting any younger, so—"

"Poop or get off the potty seat," Gloria said.

When I made it back to my house, it was family-free for a change. I started singing a spirited if slightly off-key version of "Another One Bites the Dust" to fill the silence. I headed straight for my bedroom, kicked off my shoes in the general direction of my closet.

I unbuckled the thick faux leather strap of my watch to officially put it away for the summer. My students loved its oversize analog face and delighted in pointing out the numbers they recognized. Occasionally one of them even made the connection that both hands pointing to the twelve meant it was time for lunch. Not a few parents over the years had insisted that their brilliant preschool progeny could tell time. The truth is that knowing the numbers on the clock is one thing. Con-

ceptualizing time and doing the math is another thing
entirely. Most students don't master it until seven or
eight, and it's not unusual for kids to be pushing nine
or ten before they really get it. One thing I'd learned as
a teacher was that parents love to give their offspring
imaginary superpowers.

Instead of tossing the watch on top of my dresser
the way I usually did, I decided actually putting it away
in my jewelry box would add a nice end-of-the-school-
year ceremonial touch. I shoved a pile of clean underwear that had never quite made it to my underwear
drawer off to the side and unclasped the carved wooden
lid.

My mother's favorite butterfly brooch glittered up
at me. It was made out of rhinestones that ranged from
aqua blue to peridot green—mostly round but with
teardrop-shaped stones set into the four points of the
wings. It was a lovely vintage piece, but I was always
afraid to wear it. Anything could happen.

I lifted it out of the jewelry box. I sat on the edge of
my bed and held it carefully in both hands. My mother
had believed in my superpowers, too. She'd never
thought a challenge was too far over my head, a situation couldn't be made better with my touch.

Once when I'd found a baby bird limping around the
front yard, she'd let me keep it in a shoebox and feed it
bird food and water. "What if I can't fix it?" I'd asked,
the weight of the responsibility heavy on my six-year-
old heart.

"It's okay," she'd said. "What matters is that the rest of its little life will be better because it has you in it."

I squeezed her butterfly pin tighter, the tarnished silver pin poking my palm. When I closed my eyes, Painted Lady butterflies fell from the sky like a rerun of an old television show. I heard the screams of the tiny graduates and their families all over again. Hot tears ran down my cheeks.

"I'm sorry I let you down, Mom," I whispered.

Five

Michael was pushing one grocery cart, and Annie and Lainie were pushing another. I was wearing my darkest sunglasses and my floppiest hat in the hopes that I wouldn't be recognized. And possibly tarred and feathered and run out of Marshbury for butterfly abuse.

"How are we doing on milk?" Michael asked as he held up a gallon.

"Shh," I said. "Don't talk so loud."

My head hurt. I wasn't a big drinker and two pomegranate martinis on an empty stomach yesterday had definitely not been my most brilliant move.

We turned the corner. One of the Bayberry students, who wasn't even in my class, pointed at me from the other end of the cereal aisle. His mother scooped him up and turned away as she averted her eyes, pretending they hadn't grazed mine first.

"Great," I said. "Young, impressionable children are no longer allowed to look at me. And they're out of Cheerios, too."

"They can't be out of Cheerios," Michael said. "Nobody's ever out of Cheerios." He located the Cheerios and dropped them in next to the milk.

"Show-off," I said.

My cell phone rang in the middle of the aspirin aisle.

I finished wrestling the childproof cap off a bottle and counted out a double dose. "What," I said to my phone as I headed for the seltzer aisle to find something to wash them down.

"What were you *thinking*?" My sister Carol's voice collided with my headache somewhere in the vicinity of my right temple. "Next time try bubbles. Bubbles don't die."

"Who told *you*?" I asked.

"Oh, please. It's all over town."

Another call beeped in.

"Way to go, Sarah," my sister Christine said when I used her for an excuse to ditch Carol. "I've got two words for you: white doves."

"Listen, Christine, I have to go. I'll talk to you later."

When Michael spotted me, I was just standing there with a half-chugged bottle of seltzer clutched in both hands waiting for the aspirin to kick in. He picked up the speed on his shopping cart and rolled toward me. Annie and Lainie barreled around the corner at the

other end of the aisle. My brother and nieces surrounded me with their shopping carts like stagecoaches in an
old Western.

"Are you all right?" Michael asked.

I shook my head. "I'll meet you in the car, okay? I
think I need to lay low until things die down."

"You mean the butterflies?" Annie said.

I scrunched my eyes shut. "How do *you* know?"

"We helped start a memorial page on Facebook,"
Annie said. "It has over three thousand likes already."

Lainie bowed her head and made the sign of the
cross. "Poor butterflies. My friends and I are writing a
song about them. We're going to put it up on YouTube
and get famous."

I was rubbing my throbbing forehead and letting it
sink in that my biggest teaching gaffe was out on the
Internet for the whole wide world to see, when Michael's wife, Phoebe, pushed a shopping cart around
the corner.

Phoebe froze. The good-looking guy with his hands
next to hers on their shared cart froze, too.

"Mommy!" Lainie yelled.

"Hi, Mom. Hi, Uncle Pete." Annie said.

"Loveyouhavefunwithdaddy," Phoebe said. By the
time the last fast syllable was out, she'd backed her way
to the end of the aisle and disappeared.

"Don't," I said to Michael.

"Don't what?" he said.

"Don't anything." I turned to the girls and switched
to my singsong-y teacher voice. "*I* know, what if we

meet you over in the ice cream aisle? Make sure you don't forget the chocolate chip cookie dough-oh."

They looked at me like they weren't buying it. Then they made a U-turn with their cart and drove off in the direction of the ice cream.

As soon as they turned the corner, I put my hand on Michael's shoulder. "Listen," I said. "Maybe there's an uncle you missed."

He shook his head as if he were trying to get water out of his ears. "That guy is no uncle." Then he let go of our cart and took off after Phoebe.

I took off after him. We dodged a cart left stranded in the middle of the aisle and headed for the front of the store. Michael bounced back and forth from one foot to the other, looking like an unkempt boxer warming up for a fight, as he searched for them in the checkout lines.

"Michael," I hissed. I tried to grab his arm, but he shook me off. A couple with a child in Lorna's class turned to look. The wife's eyes slipped past mine. She blocked her mouth with one hand and whispered something to her husband. In an instant they'd both turned away.

Michael bolted for the exit. When I followed him through, the whoosh of the sliding doors made my head hurt even more. I closed one eye against the bright sunny day trying to sneak around the edges of my sunglasses and pulled my hat down lower as I chased my brother.

Phoebe was just climbing into the passenger seat of a jet-black low-slung sports car. Randomly, I knew it was a BMW Z4, because Kevin had lusted after one the whole time we were married. *Shit, he would have to drive a nice car,* I thought as Michael lunged for the door. Like it would somehow make this a better situation if Phoebe and a good-looking guy were climbing into a beat-up old minivan.

The beamer roared to life. Michael yanked the passenger door open.

Phoebe held onto the door.

Michael pulled harder.

Phoebe let go. The low-flying door propelled my brother backward until another car stopped him with a dull thud. I took a good look at my brother, wedged between two cars, his dark hair flecked with gray and sticking out all over the place, his beat-up old half-zipped hoodie, his ancient gray sweats, his smelly untied sneakers, the heavy metal edge of a Z4 car door wedged dangerously close to his private parts.

Phoebe leaned out of the BMW and a ray of sunshine caught her freshly foiled hair. When she tilted her head up at Michael, it also played up the dark circles under her eyes.

"Leave. Me. Alone," she said. Her voice was flat and icy cold.

"I don't *want* to leave you alone," Michael said. "I love you. I want us to be together." He rubbed a fist against the corner of his eye and my own eyes teared up. "I want you to get out of that pretentious asshole's car and come with me right now."

The look Phoebe gave him brought me back to my final days with Kevin, when the rage between us was such an overwhelming *presence* that you could almost put a collar around it and take it out for a walk.

"The real problem," Phoebe said quietly, "was that you never gave me any space to *breathe*."

Michael made an ugly face. "Oh, so that's what they call it now, huh, *breathing*. Listen, if you're going to screw around on me while we're still married, at least call it what it—"

I grabbed his arm. "Michael."

He shook me off. "Stay out of it, Sarah. Say it, Phoebe. Tell me what you're going to do with *Uncle Pete*."

The driver's door opened.

Phoebe whipped her head around. "Get back in the car. Now." The car door clicked shut.

Phoebe and Michael glared at each other.

"Make sure you get the license plate, Sarah," my brother said. "So my lawyer can run a check on him."

Phoebe and I made eye contact. "Grow up, Michael," Phoebe said without taking her eyes off me. "And, Sarah, please check on the girls. My lawyer will want to know they're not being abandoned in grocery stores."

"I know," I whispered into my cell phone to John Anderson. "I know I promised I'd stay at your place tonight. But you should have seen the look on Michael's face when Phoebe tore out of the parking lot with that guy. I can't leave him—he's a mess. And now that he's told Phoebe he has a lawyer, I think maybe I should help him find one for real. And my nieces are here until tomorrow morning, so . . .."

I paused for a breath. Elementary school was still in session, and Michael always dropped the girls off at school on Monday mornings on his way to work, and then Phoebe juggled her job as a portrait photographer to make sure she was waiting for them when they took the bus home. This was Annie and Lainie's last week before summer vacation, the best week of the whole year, filled with fun end-of-the-year activities like field day and beach day. I wanted to keep things as normal as possible for them so they could enjoy it.

"So," I said, "I was hoping you wouldn't mind if I just met you at the office, and then I could stay over tomorrow night instead? If your sleepover card isn't already filled, of course."

John Anderson let out a laugh, but I had to admit it sounded a little bit forced.

I took a deep breath. "Thank you for understanding. I promise this won't last much longer."

There was a pause on the other end. "I don't think it can," he finally said.

CHAPTER

Nothing was simple. I thought about leaving my car at the Marshbury station and taking the train to Boston so my car would be waiting for me when I got back. But with my luck the train would be filled with Bayberry families on an early summer jaunt to New England Aquarium or Boston Children's Museum. And if I paired my floppy hat with my sunglasses so they'd be less likely to recognize me, I'd have hat hair when I arrived at John Anderson's office.

I considered driving all the way in to the city, but once I got through the outrageous rush hour traffic, I'd have to face an even more absurd hunt to find somewhere to park near John's office. And then later on I'd have to find somewhere else to park near his condo. John's condo only had one underground parking spot, so we'd have to drive around the block forever looking for on-street parking, and in the end I'd probably end up at a public garage or a parking lot, which would cost a small fortune. Money had been tight since I'd bought Kevin's half of the house, and even though Michael was paying for groceries since he'd moved in, we were both pretending his stay was just temporary so it's not like it made sense for him to pay rent.

So, after some serious overthinking, I decided to have Michael drop me off at a subway station on his way to work on the other side of the city. And then I was free to turn my attention to the other thing that women who reside in suburbia, where you can live out most of your adult life in yoga pants, obsess about when they go to the big city. What the hell was I going to wear?

After Annie and Lainie and Michael were sound asleep and Mother Teresa had had her final pee of the night, I'd stood in front of my closet door mirror as I tried on outfit after outfit after outfit. The thing about being a preschool teacher is that in the beginning of the year you promise yourself that you're only going to wear certain clothes to school. But then a Sunday night comes along and everything's dirty and you're tired and just don't feel like doing laundry, so you add one more outfit to the rotation. And so it goes. By the end of the school year, pretty much everything you own is covered with finger paint. It's supposed to be washable, but don't believe it for a second.

The other thing about being a preschool teacher is that most of your clothes are, well, teachery. You have to be able to bend down to pick up a fallen picture book or whisper encouragement in a child's ear. You have to be able to kick a playground ball. And it's simply not okay to let your students see your underpants at circle time.

Finally, I called my sister Carol.

"What's wrong?" she said.

"Why does something have to be wrong?"

"Uh, because it's 10:03 on a Sunday night? Hold on, let me at least get out of bed so I don't wake up Dennis."

"Never mind," I heard myself whispering, as if I were the one in bed with someone. "Just go back to sleep. I'll talk to you some other time."

"I'm already up. What do you want?"

"How do you know I want something? Couldn't I just be calling to catch up? Okay, I was wondering if you have an outfit I could borrow tomorrow. It's my first day of that consulting job—"

"*What?* You woke me up from a sound sleep with an eleventh hour clothing request? And by the way, I haven't forgotten you got Play-Doh all over that last sweater you borrowed, Sarah. You promised me you wouldn't wear it to school."

"Forget I asked," I said. "Hey, will you stop by my place and check on Michael tomorrow night? I'm not going to be here and I just want to make sure he's not, you know, lonely. Or bothering Phoebe." I had to admit keeping Michael away from Phoebe was becoming a fulltime job, and as much as I loved him, I looked forward to a brief vacation.

"Of course I will. It's already on my calendar. And listen, I'll leave that turquoise jacket you like in a bag on my front steps. The color's better on you anyway."

I hated that jacket. "That's okay. Go back to bed. I just remembered I bought a new dress for graduation. I can wear that."

My purple wrap dress looked pretty good before my eyes were fully awake. I'd sprayed it within an inch of its life with stain remover, but a crucial day or two might have elapsed before I got around to doing it. Just to be sure, I layered on a funky silver necklace to distract from any residual pomegranate martini spots.

Lainie and Annie, my visiting fashion police, even approved.

Annie looked up from her Cheerios. "Wow, Aunt Sarah, you look awesome. Can I borrow that necklace sometime?"

Lainie jumped right in. "Can I borrow those earrings? Dad, when am I going to be old enough to wear dangly earrings again?"

Michael looked at me for the answer.

"Thirteen," I said definitively. I actually had no idea what Phoebe's dangly earring rule was, but firm, clear limits made kids feel safer, especially during major upheavals in their lives.

"Oh, that's so not fair," Lainie said.

"You can take turns wearing the necklace," I said.

We all piled into Michael's car, and it made me flash
back to my own car trips as a kid, all six of us unbuckled in the back of my parents' wood-paneled station
wagon, the boys rolling around like puppies in the way
back. We'd pass the long drive to Worcester or Ho-
lyoke to visit one of our two sets of grandparents by
playing the license plate game. "Why, begosh and be-
gorrah, I do believe I see a Z," our father would yell
when we finally got to the end of the alphabet.

"Where, Dad, where?" we'd all scream.

"Right there," he'd say as he pointed. "On Mazza-
chusetts."

All these years later, I pointed. "I see an A," I said in
my cheeriest early morning voice.

"Boring," Annie said.

"Boring," Lainie said.

Once we'd dropped the girls off at school, Michael
and I were quiet for most of the ride, lost in our
thoughts. The thing about hanging out with your family is that you've given up trying to impress them and
you don't have to entertain them. It kind of takes the
pressure off.

Eventually we made it almost to Michael's office. He
stopped at a red light half a block from the nearest
subway station, so I jumped out. "Call me if you need
anything," I said before I slammed the door.

"Thanks," he said. "Knock 'em dead, sis." He
brushed a chunk of hair out of his eyes and I made a
mental note to remind him about getting a haircut
when I got back.

Michael worked downtown, which was far enough from Marshbury, but John's office was over the river and through the city and almost to the end of the red line, and by the time I got there it felt like I'd traveled all the way to another planet. It was a good thing I'd only have to make the trek once a week. The rest of the time I'd meet with the geeks where they lived—online.

I spent the subway ride standing up and fighting to keep my balance while I hung on to a metal bar, packed in with the other passengers like a bunch of dressed-up sardines. I passed the time by trying to decide whether or not it would be okay to stop by John's office before I reported for duty. On the one hand, it would be more professional to go right to the conference room where my students would be waiting and where John's boss would introduce me. On the other hand, John was the one who'd gotten me the job, so it would be only good manners to stop by first and thank him again. And after all, I was here in part to teach good manners, and modeling was one of the most effective methods of teaching. With luck John would be alone in his office and we'd have time to steal a quick kiss. Which was probably not all that professional, so maybe I should go straight to the conference room after all.

I got so caught up in my reverie that I almost missed my stop. I pushed my way past the briefcases and purses and messenger bags and made it out just before the doors swished closed again.

John was waiting for me on the sidewalk in front of the building, a soft khaki button-down shirt blending perfectly with his Heath Bar eyes. John's two-toned eyes were his best feature, a circle of chocolate surrounding a ring of toffee. He was wearing his contacts today and holding two cups of coffee. He held his arms out to the side and leaned in to kiss my cheek. He lingered for a moment and I took in the woodsy smell of his soap.

"Thanks," I said as he handed me my coffee.

"You look great," he said. "You could charm me in a second."

"You look great, too," I said. "And thank you again for setting this up."

"I had to. It was the only way I'd ever see you."

"That's not true and you know it." I took a sip of my coffee. "I have to admit there's a part of me still wondering why I let you talk me into saying yes to this. Right now I could be back at Bayberry where I actually know what I'm doing. Which is basically wiping noses and giving out hugs and time-outs."

He swung his non-coffee-bearing arm around my shoulder. "Who's to say that's not what you'll be doing here? And besides, aren't you the one who always says it's not about the subject matter? That a good teacher can teach anything?"

"What do I know." I took another careful sip of coffee, trying to minimize the spill chances. I endeavored to calm my nerves by reminding myself how much less time-consuming and more lucrative this consulting gig would be than another stint at Bayberry summer camp, where the teachers were even more underpaid than they were during the school year. Bottom line, even if it had been a bad call, I'd have money in the bank for a change and it would be over before I knew it.

But the truth was, it had been more than the money. When John first broached the idea, we were sitting at a trendy little tapas bar on Newbury Street, sipping glasses of sangria as we shared a plate of figs stuffed with warm goat cheese and wrapped in bacon.

John leaned toward me across the table. "Every time I so much as pass one of the Gamiacs in the hallway, it all comes back. I was just like that in high school. Geeky and isolated. I don't know what I would have done if my physics teacher hadn't started a model airplane club."

I smiled. "I bet that was a direct line to popularity."

"Popularity wasn't even on my radar—I was going for survival. And I didn't have the skills to get there on my own."

I flashed back to my brother Billy Jr., of all my siblings the one who'd struggled most socially when we were growing up. His nose was always buried in a book. He didn't appear to have any real friends. He was four years older than me, which should have made him an instant crush magnet for my teenybopper friends, but even they ignored him to flirt with Johnny, or my younger brother Michael.

One night I woke up to go to the bathroom, and as I passed the open stairway, I heard the sound of my parents' serious voices below. On the return trip, I tiptoed halfway down the staircase to eavesdrop.

"I'm worried," my mother was saying. "Sometimes I stand outside his bedroom door and listen, just to make sure he's still breathing in there."

Even without a name, I somehow knew she was talking about Billy Jr. I vowed to be nicer to him from now on, even if he didn't want me to.

"He'll be A-okay before we know it, hon," my father said. "Just give it time."

And then Billy Jr.'s high school English teacher talked him into trying out for a play. Before we knew it, the whole Hurlihy clan was stretched across an entire row in the high school auditorium. While a couple of lines in *Arsenic and Old Lace* might not have morphed him into Mr. Popularity, it was a turning point. When Billy took his bow, we gave him a standing ovation. All these years later, I could still picture my father wiping tears from his eyes with his handkerchief as the rest of us whistled and yelled his namesake's name.

Seven

It would be an understatement to say that the company I'd be consulting for had a colorful history. Back in the day, a funeral home had expanded to include senior housing. This may have sounded like a good idea on paper, but in the end it turned out to be too much like one-stop shopping for anyone to actually want to live there. So it promptly went six feet under.

Around the same time, an electronic gaming start-up was in the process of merging with an Internet technology company. They bought the funeral home-slash-senior housing building at auction and renamed the new company Necrogamiac. The visitation rooms, and probably some of the other rooms I didn't want to think about, were turned into conference rooms. The rest of the building was renovated into office space as the company expanded, fueled by state tax incentives and worldwide video game addiction.

John took his arm back and we maintained a professional distance as we rode the elevator up to the fourth floor. The elevator walls were paneled in dark mahogany and tufted satin that made the elevator feel like a cross between a suite in a five-star hotel and a comfy casket. Shiny lengths of old brass crisscrossed like an accordion to make the elevator door. A wooden bench, topped with a heavy brocade cushion, stretched across the back of the elevator. I had to admit I'd always had a little bit of a fantasy about making mad passionate love on an elevator stopped between two floors, so I may have allowed the thought to drift briefly by.

I took another careful sip of my coffee. Our eyes met. I blushed. "Nice elevator, huh? Like some kind of den of iniquity throwback."

John glanced over his shoulder. "I've never really noticed."

"You're kidding. I would have thought everybody who sets foot in here has the same fantasy. Somebody could make a fortune renting pillows and blankets by the hour."

He took a long drink of coffee.

Clearly this was not pre-work conversation, but I couldn't seem to shut myself up. Maybe it was new job jitters. "Ooh, and they could put a coin-operated champagne station on one wall."

He shrugged. "I guess I'm just one of those turn around and look straight ahead elevator riders."

"Never mind," I said as the elevator rumbled to a stop and the see-through brass doors opened.

"Break a leg," John said when he finished walking me to the conference room. He opened the door for me and then disappeared down the hallway as I pulled the door closed behind me. A purple foam dart from a Nerf gun sailed by, barely missing my head. I raised one hand to shield my face from a yellow foam dart coming from the other direction. The good news was that I was fully awake now.

I stopped in my tracks, hoping against hope that John's boss would materialize at this very moment. That way he could play bad cop and do crowd control, and I could hang back and be the good cop until my students got to know me a little better. First impressions were important.

I scanned the long rectangular room, which looked a lot like what might happen if the Addams Family and Ikea got together and had a baby. Three rectangular frosted glass conference tables with square chrome legs abutted each other end-to-end, their opaque tops scribbled with notes and graffiti in a rainbow of fluorescent marker. Posters took up most of the available wall space: Morticia, Cousin Itt, Wednesday, Gomez. An Uncle Fester lamp stood next to a massive funereal urn-turned-ice bucket that held an assortment of bottled water and over-caffeinated drinks. The ceiling was painted black and dotted with the kind of stick-on yel-

low plastic stars that glowed in the dark. Fake spider
webs draped down like Spanish moss. Maybe it was
more like John Anderson's Addams Family pinball machine had come to life.

Clearly, I wasn't at Bayberry Preschool anymore.

See-through Lucite chairs, each one occupied, surrounded the table. A sleek iMac sat on the tabletop
across from each seat. I didn't realize John's boss was
already in the room until he put his Nerf crossbow
down on the conference table and stood up. "There she
is," he said. "Sarah, meet the Gamiacs. Everybody,
meet Sarah."

"I'm delighted to meet you all," I said. I stood tall,
shoulders back, making direct eye contact with every
eye I could catch, an engaging smile on my face. An
orange and black foam basketball whizzed by my left
ear.

John's boss had picked up his crossbow again and
was already headed for the door. "Sarah is here to . . .
well, I'll let her tell you."

I started to ask him to wait, but then I wondered if
this might be a test. Sink or swim. Trial by fire. Maybe
even fight or flight. I had to admit right now flight was
winning by a mile—every instinct I had was telling me
to run back to my safe little preschool while I still
could.

I took advantage of what appeared to be a temporary cease-fire and walked over to stand behind the
Lucite chair John's boss had vacated. I stole another
moment to assess the students before me. About half
seemed to be deeply immersed in computer games. One

was scratching his scalp. Another was picking his nose. I reached into my bag and handed him a tissue. This strategy worked remarkably well with preschool students. If you wordlessly handed them a tissue every time they reached an index finger up their noses, by the tenth or twelfth time they would automatically reach for their own tissue instead.

"So." I cleared my throat. "Let me cut to the chase. Your boss has hired me to ramp up your social skills."

Two of the students, one male and one female I was fairly sure, looked up with mild interest.

Another student leaned back, his clear Lucite chair bending with him. "Wait. This isn't computer camp? Whoa, radical bait and switch, dude."

"Seriously?" somebody else said.

"What do you do at computer camp?" I asked. I prided myself on being a responsive teacher. Maybe I could come up with an integrated lesson on the spot, combining something they liked with something they needed, the way preschool students sang their ABCs or counted cookies before they ate them.

A boy sitting diagonally across from me, who would have been adorable if he brushed his teeth occasionally, put his hand up. I nodded.

"Well," he said, "one thing we do is as soon as anybody gets up to, like, go get some more Red Bull or go to the bathroom or anything, we change the background on their computer."

"Yeah," another student said. He was wearing a flannel shirt, possibly since flannel shirt season. "Once, somebody put a picture of Donatello on mine. So not funny. He was totally like my least favorite Teenage Mutant Ninja Turtle."

"Ha, that was me," the student next to him said. "I so got you, dude."

So much for computer camp integration. I decided I'd go back to my original plan and start with a quick baseline assessment of their social skills and then we could set some group goals. And if that didn't hold their attention, we could always finger paint on the frosted glass tabletops.

"Okay," I said. "Let's start with a show of hands. Who's a member of a social or professional group that gets together on a regular basis? Maybe Toastmasters or a meet-up group or even a book club."

The ones who weren't ignoring me looked at me blankly.

Somebody farted. There was a moment of silence, then everyone pointed to someone at the table, in what I could only assume was an attempt to guess the perpetrator. After giving them all sufficient time to register their votes, the farter stood up and bowed. Everybody clapped.

The simple elegance of teaching is that a good teacher meets her students where they are and escorts them to the next level. I chose to see this ritual as a sign of at least rudimentary social interacting potential.

"I'll take that as a resounding and aromatic no," I said. Nobody laughed. Most of them had resumed eye contact with their iMacs. The nose picker reached for his nose. I handed him another tissue.

I cleared my throat. "Next question: How many of you currently have a girlfriend or a boyfriend?"

A couple of them actually glanced my way.

"My last girlfriend," one of them said, "had the worst fucking taste in manga."

"Hey," somebody else said. "Guess what I found out? If you stick toothpicks in two Peeps and put them in the microwave facing each other, when you turn on the microwave, it looks like they're jousting."

"Die," the flannel shirt student yelled as he hunched over his computer. "Die you bastards, die."

A purple foam dart hit me right between my breasts. Finally, everybody looked at me.

I looked down. Under the bright light of the overhead LED bulbs, pomegranate martini spots dotted my purple wrap dress like a constellation. I moved my necklace back to center.

"Whoa, dude, direct hit. Hey, did I draw blood? Tactical error fully acknowledged."

There comes a point in every school year or summer camp session when the honeymoon's over and you have to let them know who's boss. Nine minutes in was early, but the signs were indisputable.

"Unhand your weapons," I said.

They ignored me.

I clapped my hands.

They ignored me some more.

I put two fingers in my mouth to whistle the way my father had taught us when we were kids, sitting out on the back deck on a sticky summer's night, the air thick with the smell of low tide, waiting for the coals to get hot enough to blister the hotdogs and hamburgers within an inch of their lives. All six of us would be gathered around him as if he were the Pied Piper while my mother finished assembling the coleslaw and potato salad inside.

"'Tis top secret, the family whistle," he'd begin, "so you've got to swear on your sainted ancestors' souls that you'll never let it leave this circle."

"I swear, Dad," we'd all say.

"How many times have I told you kids not to swear," he'd bellow.

We'd laugh and laugh, like this was the first time we'd heard it instead of the hundredth.

"The trick," he'd continue, "is to wet your whistle first." He'd reach for his beer and take another drink, then he'd look over his shoulder to make sure our mother was still in the kitchen. If the coast was clear, he'd pass the can around. We'd each take a sip and use our fleeting moment in the spotlight to follow it up with something dramatic—a blissful swoon, a throat-searing gag, or a Shakespeare-worthy death spiral to the splintery wood deck.

When we'd all finished, he'd nod his head in approval and take his beer back. "God bless you and keep you. Chips off the old block, every last blessed one of you." He'd pause here for his own sip. "Next, you've got to leave enough space between your fingers for the whistle to get airborne, but not so much that it gets distracted and forgets where it's going."

We'd put our fingers, still tasting of cold aluminum, in place. My father would walk around the circle, inspecting us one by one, nodding solemnly or adjusting a finger.

"And then you say a quick prayer to Al O'Whistles, the patron saint of whistlers."

We'd bob our heads, hanging on his every word.

"On your knees," he'd roar.

"Da-ad," the older kids would say, but we'd all get on our knees anyway, fake a quick prayer, cross ourselves.

"And then you simply let her rip." And he would—a shrill, piercing, ear-clamping whistle that I used to imagine the angels could hear all the way up in heaven.

We'd join in for a group whistle, our imperfect family harmony filling the air.

Then our father would drain the last of his beer. "Boyohboy," he'd say, "Irish I had a Schlitz." And we'd all race to the kitchen to get him one.

I blinked myself back to the present. I let out an eardrum-denting whistle.

That got the Gamiacs' attention.

"Take your hand off your mouse and stand up," I said. "Slide your chair under the table."

They looked at me in disbelief.

"Now," I said.

They stood. The sound of metal chair legs on marble floor was not pretty as they slid their chairs back in, but at least they did it.

"Wow, this is like when Bart almost has to go to military school on *The Simpsons*," somebody said.

I made the universal teacher sign for zipping your lips. "IPhones on the table and line up by the door. Single file. We're going out."

This time they looked at me in sheer terror. I wasn't sure if it was iPhone separation anxiety or fear of the outdoors, but I crossed my arms over my pomegranate martini stains and held firm.

There were too many of us for the elevator, and I didn't trust them not to bolt if we broke into two groups, so we all clomped our way down four flights of stairs together. I pushed open one of the heavy double doors and did a head count as they filed out to the sidewalk. Like every good teacher on a field trip, I'd count and recount along the way to make sure I didn't lose anybody.

I followed the last student outside. They clumped together like moles, blinking in the sunlight.

Eight

After we'd made love, sometimes John would just look at me and say, "Sarah." The way he said it, it was a complete sentence, both present and future tense, filled with everything you needed to build a life with someone.

I really sucked at this kind of thing, but it seemed only fair to give it a shot. We were stretched out on our sides facing each other, the covers a tangled mess at our feet. I traced the letter *J* on his chest gently with one fingernail as I looked into his eyes. "John. I mean, Jack. You know, I really think we need to solve the name thing. In a way, it might be kind of cool to have a family nickname."

"Or I could go out on a limb and have it changed legally. As a show of solidarity or to pledge my troth to you."

"Sure, and maybe I could cut off an ear for you or something."

He kissed the ticklish spot behind my left ear. "Maybe we should pick the name that sounds better in the heat of passion."

I hooked one ankle around his. "That makes sense. Okay, here goes." I pushed myself up on one elbow and threw my head back. "Oh, John, oh, John, oh, John."

He rolled over to his back and looked up at the ceiling while he considered. "I think that one has real potential."

"Wait. Don't decide yet." I fluffed my hair and threw my head back again. "Oh, Jack, oh, Jack, oh, Jack."

He stared at the ceiling some more. "This is tougher than you'd think it would be. Can I hear them both one more time? It's an important decision and I wouldn't want to rush it."

There was a low growl on the other side of the bedroom door.

"Uh, oh," I said. "Is that Horatio?"

"No, that was me."

"Good. I like a man who growls."

Horatio had growled at me for the first time today when we'd picked him up at Happytails Puppy Play Care. John had taken a half-day off so he could leave with me when I finished my session with the Gamiacs. We'd wandered the streets for a while, hand in hand,

and then stopped for lunch at a Thai restaurant. We'd gazed at each other over our pad thai, our sexual tension feeling like the dessert we knew was ahead, couldn't wait to get to, but also wanted to enjoy the sweet anticipation of just a little bit longer.

John paid the check. As he wrote in the tip, I read the amount upside down, happy that he tipped not the exact fifteen percent you might expect from an accountant but like a pinball wizard who knew what it was to have a dream that might need some support. Kevin had been a stingy tipper, always looking for reasons—slow service, overcooked meal, delayed plate clearing—to undertip our server. I'd ended far too many restaurant meals over the course of my marriage pretending I'd forgotten something so I could run back and leave a few more dollars on the table.

"I bet," I said, as we walked back toward John's office to pick up his car, "that our waitress was really a songwriter. She plays guitar in a midlife girl band on her nights off and she's saving up for her first recording session."

John nodded. "I like it. She has the soul of an aging rock star but the bills of a waitress."

"Do you hate being an accountant again?"

"Not really. I'm good at it, and it's a cool place to work. Plus, I like having an office with actual people in it to talk to, as opposed to a roomful of pinball machines." He sighed. "Especially when I'm alone so much since my girlfriend is constantly blowing me off."

I reached my arm through his. "I am not."

"Well, that remains to be seen. But back to the subject at hand, I think the reality is that very few people are as lucky as you are, Sarah, to have their passion and their day job all rolled up into one tidy package."

"Ha," I said. "Not too tidy. I wiped out an entire generation of Painted Lady Butterflies, traumatized a preschool full of students, and you should have seen me today dodging Nerf darts with the Gamiacs. I'm not sure yet how much I'll be able to accomplish, but I like them. They remind me of supersized toddlers one minute and wise old souls the next."

I let go of John's arm so we could walk around three laughing women blocking the sidewalk. He swung his arm around my shoulders when we found each other again.

"Hard to believe most of the Gamiacs are in their mid-twenties," he said as we matched our strides again. "I have a theory that hovering parents and a crashing economy combined to create a generation of boomerang kids living an extended adolescence."

I nodded. "I know. It's so not fair that childhood lasts longer these days."

"Uh-oh. You said 'these days.' That means we're officially old."

"Speak for yourself. Anyway, I like them. We're really going to have to work on hygiene. And farting. Nose picking's coming along swimmingly though."

"See. You're completely into it already. You'll be drawing up lesson plans and making gamer finger puppets so they can practice their manners."

"Wait." I reached into my purse for the little note-book I carried everywhere. "Let me write that down."

Back at John's condo, Horatio growled again.

John sat up in bed. "Horatio, place."

Horatio barked and slammed himself into the door with a bone-shattering thump.

"Horatio, place," John said again. This, according to the training manual John kept on his bedside table, was supposed to send Horatio to the doggie equivalent of the time-out chair, a fluffy little faux fur bed with *Horatio* embroidered on it in loopy cursive letters that was nestled in front of the tall condo window with the best view.

We heard another bark and thump. Bark and thump. Bark and thump. Some serious scratching followed, which sounded exactly like fingernails on a blackboard to me.

I put my hands over my ears. Horatio barked some more.

John dangled one leg over the edge of the bed. "Okay with you if I let him in? I'm thinking maybe if we have a group cuddle afterward, he won't feel so bad about being kicked out of the bedroom."

"Or you could be reinforcing his door-scratching behavior," I said. A flash of déjà vu hit me, as if I'd suddenly found myself doing a parent-teacher conference in the nude.

John was already halfway to the door. I reached for the covers and pulled them up to my chin.

As soon as the door opened, Horatio exploded into the room, a gangly barking whirlwind of long legs and tricolored fur. John scooped him up in his arms. Horatio covered John's face with kisses so thoroughly and enthusiastically that I wondered if I should be taking notes.

John flipped his puppy over in his arms so that he was cradling him like a baby and began scratching his belly. Horatio's tongue dangled from one side of his mouth and his extreme panting made his chest go up and down in short even bursts. I watched them, not really jealous, but not really not jealous either.

I was just contemplating a brief nap to pass the time when John remembered me. He smiled and walked Horatio across the room and placed him on the corner of the bed.

"Say hello to Sarah, Horatio."

Horatio crossed the bed in a single leap. His greyhound half had given him height and speed, his Yorkie side determination and a bad attitude. He stopped, inches from me, and started barking his head off. His bark somehow managed to be both yappy and ferocious.

I held out one hand as a peace offering.

He snapped at me, his teeth grazing my fingers.

"Ouch," I said. I inspected my fingers, counted them just to be sure.

"He didn't bite you," John said. "If he really wanted to bite you, you'd know it."

"Why do people always say that? It's a really stupid thing to say. How do you know he just doesn't have bad aim? Or need glasses?"

"Did he break the skin?"

I flipped my hand back and forth and inspected my fingers some more. "Not really."

"See. My point exactly."

We looked at each other over the wall of furious puppy that separated us.

I wiggled one toe under the sheet. Horatio took his barking up an octave.

I shook my head. Horatio crouched low over his front paws, his butt sticking up in the air, and growled a really mean growl.

"Do something," I said.

"He's playing."

"He's not playing. His fur is sticking straight up." I gave Horatio my strictest teacher look. "Do not raise your hackles at me, young man."

Horatio dove for me, barking like a maniac. John lassoed him with his arms just in the nick of time.

I jumped out of bed, grabbed my oversize shoulder bag in case I needed a shield, and made a run for the master bathroom.

I slammed the bathroom door behind me. When Horatio hit it with a vengeance, the door actually shook.

Horatio barked and scratched, scratched and barked, hit the door again.

"Horatio, place," John said from the other room.

Horatio let out another bark, but I knew what he was really saying, loud and clear, was *Sarah, place.*

I felt the cool travertine tiles of John's bathroom under my feet, took in the frameless glass-enclosed double shower, the fluffy white towels. The brushed chrome fixtures were a perfect match for the twin contemporary mirrors topping his and her sinks. It was a nice bathroom, but I wouldn't want to spend my life hiding in here.

I splashed water on my face and located my travel pack of makeup remover sheets in the bottom of my bag so I could wipe away the mascara that now ringed my eyes and made me look like a post-coital raccoon. I'd yet to leave any toiletries in John's bathroom, any clothes in his closet. Besides the fact that Horatio would probably have chewed them to pieces by now just to spite me, leaving a mere toothbrush behind felt like such a brazen declaration that I'd be coming back.

An extra robe or a T-shirt was even worse. It was the kind of thing that could jinx the chances for a long-term relationship. Not to mention that it just reeked of those clichéd things you read about women doing to get one foot in the door, to be partially moved in before the poor unsuspecting guy realizes it.

Still, it's not like you could show up to teach geek charm school rolling a cute little suitcase filled with fresh undies. So to save myself from doing a walk of shame back to Marshbury—same clothes, new day—I'd buried the bare essentials way in the bottom of my biggest shoulder bag. It was appropriately named, since by the time I finished lugging it all over the city, I could feel the weight of it wearing a new groove in my shoulder.

Horatio hit the door again.

"Let me know when you're ready to come out," John yelled, "and I'll make sure I'm holding him. Maybe that will help."

Relationships, two-footed and four-footed alike, were just too damn complicated. For the first time it occurred to me that this could be a really long season. It was only June and we'd already hit the dog days of summer.

CHAPTER

Nine

My father was girlfriendless for Sunday dinner. This was far more unusual than having a strange woman, or even two or three, open the heavy oak door to welcome me into my family home.

I let myself in with the tarnished brass key I'd had since junior high and headed straight for the kitchen. I knew I'd find everyone there. Sure enough, my father was hunched over his ancient manual typewriter at the old pine trestle table, two-finger typing on a thick sheet of ivory paper. I kissed him on the top of his head.

"Sarry, my darlin' daughter, it's good to see your smiling face," he said without looking up. "Can you check a wee bit of spelling for me once I've finished?"

"Sure, Dad," I said. "I'd love to."

Christine looked up from snipping a stalk of rose-
mary over the pork roast with the kitchen shears.
"Why does Sarah get to check your spelling? I'm the
one who placed three times at the state spelling bee."

Carol looked up from the potatoes she was peeling.
"And she still has the trophies to prove it."

Christine glared at her. "What's wrong with that?
We have a trophy case. It came with the house."

Carol rolled her eyes as she turned to me. "Where's
Jack?"

"He wanted to spend some time with his dog," I said.

Everybody turned to look at me.

"Don't say it," I said.

"We wouldn't think of it." My brother Billy shook
his head. "But I can't believe he calls you his dog.
That's harsh. I mean, his teddy bear maybe—"

"Or even his honey bunny," Christine said

I was still watching my father. "Dad, don't you think
it might be time to upgrade to a computer? You know,
try a little email . . .."

He combed one hand through his long white mane.
"Never. Not as long as a single solitary mailman is still
reporting for duty—"

"But," I said.

He hit another key, back-spaced, then hit it again,
harder. "Trudging through rain and snow and sleet
and hail—"

"But," I said again.

"Just because the rest of the world has gone to hell
in a hand basket, my darling daughter, doesn't mean
Billy Hurlihy has to jump on the next train. Jesus,

Mary, and what's his name, where in tarnation did that W go?"

I glanced over at the rest of my family, thinking a little bit of backup on the computer issue might be nice. Michael was busy chopping onion, tears streaming down his cheeks. I could only hope it would be thera-peutic.

My niece Siobhan was peeling carrots next to him. "Uncle Michael, I'm not kidding. Wearing socks with your topsiders is social suicide. You'll never get a date."

We all stopped what we were doing to look at Mi-chael's feet. A glimpse of white tube socks was clearly visible in the space between the tops of Michael's boat shoes and the hem of his jeans.

"Who knew," Billy said. He was licking one of the beaters while his wife Moira poured chocolate batter into two round cake pans. "And here I would have thought Mikey's breath would have been his biggest date obstacle."

Michael put his chopping knife down and wiped his eyes with the back of his hands. Then he lunged at Bil-ly, hitting him at waist level with one shoulder as he circled his arms around Billy's thighs and threw him over his back. The half-licked beater went flying and hit a lower cabinet with a chocolate-covered thwack.

Michael danced Billy around in a circle. Billy wig-gled free and knocked Michael to the ground. They rolled around the speckled linoleum floor like puppies. Mother Teresa galloped in to the kitchen and started barking. Michael hooked an arm around her neck and pulled her into the wrestling match.

"Don't come whining to me when you throw out your back like you did last time," Moira said as she threw the wayward beater in the kitchen sink. Billy had been married to Moira for ages, but every time I saw them together, my heart still lifted that he'd found her. Moira was as social as Billy was awkward, and from the moment we'd met her, my whole family had welcomed her with open arms. She was one of us.

"Remember," Carol said as she bent down to wipe the cabinet with a sponge, "when Johnny and Billy were fighting and they broke Mom's favorite gravy boat. And we all helped them put it together with Elmer's glue and then they snuck it back into the china cabinet."

"And," I said, "Mom didn't say a word—"

"She just filled it with gravy the next Sunday and put it on the dining room table," Christine said.

Michael let Billy out of a headlock so he could talk. "And we all had to sit there and pretend we didn't notice the gravy leaking all over the tablecloth."

Johnny walked into the kitchen with a gallon of ice cream and put it in the freezer. "Yeah, and she kept saying 'Gravy anyone?' And then Dad finally reached over and picked up the gravy boat and the whole thing collapsed."

We all burst out laughing.

Our father looked up from his typewriter. "Your mother," he said, "was the best gosh darn straight man ever. Gracie Allen had nothing on Marjorie Hurlihy."

I was just about to go find a place to hide before anybody noticed I didn't have a meal prep assignment, when Carol caught my eye and jerked her head, sister code for *meet me in the hallway*. Since this usually meant she was about to make me do something I didn't want to do, I ignored her. She scraped the potatoes off the cutting board and into the pan. Then she grabbed me by the elbow.

"Ouch," I said as she pushed me into the hallway. "That pinches."

She dragged me about halfway up the stairs until we reached the step that, after years of childhood trial and error, we'd all discovered was low enough to spy on the floor below but high enough to keep the conversation private.

"Do you know," she said as soon as we were seated, "that the *Marshbury Mirror* doesn't even have a personals section in the print edition anymore? They're still taking Dad's money, but they're running his ads in the home improvement section now. As in between the drywall guy and the wallpaper lady."

"Ha," I said, "that's actually kind of cute."

Carol glared at me. "Sarah, his freezer is almost empty."

I could feel my jaw literally drop as this registered. Our father's dating escapades may have been responsible for varying levels of discomfort in his six adult children, but he'd yet to connect with a woman who hadn't contributed at least one casserole to sustain him against the ravages of widowerhood.

Carol nodded. "Yeah, exactly. When it's empty, you know who's going to have to cook for him. And let's be fair. I mean, you're the one with the summer off, so I think you need to take the first shift."

"I do not have the summer off. I—" I stopped, visions of casseroles dancing in my head. Other than one scary concoction of ground beef, raisins, and some other unidentifiable ingredients, they were all pretty good. Tuna noodle casserole sprinkled with crushed cornflakes, American chop suey, chicken tetrazzini, corned beef and cabbage roll-ups.

Kevin had done most of the cooking when we were married. Since my divorce, my father's date-baked casseroles had not only saved me from cooking for my father, they'd pretty much saved me from cooking. His freezer had become my free 24-hour grocery store. Not only that, but I was sometimes able to pass them off as my own creations. Even my brother Michael was starting to think I was a good cook.

I shook my head to clear the casseroles. "Why do you think he has a shortage?"

Carol shrugged. "Well, obviously, his ads are no longer hitting his target demographic. All the single seniors are online now."

"But what can we do? You saw how he blew me off when I brought it up—we'll never get Dad to give up his typewriter. We can't even get him to plug in the laptop we all chipped in on. What was that? Two Christmases ago?"

Carol leaned forward to make sure nobody was spying on us from below. "Okay, here's the plan. We kill two birds with one stone and get Dad and Michael dating together."

"I thought you said Michael wasn't ready to date yet."

"Sarah, get with the program. *Phoebe* is dating."

"So that means Michael is ready?"

"No, it means we want him to get over Phoebe. So we've got to bump him up to pre-ready. And he might as well get all his near misses and rebound relationships over with anyway. That way, when he's really ready, he can move right along."

I buried my head in my hands. "Oh, please, don't ever make me go back out there again."

"Sarah, this isn't about you, so get over yourself. While the roast is cooking, I'm going to take Dad aside and convince him he has to do it for Michael. And you'll take Michael aside and tell him he has to do it for Dad."

The thing about my sister Carol was that even though she was way too bossy, she came up with some pretty good plans. "How long do roasts take to cook again?" I asked, just so she'd know I was contemplating the variables.

She shook her head. "Clearly you need those casseroles." She pulled herself to a standing position with the worn mahogany banister we all used to slide down as kids. "Focus. And we'll check in with each other later."

Carol disappeared back into the kitchen. I reached over to yank myself to my feet with the banister.

"Aunty Sarah," Lainie yelled. "Can we do a dress rehearsal for you?"

Annie and Lainie came running into the hallway. Maeve and Sydney, their youngest cousins, followed right behind them.

"Sure," I said. I plopped back down on the stairs, getting ready to watch them bust some moves or do a one-act play. Over the years, the wide center hallway with its stairway seating had been the stage for everything from magic shows to hula-hoop exhibitions.

My nieces lined up, side-by-side, oldest to youngest, and began to sing.

If I were a butterfly
And you were a ladybug
Would you marry me anyway
And have butterbug babies

If I crashed and fell
On all the little children
Heading straight for hell
Would you put me back together again
So we could fly to heaven.

If I were a butterfly
And you were a ladybug
Would you marry me anyway
And have butterbug babies

CHAPTER

Ten

I just sat there for a while after my nieces left to go sing my butterfly humiliation around some more. Dozens of family photographs surrounded me like a group hug. Mismatched frames stretched along both sides of the staircase all the way up to the second floor.

My eyes went, as they always did first, to my parents' sepia wedding photo. A thin and dapper version of my tuxedoed father that was both so him and so not him all at the same time. My mother in her wedding gown with the impossibly elaborate lace bodice, the look in her eyes saying how did I get lucky enough to marry this handsome guy. Her cat's eye glasses with little rhinestones that I would give anything to get my hands on now and which were just flashy enough to make me wonder if I'd ever really known her.

My grandparents' wedding photos were up on the wall, too, as well as my brothers' and sisters'. I'd taken down Kevin's and my wedding picture the day our divorce had become final in a ceremony that involved my father's biggest hammer and the sound of breaking glass while my family cheered me on. There were so many photos that you might not notice the empty space unless you knew where to look. I kept meaning to bring another picture over to take its place, but somehow I never seemed to get around to it.

Michael came into the hallway before I even had to track him down. "That old coot. Do you believe he can sing Mom's praises at the same time he's typing out a personal ad?"

I sighed. "Yeah, sometimes I feel that way, too, at least a little bit, but she's gone, Michael. What's he supposed to do, bring flowers to her grave once a week and mope around the other six days?"

Michael shrugged. "I don't think I could do it, that's all."

"You'll get there. Give it time." I didn't have the heart to tell him that with Carol on my back, *time* meant about five minutes.

I followed his eyes to his wedding picture, taken on the front steps of the church in Savannah where Phoebe grew up and where they were married. Michael with a fresh haircut and shiny brown eyes, dapper in his tux. Phoebe in a strapless white dress looking blond and fragile and like someone who didn't quite belong to this dark-haired family with their big smiles and shiny brown eyes, like the old *Sesame Street* game about which of these things is not like the other.

I had a sudden urge to go get Michael the hammer, but I knew he wasn't ready yet.

He ran one hand through his scraggly hair.

"Hey," I said. "Let's sneak out and get you a quick haircut while the roast is in the oven."

He sighed a long sigh, like a simple haircut might be beyond him. "Yeah, okay. Let me just tell Annie and Lainie that I'll be right back. It could take me a minute. They've got some song they want me to listen to."

"Great," I said.

Michael drove, his Toyota 4Runner starting right up the way it always did, even though it had passed the hundred thousand mile mark and then some. I adjusted the beach towel he kept draped over the cracked vinyl of the passenger seat. Mother Teresa poked her head between our shoulders. I reached for a tissue to wipe some drool dribbling from the corner of her mouth.

We headed in the direction of the nearest walk-in sports cut place. If I were a better sister, I probably would have thought ahead and called someone to get a referral to a cutting edge salon and then made an actual appointment, but at this point even a buzz cut would be a step up for my brother.

"You know," Michael said, "if Phoebe wanted me to drive a nicer car, she should have said something. I thought we'd agreed that it made more sense to stay on track with the girls' college fund."

"Listen," I said. "We've been over this a dozen times already. It's not about the car. We have no idea who this guy is or if they're even dating. He could be a client. He could be gay."

"Right," Michael said. "Or he could be banging my wife."

On the one hand, I wanted to make Michael feel better. On the other hand, I wanted him to get over Phoebe. There didn't seem to be a lot of overlap, so I had a tendency to bounce back and forth between the two, trying to find a balance.

I nodded carefully. "Or they could be screwing around together. When is your next session with the marriage counselor?"

"Tuesday. But Phoebe will probably cancel again." He shook his head. "She'd better not. It's our last session before she takes the girls to Savannah to visit her parents."

"Don't anticipate," I said. "Maybe she just needs some time."

"Time." Michael stopped at a stop sign. He waved one car ahead of us and then another. Maybe he was trying to build up some good karma.

Finally, we had the intersection to ourselves. Instead of continuing in the direction of a potential haircut, Michael put his foot on the gas pedal and made a U-turn.

"Don't do it," I said.

He ignored me.

"Michael," I said.

He ignored me some more. We followed the tree-lined streets toward the west end of town. I knew exactly where we were going. Since we'd run into Phoebe and Uncle Pete at the grocery store, this was at least the third drive-by Michael had taken me on. I could only imagine how many trips he'd made without me.

"It's still light out," I said. "She'll spot you right away."

He didn't say anything.

"If we don't hurry, the sports cut place will be closed by the time we get there. Come on, Michael, haircut first. That way if Phoebe calls the cops on you, at least you won't look like a criminal in your mug shot."

He leaned forward over the steering wheel and pushed down harder on the gas pedal.

I put on my perky teacher voice. "How about this? We get you a haircut, then we go back and have a nice yummy dinner, then we leave the girls with Dad for a little while. Or we could even ask Dad to drive them back to my house and meet us there. And then, when it's good and dark, you and I can drive by as many times as you want, if you think it will make you feel better. But I don't think it will, Mikey."

Mother Teresa licked my cheek.

I reached back to give her a pat on the head. "Fine, you can come with us, too, girl. But, I have to tell you both I don't think this is a very productive way to spend our time."

Michael took a left, and then slowed to take a quick right onto his street. I held my breath, hoping we wouldn't find Phoebe standing in the front yard, making out with Uncle Pete.

The BMW was in the driveway, parked directly behind Phoebe's minivan, so close their bumpers were practically touching.

Mother Teresa saw them first. She let out a big St. Bernard bark.

"Shhhh," I hissed. I hunched down in my seat and closed my eyes, the way a preschool student might try to make herself invisible. "Come on, Michael, let's get out of here."

My brother ignored me and slowed to a crawl. I opened my eyes. Phoebe and Uncle Pete were standing in the front yard, shoulders practically touching. In front of them was a hedge of bridal wreath spirea whose flowers had mostly gone by, leaving only the occasional pop of white against spent brown blooms. Uncle Pete was holding big orange-handled clippers and Phoebe was gesturing with one hand to show him how low he should cut the hedge. She was also wearing a really short white skirt with turquoise espadrilles, and her legs appeared to have been spray tanned.

They were so focused on the hedge that I'm not sure either of them would have noticed us if Michael hadn't pulled into the driveway.

"Michael," I screamed as the front bumper of his 4Runner came way too close to the back bumper of the Z4. I covered my ears and waited for the crunch of impact. It never came. When we stopped moving, several inches of Michael's bumper hovered over Uncle Pete's, the way a dog puts his head on top of another dog's to show who's the alpha.

Mother Teresa buried her head in my neck.

Michael jammed the car into park and unbuckled his seatbelt.

"Don't you dare open that car door," I said, like that was going to work.

Michael jumped out.

"Get your hands off my clippers," he yelled.

Mother Teresa made a sound like a cross between a yawn and a sigh.

"I know, I know," I whispered. "Definitely not his best line."

I tried to decide whether my smartest move was to hide out in the car or jump into the fray. On the one hand, hiding out would be my preferred option. But on the other hand, the car door was wide open, so it really wasn't much of a choice.

My phone rang. I dug it out of my purse and checked the display. John.

I tapped the Answer button. "Hey," I whispered. "Can I call you back in about ten minutes?"

"Sure," he said.

I pushed the End button and put my cell back in my purse. "Okay, we're going in." I clicked open my door and slid out of the car. I opened the back door and reached for Mother Teresa's leash.

She almost bowled me over on her way out. She lumbered across her former front yard, dragging me with her. She stopped at the base of the spirea hedge for a long, luxurious pee right next to Uncle Pete's left foot.

"Good girl," I said.

"Michael," Phoebe was saying, "it's a hedge." Mother Teresa walked over and leaned into Phoebe's thigh. Phoebe reached down and patted her head.

"It's *my* hedge," Michael said. "I planted it and if it needs to be cut, *I'll* cut it and not this loser."

"Or we could go get a haircut," I said.

"It was here when we bought the house," Phoebe said.

Phoebe and Michael stared at each other.

"Cut the hedge, Peter," Phoebe said.

Mother Teresa slumped to the grass and buried her nose in her paws.

"You let this idiot touch my hedge," Michael said without taking his eyes off Phoebe, "and I won't give you permission to take the girls to Savannah."

Phoebe grabbed the clippers and hacked a big hunk right out of the center of the hedge. She stabbed the points of the clippers into the ground about an inch away from Michael's toes.

"Are you happy now?" she screamed as she ran for the house.

CHAPTER

Eleven

John wasn't waiting for me on the sidewalk in front of the Necrogamiac building holding two coffees from Starbucks. He wasn't even in the lobby.

When the elevator door opened, I expected him to magically appear and tell me that he'd come in early so he could get enough work done to spend the rest of the day with me. He'd say he was sorry he lost track of time. I'd respond that it could happen to anyone and assure him that I completely understood. I'd apologize again for forgetting to call him back last night. Apologies out of the way, we'd gaze at each other longingly as we rode the elevator back upstairs together.

It didn't happen. The only other passenger on the elevator was a youngish woman with light hair. And dark roots that appeared to be intentional as opposed to sloppy. She was sitting on the cushioned bench like she owned the place.

I smiled at her.

She smiled back. "Do we know each other?"

I squinted. She did look vaguely familiar. Or maybe she just looked like someone I wished I looked like. Long legs, tight black pencil skirt, high heels, short jacket, cute haircut, a smile that said *I'm sexy and I know it.*

The jacket and pants I'd thought were appropriately businesslike as well as moderately stylish when I put them on this morning turned dowdy on the spot. I resisted an urge to tell this perfect stranger that I had better clothes at home. And then to beg her to take me shopping immediately.

"Don't tell me," she said. "Tennis, right?"

"Um," I said. "Actually, I don't—"

She laughed an adorable laugh. "I know, Zumba! Back row, I see you when we turn around?"

A muffled buzzer went off. It sounded like a test of the Emergency Broadcast System. She dug her phone out of her purse and pushed a button. "Mom, listen, I can't talk about it right now. I'm in the middle of an important meeting."

I held up one hand and said, "It's fine," as if we really were in a meeting.

She ignored me. "Mom, listen, I mean it. Stop calling me at work. I'll call you one night this week. Or as soon as I can."

She hung up and rolled her eyes. "Mothers."

"Nice ring," I said, mostly to change the subject.

"It's called 'Mom Alert.' I'll email you the link if you want."

"That's okay," I said. A bell rang. For a moment I thought she had a call from someone else, but it was only the elevator stopping. The crisscross of brass doors opened.

"My floor already," she said. "I hate that." She reached out to keep the door from closing. "In my next life I'm going to be an elevator operator so I can ride this elevator all day long."

I took a quick glance around. It still looked like a five-star hotel room to me.

"It's pretty amazing," I said.

"I know, huh?" She stepped out of the elevator and leaned back in again. "It's my happy place. I like it so much I even use *elevator* as my password." She opened her eyes wide. "Oops, you're not an identity thief or anything, are you?"

I laughed. "Nope. Sometimes I'm not even sure I *have* an identity."

"Good to hear. Oh, if you ever get the chance to practically spend the night in there, totally do it. It's like the most romantic place ever."

We were seated in a circle on a brick courtyard tucked behind the Necrogamiac building. Freshly planted petunias and salvia and feathery asparagus ferns filled ancient-looking urns and gave the court-yard a stately, formal feel. A distressed wooden coffin filled with daylilies was an unmistakable holdover from the building's funeral parlor days. A huge ultra-modern fountain, cement and square, was all sleek contrast and took over one corner of the courtyard. Water poured down the side of the fountain and crashed onto a river rock base, muffling the sound of traffic.

I'd strategically seated us as far away from the fountain as possible, and hoped none of the Gamiacs happened to be packing squirt guns.

I pulled a red drawstring pouch out of my enormous shoulder bag, careful not to dislodge any of the items I'd packed for an overnight with John Anderson. Last night, after finally dragging Michael away from harassing Phoebe, I'd put down my foot and insisted he get a quick haircut. Then we'd rushed back to our family home for Sunday dinner.

On the way back to my house after dinner I stopped by Bayberry Preschool to borrow a few things from my classroom for today. By the time I'd helped Michael get Annie and Lainie and Mother Teresa settled in on the air mattress in my former master bedroom-slash-office, picked out an outfit to wear, and brushed my teeth, I was exhausted. I conked out almost as soon as I crawled into bed.

I'd completely forgotten about John's call until I woke up this morning. I called him right away to apologize, but his cell rang four times and then went to voicemail. "Hey," I said, "I'm really sorry I forgot to call you back last night. I'll tell you all about it when I see you. Okay, well, bye."

The glint of sunlight on a cell phone caught my eye, bringing me back to the courtyard. One of the students, his hoodie pulled low over his forehead to block the sun, had pulled the sleeves of his sweatshirt down over his hands to camouflage his phone. His thumbs were going a mile a minute.

"Excuse me," I said. "Timothy?"

"That's Timmy," the boy who needed to brush said. "I'm Timothy."

"And that's Tim," the girl next to me said, pointing to the nose picker. I handed him a tissue.

I made a mental note to bring nametags next time. I'd posted a simple assignment for them (go outside once a day with someone else in the group) in a private work chat room after our first meeting and found it much easier to tell them all apart by their IDs: RavenSureSong, ObscureEssence, DarkShadow, ObsidianDream . . ..

Timmy's thumbs were still dancing away. I cleared my throat and held out my hand. "I'll take that. You can pick it up at the end of the session, Timmy. And let me remind you all that this is an electronics-free zone."

"Well, that sucks," Timmy said, but he handed over his phone.

I tucked it under a corner of my shoulder bag, hoping out of sight would, in fact, be out of mind. I rolled down the sides of the drawstring pouch so the contents were revealed.

The chorus of *cool* and *dude* and *off the hinges* that followed was music to my ears.

I gestured to the contents. "Choose a finger pup-pet."

They were like new Gamiacs. As soon as their index fingers were covered, they all started actually socializing. The girl with a blank stare and a magenta streak in her hair, who was either Megan or one of the Caitlins, put on a Bo-Peep puppet with a big lacy bonnet and a long wooden shepherd's staff.

"Boohoo," she said in a girly voice. "Has anybody seen my littlest lamb? She's lost and doesn't know how to find her way home."

The nose picker, who was seated next to her, slid his picking finger into a bright green tortoise puppet. I made a mental note to spray all the puppets thoroughly with Lysol before I returned them to Bayberry. "I'll help you, Bo-Peep," he said in a deep, manly voice. "I might be slow, but I won't give up until your littlest lamb is home safe and sound."

A good teacher knows when to stay out of things.

Cinderella and Pinocchio perched on index fingers and faced each other.

"I hate my nose," Pinocchio said.

"It's not that bad," Cinderella said. "Hey, do these rags make my stomach look fat?"

"Not really," Pinocchio said. "Plus all that sweeping probably works practically as good as iFit."

I felt a tap on my shoulder. When I turned around, a tiny Prince Charming handed me a pink petunia. Above the prince, Timothy's eyes met mine.

"Why, thank you so much, kind sir," I said. "But I think you might want to give that to another puppet."

A cloud of hurt passed over his face. "It was for you," he mumbled.

This was a new wrinkle, and yet not so new. As a preschool teacher, I'd had my share of marriage proposals from three-year-old boys, as well as the occasional three-year-old girl.

I reached for the flower and smiled a teachery smile at Timothy, warm and nurturing, but not at all crushworthy. He turned and stomped off in the direction of Cinderella, still holding the flower.

"Quack-quack-quack." Across the courtyard, the ugly duckling ruffled its feathers.

"Breakfast!" the red fox yelled as it lunged for the ugly duckling's neck.

The ugly duckling's puppeteer jerked the ugly duckling away. "You frackin' ass quack," the ugly duckling said. The red fox dove for its neck again.

It was time to redirect. I held up one hand. "Freeze," I said.

They froze.

I waited a moment to make sure I had their attention.

"I want you to go around the circle and count off by twos." I nodded at the girl holding Bo-Peep.

"One," she said.

"Two," Bo-Peep said.

I didn't have to be a math whiz to know counting off wasn't going to work if the ones and the twos were attached to each another. "Okay," I said, "let's try this. You and your puppet will share a number. I'll tap you on the head and give it to you, so all you have to remember is whether you and your puppet are a one or a two. Got it?"

Nobody said otherwise, so I walked around the circle and tapped the students on the head, alternating ones and twos. If this didn't work, I figured we could just segue into a quick game of duck-duck-goose.

"Now," I continued, "I want all the ones to stand up and take three giant steps to an unoccupied space on this courtyard."

A hand shot up. "Us or the puppets?"

"Both of you," I said.

"So, that's like six steps, right?" somebody said.

And I'd thought preschoolers had their challenges. I let out a puff of air. "Sure. Six steps—three big ones and three tiny puppet ones."

They took their steps. I redirected a couple of them away from the fountain.

"Okay, when you hear this . . .." I pulled a tambourine out of my shoulder bag and shook it. "I want the twos to walk your puppet over to stand in front of a one puppet and ask it three questions."

"Can I play the tambourine instead?" the nose picker asked.

"Not today," I said.

"Okay, the first question is: *If you had three wishes, what would they be?* The second question is: *If you could be any kind of dog, what kind would you be and why?* And the third question is: *Where would you like to go for lunch today?*"

I jangled the tambourine. I watched as their puppets all partnered up with new puppets and asked their questions.

Even though a couple of them seemed to be speaking in accents straight from *Downton Abbey*, they made eye contact. They laughed. They took turns speaking.

I shook my tambourine. "Okay, now ones, it's your turn to ask the twos the same questions."

When they finished, I shook my tambourine again. "Twos, stay where you are. Ones, find a new puppet," I yelled.

They found new partners without a hitch. They were fully engaged now, and as a teacher there is nothing better than seeing an activity take on a life of its own. The buzz of laughter and conversation blended with the crashing of the water in the fountain and the background roar of the traffic.

Scratch the surface and the Gamiacs were like lumps of clay, soft and malleable. Maybe deep down inside we were all still in our formative years. Maybe it was never too late for any of us to change.

CHAPTER

Twelve

The door to John's office was closed.

I slipped a dog puppet over my index finger and knocked.

There was a beat of silence, followed by a business-like "come in."

I opened the door a crack and wiggled my finger puppet through it. "Ruh-oh," I said in my best imitation of Scooby Doo. "You're mad at me because I didn't call you back last night, right?"

I jumped as the door swung open to reveal the woman from the elevator smiling at me from about a foot away. Her teeth were flawless.

"Hey," she said. "You again. I'm Keli. With one *l*. And an *i*."

"Sarah. One *r*. One *h*." I shook my hand like a tambourine. "And one puppet."

"I love puppets. Except for the kind with the strings."

"Marionettes," I said.

"That's a cute name," she said. "Mine was Flossie. Like dental floss. But I think I gave her the name after I got rid of her." She turned to look over her shoulder. "What year was dental floss invented, Johnny?"

She flipped her hair as she turned to him. John Anderson shrugged and shook his head.

"He'll think of it. He knows everything." Keli giggled. "He reads every big boring book he can get his hands on. And don't ever get him talking about old pinball machines." She crossed her eyes and somehow managed to still look adorable.

I didn't know where to look, so I focused on the puppet. You knew what you were getting with a puppet.

"Hey," Keli with one *l* and an *i* said. "I've got an idea. Let's go out to lunch. Or we could work first and then have drinks. There's a new bistro down the street with super cute guys."

When I realized she was talking to me, I gave John a quick glance, but he was busy rearranging some mechanical pencils in a holder on his desk. "Thanks so much," I said, "but I think I might already have plans."

Keli flipped her hair and looked over her shoulder again. "Johnny?"

He glanced up. "Thanks, but I've already met my quota of super cute guys for the week."

Keli giggled. "Actually, I think I might already have plans, too. Maybe they're the same plans and we'll see each other there. Or we can do it next time."

The Mom Alert buzzer went off on her phone. She sighed, reached into her purse, made it stop.

She turned back to me. "It could be the grocery store. Do you shop at the Trader Joe's down the street from my tennis lessons?"

"Possibly," I said. "Hey, don't you think you should have answered that? It might be important."

She rolled her eyes. "With my mother, it's never important. Wait, I completely forgot I brought a present for my boyfriend."

John Anderson and I looked at each other across the long expanse of quiet office. I swallowed back another *ruh-oh*.

Keli pulled a professionally wrapped present out of her purse, stretched sexily as she handed it to him.

"Thank you," John said.

"You're welcome. I hope the big guy likes it."

For a split second half of my brain thought Keli was referring to John's penis. This was the half that wasn't still trying to figure out *boyfriend*. In my defense, I'd grown up with three brothers who all had names for their penises. If you put *the big guy* next to *Duckie* or *Mr. Murphy*, it wouldn't even stand out all that much.

"Uh-oh," Keli said. "I just remembered I have lunch plans. Maybe I'll see you there."

"Thanks again," John said as he closed the door behind her.

Silence filled the room.

"The big guy?" I said casually.

John shrugged. "What can I say? The two of them have a bit of a love fest going on."

"Excuse me?"

"They've only met a few times, but she's always buying him little presents."

Presents? What do you even buy for a penis? A scarf? Or maybe some variation on those knitted nose warmers from the '80s?

John put the package next to his messenger bag. "I guess I'd better wait and let Horatio open it."

"Horatio," I repeated.

"Seriously?" John Anderson said as we strolled down the street. "You did speed dating with puppets?"

"Ha," I said. "Genius, if I do say so myself. But the finger puppets were your idea, so I'm willing to split the credit right down the middle. Anyway, we were a bit short on girls, but I don't think anybody really noticed. And it was actually more like speed pre-dating, though I'm happy to report that lunch plans were in fact made by the end of the session."

It was a gray murky day. The temperature was climbing and the air was sticky and getting stickier. John and I walked toward the restaurants that clumped around the square. We were going through all the conversational motions, but we didn't hold hands. Awkwardness hung over us like a rain cloud threatening to let loose any minute. Had my not calling him back last night made him pull away from me? Or maybe it was Keli. I wasn't stupid. I mean, what woman buys presents for a guy's dog unless she has ulterior motives? She was too young for him. I hoped he knew that. And at the risk of being unkind, my first impression was that she wasn't the brightest crayon in the box.

I stopped to swing my shoulder bag up a little higher on my shoulder. It seemed way too big today, like a neon billboard flashing: *Toiletries inside! And a fresh change of underwear!* The thing about being in the city without a car was that you had to carry everything with you. If I were back in the 'burbs where I belonged, my car would be close by and my bag would be in it. That way if it turned out I didn't actually need it for an overnight, no one would have to know I'd even brought it with me. A car was a sidekick, always waiting nearby, Tonto to your Lone Ranger. A car was a security blanket. The city separated you from it, exposed you, made you vulnerable.

"Here, let me take that." When John reached for my shoulder bag, our hands touched and sparks flew. Whether the sparks were caused by static electricity or love or the uncertainty I'd been feeling since I watched Keli wiggle her butt out of John's office, I wasn't sure.

Our eyes met. He was such a nice guy. Sweet. Fun. Smart. Generous. Gainfully employed. Healthy as a horse. And far more patient than I had any right to expect him to be. I should have called him back last night. Actually, I shouldn't have. I should have talked to him when he called. I could have closed the door of Michael's 4Runner and had the conversation right there. Michael was a grown man. He could have messed up things with Phoebe all by himself. And then once John and I had finished our conversation, I could have picked up the pieces. It wasn't like I had to turn my back on my brother in his time of need. I just had to balance things a little better.

"Hey," I said. "Do you want to skip the restaurant and just grab a pizza and take it back to your place?"

"It tastes so much better this way," I said. I reached across John's naked body for another piece of pizza.

He laughed. "It's all about working up an appetite. Red pepper flakes?"

"No thanks. You were hot enough."

He laughed again, put the jar of red pepper flakes down on his bedside table, slid a little closer to me. It wasn't the world's best line, but it was pretty flirtatious if I did say so myself. In a relaxed, carefree kind of way. *Insouciant* came back to me from my college French class of a zillion years ago. *Sarah est une jeune fille insouciante.* Maybe I could find a way to slip it into the conversation. Although I guess I'd have to upgrade it from *Sarah is a carefree young girl* to *Sarah is a carefree no longer young woman.* I took a bite of my pizza, put it down on my paper plate on the bedside table. Reached for my seltzer.

Out of the corner of my eye I saw John glance over at his bedside clock.

"Am I boring you?" slipped out of my mouth. So much for carefree.

John sighed. "I was just thinking about Horatio. I'm sure he'll be fine though. He's usually at puppy play care later than this anyway."

I swallowed back my own sigh. Horatio was a dog. I loved dogs. Ergo, eventually I would come to love Horatio, too. Of course, it would be helpful if he'd stop trying to chew me to pieces, but I had skills. I'd worked with some difficult preschool students over the years, and come to think of it, some of them were biters, too. A combination of redirection, and firm, consistent time-outs usually did the trick. And just for the record, no matter how tempted you are and what the old wives' tales say, biting back doesn't work. It only reinforces the inappropriate behavior. And makes you look like an idiot.

I reached for my pizza and took another bite. Then I leaned over and hoisted my shoulder bag up onto the bed and started rummaging for the T-shirt and yoga pants I'd buried in there.

"Do you have somewhere you have to be?" John asked.

I smiled. "I was just thinking maybe we could go get Horatio."

His face lit up.

The sun had come out, and while there wasn't actually a breeze, leafy green trees lined the sidewalks and acted a little bit like beach umbrellas. The tall buildings created more shade. The sidewalks bustled with sweaty people who had places to go and things to do. Maybe they were picking up their dogs early today, too. Or even their kids.

"I've been doing some research," John said as we walked hand-in-hand to puppy play care, "and apparently Horatio sees you as a threat to his place in the pack."

"Interesting," I said. I'd had more than my share of parent-teacher conferences that went something like, "But Aubrey feels threatened when we try to tell her when to go to bed." I mean, come on, Aubrey is *three*. She doesn't even know what *threatened* means. She shouldn't get a vote on bedtime.

I chose my words carefully. "And I see the two of us as people and Horatio as a dog. Which means that essentially we're in two *different* packs."

John turned to look at me. "It doesn't work like that for a dog. There's one pack and it's all about the pecking order within that pack. You're either above Horatio or below him."

I stopped walking. I let go of John's hand and put my own hands on my hips. "And your preference would be?"

He grinned. "Relax. Obviously, he needs to accept that you're above him in terms of hierarchy."

I wiped the back of my hand across my forehead. "Well, that's a relief." I was kind of kidding and kind of not kidding.

"And he needs to know that it's not acceptable for him to challenge your superiority."

"I like the sound of that. Okay, so what do we do?"

He put his arm around my shoulders and we started walking again. "Well, according to everything I've read, walking is the most effective way to establish pack order."

I slid out from under John's arm and took a quick series of steps out ahead of him. I channeled Keli with one *l* and an *i* as I wiggled my hips, then executed a pretty respectable model's runway turn until I was facing him.

"Ta-*dah*," I said as I extended both arms, palms up. "See, I've totally got walking down. The trick is going to be to keep Horatio from attacking me *as* I walk."

CHAPTER

Thirteen

Dale Evans and Roy Rogers serenaded us with "Happy Trails to You" from outdoor speakers hidden somewhere up in the trees. John and I joined in as he held the gate open for me. Our voices sounded pretty good together.

Happytails Puppy Play Care seemed a lot like a Bayberry Preschool for dogs. Puppies barked like crazy and ran around all over the place. They rolled in the grass. They knocked one another over. The only thing they didn't do was cry and ask for Band-Aids to put on their boo-boos.

When I looked more closely, I realized *puppy* was actually a stretch for some of them. One black Lab racing around with a plastic squirrel in his mouth even had some gray whiskers embellishing his muzzle. This made me feel a little bit better about the age of some of the Bayberry kids, usually boys, whose parents didn't want them to head off to kindergarten until they were sure they were going to be the biggest and brightest in the class. Lorna and Gloria and I joked that if this trend continued, the preschool students would eventually be older than some of the more recently hired teacher assistants.

Happytails even had some of the same playground equipment as Bayberry. A tri-colored corgi pup with impossibly short legs dribbled an orange foam playground ball around like a soccer star. A golden retriever and a puppy of indeterminate origin pulled opposite ends of a purple-striped hula-hoop, both snarling dramatically. When the golden opened its mouth to bark, the other puppy raced off, bumping the enormous hula-hoop along beside her. Puppies ran and crawled and wiggled their way through the exact same foldable green nylon play tunnel my own students couldn't get enough of.

Horatio poked his head through the flap of a doggie door at the top of some cement stairs leading up to a building. He flew down the stairs and ran toward us, barking like a maniac, and then hurled himself at John.

When John bent down to greet him, Horatio covered his face in puppy kisses. I watched them, smiling until my face hurt. Then I tapped one foot for a while. I mean, how long does it take to say hello to a dog? I killed some more time looking around the fenced-in play area, wondering what kind of puppy I'd choose if I ever decided to commit to a four-legged someone of my own. A dog is a big responsibility. At least with a husband, he can trade you in for a chatty younger woman with most of her eggs still in place. When a dog is over you, it can't just sneak off to go looking for a new owner. There are leash laws.

A woman wearing a Happytails T-shirt waved as she walked in our direction. Her wiry red curls, short forehead, and long nose made her look remarkably like a cocker spaniel. When she handed Horatio's leash to John, it finally broke up their love fest.

"Who was a good doggie today?" she said it a high-pitched, goofy voice as she bent down to scratch Horatio's chest. "Were *you* a good doggie today?"

Horatio looked up at her adoringly. Before John could introduce us, Cocker Spaniel Lady ran off to rescue a big mixed breed puppy with floppy ears that had been backed into a corner by a yappy little ball of strawberry blond fluff I was pretty sure was part Pomeranian.

John waited until we got to the sidewalk to hand me the leash. Horatio looked up, as if noticing me for the first time. He growled, low and mean.

"Good boy," John said, like wishing could make it so.

Horatio wagged his tail.

"Good boy," I echoed. I didn't believe it for a second, so I reached my non-leash-holding hand behind my back and crossed my fingers as I said it.

Horatio lunged at me with a burst of speed from his greyhound genes. Then he tried to separate my hand from the leash like a Yorkie gone wild.

I threw my end of the leash at John. It dropped to the sidewalk, short of its mark.

Horatio darted down the sidewalk like a rocket.

I gasped.

John took off after Horatio. He executed a super hero lunge and managed to land on the leash with both feet.

"Sorry," I said, once I'd caught up to them.

"I know you are," John said, "but it's a busy street. I don't even want to think about what could have happened to him."

"But he attacked me," I said. I looked down at my hand, hoping for blood.

"He didn't attack you. If he attacked you, you'd know it."

John and I looked at each other. I wanted to stamp my foot, take my toys and go home. I had a funny feeling John wanted me to do the same thing.

Horatio wagged his tail in triumph.

Horatio gloated and led the way while John and I walked quietly behind him. We turned off the busier main road a few blocks from his condo. Then we cut down an alley.

"Where are we going?" I asked. I didn't think Horatio would be able to talk John into dragging me down a dark alley so he could do away with me, but it never hurt to ask.

"We're approaching the condo from another direction," John said.

"Okay," I said, as if that made sense.

"It's important for Horatio to think that he has no choice but to follow you into uncharted territory."

I wanted to explain that this was uncharted territory for me, too. Dogs loved me. Kids loved me. Basically, everybody loved me. Well, not everybody, but there was enough of a consensus that I shouldn't have to feel like a pariah just because one poorly behaved puppy had it in for me. I mean, how many people loved Horatio? As far as I could tell, only one: John Anderson. Maybe two if you counted Cocker Spaniel Lady, but it was her *job* to love him. Okay, three if you counted Keli.

Could you actually lose a guy to another woman because his *dog* liked her better? It seemed far-fetched. Ha. Far-*fetched*. I smiled at my accidental dog pun. I'd have to remember to write it down so I could try it out on John when things were a bit less stressful.

The alley turned out to be fairly well lit. It led us to a quiet side street. There was nobody else in sight on the sidewalk and practically the only cars on the street were parked. I still didn't want to take the leash again. I could tell John wasn't quite sure he wanted to trust me with it either.

What I really wanted was a do-over. Not of John handing me Horatio's leash as we left Happytails, and me actually hanging onto it this time. Not even to being back in bed, surrounded by pizza crusts, when instead of suggesting we pick up Horatio early, I'd just keep my big fat mouth shut.

If only we could rewind all the way back to just before John got Horatio. I remembered it so clearly. We
were at the holiday symphony, standing in the little
foyer behind the first balcony, checking up on my father and taking a little break from the rest of my family. Every relationship that moves forward has that first
big turning point, and this was ours. We'd just finished
a sweet, optimistic kiss, and we'd decided we were going to try to make things work.

And then John mentioned that Clementine, the per-
sonality-challenged Yorkie that lived in his building,
had just had puppies. He was thinking of getting one.
He wanted to run it by me first.

This time I'd say, not yet. Let's figure out how to
become our own pack first. Maybe quit our jobs, move
to a deserted island, or a place where we don't speak
the language, where we don't have to decide whether to
be city mice or country mice. Where my family can't
change your name, where your lack of family doesn't
make me feel self-conscious about my surplus. Where
we don't get so tangled up in the details of our lives
that we start to forget the crazy wonderful miracle of
finding each other at all. And this time we really would
put all our focus on trying to make it work.

John stopped walking. "Okay, I'm going to hand you
the leash now, and I want you to hold on tight and
make sure Horatio stays behind you all the way back to
the condo."

Horatio and I looked at each other.

"In a nutshell," John continued, "the trick is that
you've got to own it. Shoulders back. Head up. No ten-

sion in the leash because Horatio might interpret it as fear or doubt."

"No fear, no doubt, no worries," I said. "We got this. Right, little guy?"

Horatio let out a bratty growl. I wondered if I could bribe his mother into taking him back. John reached down to pat him, which it seemed to me was only reinforcing his penchant for bullying.

John tore himself away from Horatio to look at me. "Don't forget, you've got to show him that you're completely confident he'll follow you anywhere."

"Should I blow in his ear first?"

"Excuse me?"

"Never mind. Old joke."

John didn't even smile. "Whatever you do, don't let him pull in front of you."

I threw my shoulders back and lifted my head up. "Just let him try."

John handed me Horatio's leash. Actually he wrapped it around my wrist twice and then helped me thread my hand through the loop. Then he made sure I was gripping it hard enough to turn my fist purple. I was no expert, but it seemed to me that if Horatio tried to take off, a broken wrist was a real possibility. I had a quick scary image of my hand dangling uselessly from a mangled wrist and John saying *Don't be ridiculous. If he wanted to break your wrist, you'd know it.*

"Ready?" John asked.

I swallowed. "Ready as I'll ever be."

John walked ahead of us.

"Heel," I said when Horatio tried to take off after him. I threw my shoulders back, attempted to keep the leash tension-free, which is a hard thing to do when a dog is trying to leave you in the dust.

I took two steps forward. Horatio pulled in front of me.

"Heel," I said again. I yanked him back. I took another two steps. Horatio surged ahead.

I pulled him back again.

Two steps forward.

Yank.

Release.

Two steps forward.

Yank.

Release.

Rinse. Repeat.

I had my doubts, but we eventually made it all the way to John's condo. John pushed himself off the front steps, where he'd been waiting for us. He held the door open. "Make sure you walk through the door first," he said. "That's key."

I managed to get one foot in the doorway first. Horatio jumped over my foot and darted in front of me. He made a beeline for the stairs.

Unfortunately, his leash was still attached to my wrist.

Fourteen

"So then what happened?" Lorna asked.

It was the first leg of our annual spending of the end-of-the-year teacher gift certificates. Certificates to nail salons outnumbered local restaurants two to one this year, perhaps because of the recent opening of a new Marshbury manicure place called In Good Hands. It was a lovely thought that the parents of our students believed they were in good hands, but it could just as easily have been symbolic of the fact that, once again, the Bayberry teachers had spent an entire school year working their fingers to the bone.

I sighed and adjusted the Ace bandage on my wrist. "Well, let's just say we went straight from romance to R.I.C.E."

"You did the right thing," Gloria said. "You have to give props to all those painful first aid classes they force us to take every year. Gotta love R.I.C.E.—rest, ice, compression and elevation will do it every time." She reached over from her pedicure chair to elevate my hand a little higher. "And as soon as we move on to drinks, I fully intend to donate my ice cubes to the cause, honey."

"You're too kind," I said.

Lorna leaned over and patted my good hand. "I think you should have made dog lover take you to the hospital, just for the drama of it. And to shame that nasty little mutt of his, of course."

"He's not nasty," I said. "Just nasty to me."

"Which one?" Gloria said. "The dog or the dog lover?"

"The dog," I said. "The dog lover, I mean, *John* is a little bit like one of those parents whose kids can do no wrong though. If he had to choose between the two of us, I'm not sure I'd put my money on me."

Our pedicure chairs were three in a row, set up on a tiled platform raised slightly higher than our footbaths. Our three pedicurists sat on stools below us, focused on our feet and completely ignoring the rest of us. They talked amongst themselves, atonal syllables bouncing all over the place, in a language I couldn't place, though occasionally I'd recognize something like *Disney World*. I glanced around the salon, hoping for a flag I could identify from our Flags Around the World unit at school.

"Clearly, you need to put him on a program," Lorna said.

I turned in her direction, careful not to move my toes or my wrist. "Which one?"

Lorna twisted in my direction. Her pedicurist yanked her back by the ankle. "Ouch. The dog. What's his name . . . Hamlet."

"Horatio," I said.

"Nothing pretentious there," Lorna said.

"Be nice," Gloria said. "It's the ultimate loyalty name. Remember, Horatio was willing to drink the rest of the poisoned drink that was meant for Hamlet?"

I shook my head. "*This* Horatio would find a way to make sure I got the poison."

"Maybe the mutt's trying to beat you down until you pull an Ophelia," Lorna said.

"Never happen," I said. "Too many swimming lessons in my formative years. Plus, I'm a floater."

Lorna cleared her throat. "As I was saying before we went all Shakespeare, what you need to do is put the canine on a behavior mod program." She lowered her voice almost to a whisper. "Remember Spartacus Mac-Leish from, what, three years ago?"

Gloria burst out laughing.

"Cut it out," I said. "Sparty was a good kid. At least eventually."

"*Sure* he was," Lorna said. "All it took was getting him to stop biting the other kids, plus that poor guinea pig."

"And," Gloria said, "let's not forget peeing in the sandbox—"

"Give him a break," I said. "He had a cat at home. He thought it was the boys' bathroom."

"*Riiiight*," Gloria said. "His parents might have bought that line, but you're better than that, honey."

"Anyway," Lorna said. "Remember, we finally got all the adults in the building to watch him nonstop, and every time he'd accidently do something right, we'd praise the living shit out of him."

"Ohmigod," I said. "Remember how confused he was? After a while, he couldn't tell bad from good and he just did what we told him to."

Across from us, a woman peeked over her magazine at us. Lorna looked at me. I looked at Gloria.

Lorna cleared her throat. "Doesn't it just make all the hard work and endless dedication worthwhile when a child's internal monitor clicks into place?" she said loudly. "There is nothing more rewarding then sending a future good citizen out into the world."

"Here, here," Gloria said.

We were quiet after that. I watched my pedicurist paint a clear topcoat over my summery pink toenails. Then she reached for a sample board and held it out to me.

"Decal or not?" she said.

I wasn't a decal kind of girl, but I took the board from her anyway, just to be polite. Tucked in the middle of shooting stars and leopard spots and paisleys and posies was the perfect little dog print.

I pointed. "I'll have that one, please. Actually, I think I'll have ten of them."

I sipped a cup of herbal tea that tasted like freshly mowed grass while I waited for Lorna and Gloria to come out of their massage rooms. My own massage had been a disappointment. Halfhearted, to say the least, and made more awkward by the fact that my ace-bandaged wrist was propped up on a pillow. Clearly Stefan did not have the soul of a masseuse. He was going through a tough time with his partner though, so I probably needed to cut him some slack. They were almost definitely finished for sure this time, and not only would they have to figure out who got to keep their apartment, but they also owned a time share together in Las Vegas they'd have to unload.

"Couldn't you just share it?" I asked. Stefan was pounding my back, so it came out with extra syllables.

"Oh, he'd like that all right." He dragged the heels of his hands down either side of my spine, added some more beach rose massage oil, dragged them again.

"And he has the nerve, the *nerve*, to say this is all my fault."

I didn't say anything.

"Do you want to know *why*?"

I let out a soft, noncommittal sound, while I wondered what it was about me that caused perfect strangers to overshare their personal lives. Kind eyes? Broad shoulders? A visible masochistic streak running, skunk-like, down the center of my back?

My eyes were closed and I was trying to pretend I was walking through a field of lavender, maybe in Pro-

vence, without a care in the world. *Sarah est une jeune
fille insouciante.* I mouthed the words over and over
like a mantra to try to tune out Stefan. When that
didn't work, I switched to the old dishwashing deter-
gent commercial. *Calgon, take me away. Calgon, take
me away.*

"Because I like to go out, and he likes to stay in. Because I like to make plans and he likes to go with the
flow. Because I like to travel and he's a freakin' home-
body. Which means. Stay home. And do. Nothing."

"Ouch," I said as Stefan found a sore spot behind my
right shoulder.

"Stress," he said.

Yours or mine? I wanted to ask, but I didn't. Instead
I spent the rest of my massage wondering, not for the
first time, how anybody ever stayed with anybody and
how they somehow, against all odds, managed to make
it work.

"Enough with the inner and outer fluffification,"
Lorna said as we all flipped through our gift certificates. "Let's eat."

I propped my elbow on the little picnic table we'd
commandeered. It was strategically located between
the salty breeze off the harbor and a packed row of waterfront restaurants.

I struggled to place some gift certificates on the table with my left hand. Ambidextrous I was not. "I've

got a pair of Oceanside Taverns and a pair of Seaside Seafoods. And I'm happy to share."

"Either works for me," Gloria said. "I've got one of each."

"Three of a kind," Lorna yelled as she slapped three Oceanside Taverns on the table. "I win!"

"Good job, honey," Gloria said. I was pretty sure Gloria praised everyone she ran into all day long, like a switch she couldn't turn off. The clerk at the grocery store when he gave her the right change, the UPS delivery person who managed to find her address. *Good job, honey*, I imagined her saying to her husband after they finished having sex.

"What's so funny?" Gloria asked

"Not a thing," I said. "Okay, Oceanside Tavern it is."

Lorna was still flipping through her certificates. "Teacher Depot? Like I don't spend enough of my own money on school supplies as it is. Now you're going to give me a *gift* that I have to spend on your kid?"

"I got one, too," Gloria said. "But I'm okay with it. I can always spend it on my own kids." Gloria taught all day and then went home to her four kids. Sometimes I wondered how she did it and was relieved I didn't have to. Sometimes I was simply jealous that she had kids and I didn't.

Lorna waved her Teacher Depot certificate in Gloria's direction. "Here, take mine. On principle alone." Lorna's kids were grown and gone. Her après school life seemed to consist of trying to get her husband,

Mattress Man, to put down the remote and get out of bed.

I handed Gloria a gift certificate to an ice cream place called Sprinkles. "Allow me to contribute to your kids' dentist bills."

Lorna flipped over another gift certificate. "A knitting store? Like I have time to knit. It's beach season."

"Maybe you can buy a finished sweater." I squinted until I could read the amount upside down. "Or at least a headband."

"Good point," Lorna said. "And last year they gave me a mug, so I guess it's a step up. I mean, come on, they have his and her Land Rovers and their nanny makes better money than I do. And don't think I didn't trick her into telling me."

"Oh," I said. "All these gift certificates just reminded me. There's this woman at John's office who gave him a present for 'the big guy'."

"She gave him a present for his penis?" Lorna said.

"Thank you," I said.

"Penis presents are not okay," Gloria said.

"Agreed," I said. "But it turned out to be a doggie painting kit for Horatio. Get this: you sprinkle some paint on the paper, cover it with this plastic thing, and let the dog walk all over it and, *voila*, you have a canine masterpiece." I shook my head. "Pathetic."

"What kind of plastic thing?" Lorna said. "I mean, maybe we could adapt it for the classroom. Can you imagine how much easier the school year would be if we didn't spend half of it scrubbing paint off the kids?"

"Ooh," Gloria said. "Here you go, honey." She handed me a gift certificate to Foofoo's Four Footed Bakery. "Not that I think you have anything to worry about."

"Yeah," Lorna said. "But just to be on the safe side, next time you go over there, you might want to dab some peanut butter on your ankles."

Fifteen

I was sitting on my couch, my father and my brother Michael on either side of me, Mother Teresa draped across our feet like a furry blanket. We were all wiggling our toes gently, rocking her to sleep.

"Thanks for bringing dinner, Dad," I said.

"The pleasure was undeniably mine." He reached over and patted me on top of the head. "And might I add, my darlin' daughter, you heated it to perfection."

"Thanks." I sighed. "I can't believe that was the last casserole."

"You didn't make it?" Michael said. "And here you had me almost convinced you could actually cook."

"Spaghetti pie?" I said. "Like I could pull that off."

Michael reached for his phone on the coffee table and checked for messages. It was at least the third time in the last five minutes.

"I don't trust those namby-pamby little things," my father said. "I'm no telephone operator, but it seems to me that when you cut off the wires, you've got to figure some of the messages are going to get derailed before they reach their final destination."

"Ohmigod," I said. "Remember that first cordless phone we had? The beige one shaped like a brick with the long antenna? It took two hands to hold it, and it picked up all the neighbors' conversations?"

My father shook his head. "I got a juicy earful or two from across the street one time when the mister got a ring on the ting-a-ling, I'll tell you. Nice people, but a wee bit too hot roddy for the likes of your mother and me."

Michael just shook his head and checked his phone again. Phoebe and the girls had been in Savannah for close to a week, and other than one text from Phoebe to say they'd landed safely, and a phone call from the Savannah/Hilton Head airport from the girls right after that, there'd been radio silence.

"No news is good news," I said. "If Annie and Lainie were bored, you know they'd be calling you every five minutes. Promise me you won't leave another message until tomorrow, okay? Once a day to say I love you is enough. After that, it gets a little creepy."

"I'm not an idiot." Michael tossed his phone and it landed with a *thunk* on the coffee table. "But if I find

out that bitch is keeping my daughters from calling
me—"

"Michael Aloysious Hurlihy," my father boomed.
Over the years, our father had been known to bungle
our first names as often as not. *CarolChristineSarah*,
he'd say, rattling off my sisters' names as a way to get
to mine. *ChristineSarahCarol. JohnnnyBillyMichael.*
He'd given up entirely on trying to come up with our
middle names. He used middle names only when he was
angry or to make a point. The boys were all *Aloysious*
and the girls *Penelope*. Even at my age, when I heard
Sarah Penelope Hurlihy, I knew I was in trouble.

Mother Teresa looked up groggily at the sound of
angry voices.

My father reached down to pat her as he yelled at
Michael. "That bitch is the mother of your children.
And married or not, you will treat her with the respect
she deserves and find a way to do right by those daughters of yours until death do you part."

Michael ran his hand through what was left of his
hair, then rubbed his eyes. "I know, Dad, I know."

"Phoebe would never try to keep the girls from calling you," I said. "She knows how much they love you.
It's going to be okay, Michael. You'll get through this
part and then you'll move on."

Michael shook his head. "God, I remember saying
almost the exact same thing to you when that asshole
husband of yours left."

"Michael Aloysious," my father said.

"Sorry," Michael said.

"It's okay, Dad," I said. "He *was* an asshole."

"There'll be no more trash talking." My father put his feet on the coffee table and crossed his ankles. "And do not for one minute think that either one of you is too old to have your mouth washed out with a bar of Irish Spring."

"Ha," I said. "Remember when you and Mom were on that swear jar kick? I think we filled it to the top with quarters in like two weeks."

Michael put his feet on the coffee table and crossed his ankles exactly like our dad. Neither of them was wearing socks with their boat shoes, which I was pretty sure, by my niece Siobhan's assessment at least, meant that they were both total date bait.

"What I'd really like to know," Michael said, "is why you and I are the only ones in the family who can't hold a marriage together. What's wrong with us?"

"Thanks," I said. "I needed that."

"'Tis not the way to look at it, Mikey boy," my father said. *'Tis* at the beginning of a sentence was one of my father's tricks for weighting it with historical significance by sounding like one of his own ancestors and waxing philosophical at the same time. "You children are still four for six in the marriage department, and our very own Sunday newspaper pronounced the national divorce average as a smidge over fifty-fifty. Hence, the proper way to see it is that statistically our family is significantly ahead of the curve." *Hence* was another one of my father's trick words.

"Gee, thanks, Dad." Michael said. "I feel better already."

"Yeah, no kidding." I put my feet up on the coffee table, too, my dog print toes a nice contrast to their boat shoes. "Now you've got me worrying about which Hurlihy marriage is going to bite the dust next."

Michael reached for the remote, turned on the TV. *Gilligan's Island: The Complete Third Season* was already in my DVD player, so all he had to do was click on the next episode.

The three of us sang along to the theme song. My father sounded a little bit like Frank Sinatra, but Michael and I weren't bad either, especially on our favorite line about the three-hour tour. It was simply amazing to me that you could go out for a sail and end up on an uncharted South Pacific island. I mean, why couldn't things like that happen to me? Although multiple boat collisions with my father at the helm in my childhood had left me feeling more comfortable on land than on sea. Plus, with my luck I'd get stranded with my family and the whole adventure would end up being just like the rest of my life.

Our singing woke up Mother Teresa again. She let out a beefy snort and wormed her head behind Michael's ankles. It was hard to tell whether she was trying to get more comfortable or to block out our singing.

"The Second Ginger Grant" started with a bang. Mary Ann and the rest of the crew were watching a scantily clad Ginger put on an island performance. Then Mary Ann hit her head.

"Oooph," my father said. "That's some smog in the noggin'."

I smiled. "Don't worry, Dad. I'm pretty sure she survives."

Sure enough, Mary Ann managed to get back up on her feet.

"Now she's cookin'." Apparently my father was going to do the whole play-by-play.

It turned out Mary Ann's fall has triggered a case of amnesia, which somehow makes her think she's Ginger.

"Like she could ever be Ginger," Michael said. "There's only one Ginger."

"Ain't that the word from the bird," my father said. "I wouldn't mind watching some submarine races with that doll myself."

"Are you two *kidding* me?" I said. "Ginger tries too hard. I mean, who wears an evening gown on a deserted island? And that beauty mark of hers looks like a total fake to me."

They both turned to look at me.

"She's way too high maintenance," I said. "Mary Ann is much more naturally attractive."

Michael reached for his phone. "Don't have a cow, sis. Mary Ann makes a great coconut cream pie, I'll give her that."

"And that's no small thing," my father said. "Given our current casserole condition."

"Men," I said.

"Your mother," my father said, "had the uncanny ability to be all kinds of beautiful at once. And she could cook like there was no tomorrow."

Carol didn't knock. She just breezed in the way she always did, like she owned the place.

She walked right by us and turned off the TV.

"Hey," I said.

"We were watching that," Michael said.

"Can you get me a glass of water?" she asked me.

"Can you get me a glass of water, *please*?" I said.

Carol smiled and opened her eyes wide. "Pretty please with sugar on top?"

I pushed myself up from the couch and stepped over Mother Teresa.

Carol sat down in my place and opened her laptop.

"I can't believe you tricked me and stole my seat," I said. "Get your own water."

"Fine," she said. "Then you can pull up the online dating profiles I made for Dad and Michael."

A flashback to my own dating days hit me with such force that a shiver actually ran down my spine. I hightailed it out to the kitchen and poured Carol a big glass of water. While I was there, I took a moment to pour another glass for myself. And to drink it. I loaded my dishwasher and rinsed out the sink. Then I opened my refrigerator and started checking expiration dates and dumping things into the trash. After that, I organized what little was left until everything was pleasingly arranged on the shelves.

I still couldn't shake the flashback. And what was even worse was that a nagging thought had risen from the deep, dark, scary parts of my brain, and I couldn't seem to get it to go away again: How did you know whether you were staying with the person you were with because you really wanted to be with him, or only because you didn't want to have to go through all that painful looking all over again?

My cell phone was sitting on the kitchen counter. I grabbed it without thinking, woke it up. A new voicemail popped up. We must have drowned out the ring with our singing. I pushed Play. *Hi. It's me. John. I'm, um, checking in to see how you are and, well, to make sure your wrist is okay. And Horatio wanted me to be sure to tell you it was an accident. Scratch that last part. I know he can't talk. Listen, what I'm trying to say is that I felt we were on the right track all the way up until the tail end. Pun intended. Okay, maybe not. What I'm trying to say is that I think we should try it again right away. That way we can build on the progress we've made. Because I think we need to work things out between the two of you as soon as possible. Horatio isn't getting any younger. Ha. I guess none of us are. Okay, so I was thinking if you didn't have plans tonight, maybe the two of us would make the ride down. We could all walk the beach, pick up some fish and chips. Call me when you get this, okay?*

I stared at my phone, wondering what it would take to get only one of them to make the ride down.

"What the hell is taking you so long in there?" Carol yelled. "Are you digging the well?"

I sighed. I brought Carol her water, sat on the arm of the sofa next to my father. I carefully avoided looking at the computer screen. "Hey, Dad," I said. "What was that thing you just said about Mom? Tell Carol."

My father didn't seem to hear me. He was hunched over Carol's laptop. He pulled his index finger back and hit the mouse pad hard, like it was a typewriter key.

"Ooh-wee," he said, "How do you like them apples. It says here she's a holy woman and a woman of simplicity. Now wouldn't that be a lovely thing in a wife, Mikey boy?"

"Dad, she's a nun," Michael said. "You hit the wrong link."

Carol reached for the laptop. "Siobhan is doing a report on saints for CCD. I was helping her with the research."

"Wow," I said. "Siobhan is still going to catechism? Impressive."

Carol shrugged. "Not really. She only pretends to go and sneaks off with her friends to meet boys, exactly like we did at her age. Dennis and I just try to make it as painful as possible for her."

My father nodded. "Your mother and I used to play tag team. I'd drop her off on Main Street near the harbor with the younger kiddos, deliver the older ones to catechism class, then circle back around to her, park the car, and we'd close in and try to catch you in the act."

"Ha," Michael said. "Remember when you caught Johnny smoking a cigarette when he was supposed to be at CCD and he swallowed it whole?"

My father slapped his knee. "It was your mother's idea to convince him that smoke was still coming out of his ears at dinnertime. We found him out in the yard, drinking from the hose, at midnight."

Carol pulled up the actual online dating site, and started scrolling through picture after picture of women. I took a quick glance. A few Gingers, a few Mary Anns. Some self-proclaimed classy ladies. A few serious cases of over-PhotoShopping.

"Holy Toledo," my father said as he leaned forward to get a better look. "You can't find this on a Smith Corona."

After my father and Carol left, I said goodnight to Michael and Mother Teresa and went into my bedroom to call John back.

"Sorry I missed you earlier," I said, even though it wasn't entirely true.

"That's okay," he said. "Tomorrow's a new day."

"Let's hope."

"Just so you know, I'll be in a meeting when you get there to work with the Gamiacs, but I'm heading in early so I can leave with you when you're done."

"Thanks." Even though it was a pretty big hop, skip, and jump from where we were now to a shared life, the pattern we'd fallen into felt like we were at least moving in the right direction. If you factored out Horatio.

"So," John said in that hazy dazy lazy way we sometimes had of continuing a phone conversation just to keep hearing each other's voices. "Where do you want to go for lunch tomorrow?"

"I kind of like where we had it the last time," I said in my sexiest voice, which wasn't all that sexy, but it got the point across.

"Why, Sarah Hurlihy," John said in his own sexy voice, which wasn't half bad. "Are you trying to talk me into bed again?"

"You bet I am," I said. "And, I'm taking the Gamiacs out for an early lunch, so I can even pick up takeout for us while I'm there."

"Sounds like a plan. And Sarah, the message I left? I think we're close. It might not seem like it, but Horatio is just on the verge of accepting you. I can feel it."

I bit my tongue so I wouldn't say, *Couldn't we have one single solitary conversation that doesn't revolve around your dog?*

"What a coincidence," I said instead. "I'm right on the verge of accepting him, too."

CHAPTER

Sixteen

I couldn't wait to get to my session with the Gamiacs. I'd talked a restaurant right down the street into opening an hour early for lunch. We'd have the place all to ourselves. We could practice holding chairs for one another, putting napkins on our laps, choosing the right utensils and navigating them correctly, chewing with our mouths closed, waiting to speak until we'd swallowed our food.

I'd filled a bright yellow gift bag with little slips of paper, each with a conversation starter typed on it like an oversize fortune from a fortune cookie. *What is the last book you read and enjoyed? What do you wish you knew more about? What are your three favorite foods? Is that a new ____ you're wearing?* They might not even need them, but it was better to be prepared, and it was important to learn that expressing interest in the other person always made for good conversation. I'd explain to the Gamiacs that once they'd internalized a few of these questions, they'd never be at a loss for words in a social situation again.

I had the rest of the day completely worked out in my head, too. John and I would make mad, passionate love and then curl up on his bed with a nice sandwich. After that I'd challenge him to a pinball game to kill some time so we didn't pick up Horatio quite as early as last time, but still early enough to impress John with my willingness, no, my *determination* to win over the dog of his life. John was right—we weren't getting any younger—so the sooner we got the dog thing squared away, the sooner we could get on with the rest of our lives.

Once Horatio was back home, I'd bribe him with the Dog Biscuit in a Bag mix I'd picked up at FooFoo's Four Footed Bakery. It came complete with a little dog bone-shaped cookie cutter and a packet of sugar free frosting mix. All I had to do was add water and then I'd bake, barefoot, with my cute dog print toes on display. I wouldn't even need peanut butter on my ankles. The smell of baking doggie treats would reel him in, and by the time they were done, Horatio would be doggy putty in my hands. It was a recipe for success, equal parts Machiavellian and Pavlovian.

Last night my sleep was dotted with crazy, happy dreams. Running through a field of daisies with Horatio by my side. Attending a childbirth class with John and Horatio and Mother Teresa and my former husband, Kevin, and his chatty new wife, Nikki. It was hard to tell who was pregnant with what, but we were all okay with it.

I woke up rested and newly optimistic. I jumped in the shower and managed to get ready with enough time left over to make coffee *and* instant oatmeal for Michael and me.

Even though I'd fed him, Michael was grumpy and sullen the whole ride to Boston. I let him pout. I had to admit he was starting to exhaust me. Carol's dating intervention had fallen flat, too. While my father scrolled through online dating sites like a kid in a candy shop, Michael had alternated staring up at the ceiling with checking and rechecking his phone for messages.

"It doesn't *matter*," he'd said whenever my father pointed out a *sweet young filly* or Carol asked him to consider a potential match she'd identified. "All I want is Phoebe."

As we approached the corner where I jumped out of his car and onto the subway, I gathered my stuff together. "I know it's hard, Michael, but try to chill. The girls will be back tonight and you'll feel much better."

Michael didn't say anything. The light turned red and we slowed to a stop.

Call me if you need anything, I started to say. But then I just didn't. Carol and Christine had both promised to stop by my place to check on him. I was off duty. And, I mean, I had challenges of my own and it's not like Michael ever asked me how things were going in *my* life anymore.

"Thanks for the ride," I said. And then I slammed the car door behind me. Even though I still had a long subway trip ahead of me, I breathed a sigh of relief that I didn't have to spend this part of my commute with my brother.

When the elevator door opened, I pushed myself up from the upholstered bench and picked up the big blue net equipment bag again. It was a lot to lug on top of everything else I had with me, but I knew it would be worth it when I saw the Gamiacs' reactions. They'd be so excited they wouldn't be able to contain themselves. I had it all worked out. We'd stop at the little park we'd pass on the way to the restaurant and I'd introduce our first activity to them there.

Catch Your Name was a team-building game I'd learned a few years ago when my boss had dragged all the lead teachers to a summer conference. The way it worked was that everybody stood in a big circle, wearing nametags. Then the facilitator introduced one object, usually a beanbag or a tennis ball, and called out the name of someone in the circle, say Jane, and then threw the object to Jane. Jane would catch it, call out the name of another person anywhere in the circle, say Jim, and throw the object.

And so it would go, until everybody had a turn catching the object. Next, the facilitator would add another beanbag, and then another, all crisscrossing around the circle at the same time, requiring full engagement, enhancing coordination, and ultimately turning a circle of strangers into a cohesive team that knew everybody by name. And if instead of beanbags or balls you used a variety of crazy objects instead, you upped the fun factor by a gazillion percent.

As an activity, it was developmentally beyond pre-schoolers, but I'd loved it enough to amass my own collection of flying objects. The whole thing had been a big hit at the afterschool program Bayberry ran for older students, as well as not a few Hurlihy family cookouts.

The door to the conference room was open a crack. I couldn't see in, but the buzz of conversation trickling out was music to my ears. I juggled the equipment bag out of my way and gave the door a hip bump.

Tim was sitting on a conference table next to one of the Caitlins, laughing as if they were well on their way to becoming a couple. I took a moment to savor the magic I'd sparked. Instead of being glued to their computers like they usually were when I arrived, the rest of the Gamiacs were seated in chairs across from them, like an actual audience.

I saw the legs first. Long, bronzed legs that shimmered with some kind of cream or spray or gel that I'd probably never be able to apply evenly, assuming I could even figure out where you bought something like that. I mean, my own idea of a good leg day was remembering to shave both of them.

And the shoes. The nude leather shoes attached to those legs had sexy red spike heels so intimidatingly high I was practically getting a nosebleed just looking at them. I glanced down at my own pathetic little wedge sandals. My perky pink toenails studded with dog prints decals peeked out like I was twelve.

"That's not bad," Keli with one *l* and an *i* said, nodding her head at Tim and Caitlin. The rest of the Gamiacs were gathered around her like a fan club, absolutely hanging on her every word. She was every popular girl who had ever upstaged me, ignored me, outshined me.

"Lean a little closer when you say that, Tim," she continued, "and Caitlin, touch his hand lightly when you answer."

Tim cleared his throat and looked right at Caitlin. "Would you like to go to a movie?"

"I'd love to," Caitlin said. She touched his hand lightly and smiled. I fought an urge to take notes.

The Gamiacs burst into applause.

"It's a date," Keli yelled as she gave a cheerleadery fist pump. She giggled adorably and turned in my direction.

"Is that a rubber chicken?" she asked.

Okay, so I'd brought a rubber chicken. And a miniature toilet plunger, a stuffed green frog, a Slinky, a rubber ring, a rubber horseshoe, and a couple of Mother Teresa's toys that she hardly ever used anymore. I had nothing to be ashamed of. It was a great team building exercise, and the wildly imaginative items, *whimsical* if you would, added to it immensely.

Keli stuck to us like glue, shedding her skyscraper heels and sliding into a cute pair of ballet flats for the walk to the park. The Gamiacs glommed on to her and completely ignored me.

"I'm next, I'm next," one of the Caitlins yelled, practically skipping she was so ridiculously excited.

"Okay," Keli said. "Cut the hair, add some highlights, play up your eyes, lose the floods."

Caitlin looked down at her jeans. "These are floods?"

"The floodiest," Keli said. "Total highwaters. Think of it this way: short is good in leggings or pants that grip the leg, but anything wider needs length."

"Can you take me shopping?" both Caitlins and Megan said all at once.

"Not a problem," Keli said. "I shop daily."

The nose picker reached for his nose and then changed his mind just as I was about to hand him a tissue. "Can I go with you?" he asked Keli. "And are my pants okay?"

"Of course you can." She pointed a finger at his cargo pants, which had been working their way down his hips as we walked, revealing about a third of his plaid boxer shorts. "Don't let just anybody see your underwear, Tim. Make them work for it."

The Gamiacs burst out laughing. I swung my equipment bag over my shoulder and wiggled my way into a tiny space that had opened up next to Keli.

"Don't you have work to do?" I said.

She made a brushing motion with one hand. "Not really. I'm in HR. I just hire a bunch of people and then hang out until they need me to hire some more. The rest of the department does all the other stuff."

Keli's Mom Alert sounded again. She let out a dramatic sigh.

"You need to answer that," I said.

"You need to get some lotion on your feet," she said. "Some lip balm wouldn't hurt either. The dry and flaky look isn't working for you."

I looked down at my paw print-decaled toes.

Keli's phone went to voicemail. She reached into her purse and handed me a little plastic pouch filled with an orange blossom perfume stick, organic orange essence lip balm, and a travel-size tube of pure blood orange lotion.

"Keep it," she said. "I haven't even opened it."

"Thanks," I said. Part of me was insulted, but the other part thought maybe she wasn't so bad after all. As I tried out the lip balm, I wondered idly whether Keli's mom looked like an older version of Keli, maybe with lower heels and a slightly longer miniskirt. Or maybe she wore jeans and T-shirts and was warm and charming and, well, motherly.

Maybe she'd even remind me a tiny bit of my own mother in a way I couldn't quite put my finger on. Enough so that if I'd passed her on the street, she might have stayed with me like a ghost for the rest of the day as I tried to figure out the resemblance. The salt and pepper hair? The tiny overlap of her front teeth? The way she nodded her head at whomever was speaking—*keep it up, you're doing just fine*—like my mother used to.

Passing a woman on the street and being reminded of my mother still happened to me fairly often. Actually, to be totally honest, it was more than just being reminded of her. It was like feeling, just for a split second, that I'd found her again. It was as if my head knew she'd died, but my heart thought she was still in reach, just around the next corner.

I'd once casually asked my sister Carol if it ever happened to her. We were sitting in my living room, our feet on the coffee table, a few weeks after Kevin had moved out for good. A bag of Trader Joe's olive oil popcorn was all we'd been able to rustle up for dinner in my lonely little kitchen. We were washing it down with the bottle of champagne Kevin and I had planned to drink on our twenty-fifth wedding anniversary.

"This champagne sucks," Carol said. "It's a good thing you didn't stay married just for this."

"Funny," I said. "So funny I forgot to laugh." When I guzzled the rest of my glassful, the bubbles escaped into my nose. "Ouch."

Carol took a more delicate sip from Kevin's honeymoon flute. "I can feel Mom cheering you on from heaven."

I smiled. "What's she saying?"

"It's about time you got rid of that asshole, honey."

I coughed and swallowed at the same time. More bubbles burned my nose.

"You are so going to get your mouth washed out with soap for that," I managed to croak.

Carol gave me a quick pat on the back with one hand as she poured the rest of the champagne with the other. Having four kids had left her permanently incapable of doing one thing at a time.

"Do you ever think you see her?" I whispered. "You know, think you see Mom?"

Carol leaned back and put her feet up again. "All the time. I see her in the look Siobhan gives me when she's not buying what I'm telling her. I see her in Trevor, the way he presses the tip of his tongue into his upper lip when he's concentrating. Remember how she always used to do that when she put on her mascara?"

I closed my eyes and tried to conjure up a picture of my mother putting on her mascara. I couldn't. It was gone, along with the all the other pieces of her I'd lost—her laugh, her sneeze, her yawn—more of her gone every day, every week, every year.

I tilted my head back so my tears would stay where they belonged. "I meant really see her. You know, like on the street?"

"Yeah," Carol said. "Sometimes. Once I followed this woman halfway across the mall parking garage, up and down the rows of cars, just to get a look at her face. She had Mom's hair and the same long tan belted raincoat, you know, the one Christine got."

"What happened?"

"She finally stopped at her car, and I was just about to yell 'excuse me' to get her to turn. Suddenly she whipped around and pointed this can of Mace at me."

"Ha. But did she look like Mom?"

"Not really. Mom was way better looking." Carol reached for her glass. "Come on, chug the rest and let's do this."

I picked up my honeymoon glass for the last time, drank it dry, waited for the bubbles to stop tickling my nose.

"One . . . two . . . three," Carol said.

"Good riddance to bad rubbish," we yelled as Kevin's and my glasses shattered against the brick fireplace.

After the Gamiacs headed back to the office, Keli followed me into the ladies room.

"Thanks again for this," I said as I unscrewed the lotion and rubbed some on my hands. "Ooh, this smells great. So orangey."

"I'm going to call my mother," she said as she washed her hands beside me. "I promise."

"I'm glad to hear that," I said. "My mother died a few years ago. I'd give anything to have five more minutes with her."

"Oh, that's so sad," Keli said. "My mother's the queen of sabotage though, always trying to fatten me up. And I'm an only child so I can't even share the calories."

"I'm one of six," I said. "I can't even imagine being an only child."

"And my father ran off when I was three. That's why I can never stay in a relationship for more than five minutes. I'm compensating for him not being there for me."

"Well, at least you understand it." I reached for a paper towel. "Sounds like you've had some good therapy."

"Actually, I saw it on Dr. Phil. But I didn't want to date him, so I'm not that far gone."

I laughed. "Sorry," I added, in case she'd been serious.

"That's okay," she said. "I'm pretty sure I was kidding. So what about you?"

"Have I ever dated Dr. Phil?"

She laughed. "No, are you seeing anyone?"

"Yeah," I said. "Actually I'm dating the big guy's owner."

She covered her mouth with one hand and opened her eyes wide. "John Anderson? Shut the front door."

I watched her carefully. "Why is that so surprising?"

"Because I have this mammoth crush on him? I mean, he's kind of geeky and kind of old, but so hot."

We looked at each other.

She grinned. "Not anymore."

CHAPTER

Seventeen

Neither John nor I had any condoms.

"But you *always* have condoms," I said as I rifled through the contents of my shoulder bag, which I'd just finished dumping out on his double vanity. I took a short break from condom hunting to roll some of Keli's organic orange lip balm on my kiss-ravaged lips.

"As do you." He shut the chrome-framed mirror that hid one of the medicine cabinets we'd decided to search once the drawer in his bedside table turned out to be condom-less. He tried to pull me back into an embrace. I caught a glimpse of us in the mirror, stark naked except for my Ace bandage. I looked okay, I thought, maybe even better than Keli looked once you got her out from under all her cute clothes. I was glad I'd set her straight about John. I had to admit she was

starting to grow on me. She was an odd choice for a
friend, but I'd probably be a really good influence on
her.

I wiggled away and opened the other mirror. One of
my favorite activities with my Bayberry students was to
help them create a timeline of their short lives on a
great big sheet of white paper, complete with photos
and drawings and the dates of important milestones. If
I were to create a birth control timeline of my own life,
it would go like this: stealing condoms from my brother
Johnny's room in high school just in case I ever needed
one; going to health services for a prescription for birth
control pills the very first week I arrived at college; actually filling the prescription two years later when I
finally had a boyfriend; semi-regular check-ups and
more pill prescriptions; switching to a diaphragm after
two years of marriage, so that there wouldn't be a waiting period when Kevin finally decided he was ready to
have kids; finding a series of holes shaped like the Big
Dipper in my former marriage diaphragm when I eventually dusted it off for post-divorce use; switching back
to condoms again.

When John and I became a couple, I considered
switching to a more hardcore form of birth control. But
people weren't always who they appeared to be, and
condoms protected you from worrying about STDs,
too. They were smaller and more portable than dia-
phragms, another advantage, and you didn't have to
remember to take them like the pill. Sure, the effec-
tiveness rate was a bit lower, but my most fertile days
were well behind me at this point anyway.

But sometimes another truth would sneak up on me in the middle of the night after a Sunday spent with my nieces and nephews, or when I saw an older mom carrying a newborn in a baby seat looped over her arm like a bracelet. *I want this*, I'd think, as a yearning so deep it almost brought me to my knees came over me. *I want a child of my own.*

Maybe the real truth was that, as a method of birth control, a condom seemed the least likely to succeed.

I stood up on my tiptoes and tried to reach the top shelf. "If we were at my house and we ran out of condoms, the car would be in the driveway and CVS would be two minutes away. Just saying."

"If we were at your house," John said, "your brother would be there and we wouldn't need a condom."

It was a good point, but before I'd decided whether or not I wanted to acknowledge that, I touched a square packet with the tip of one finger.

"Eureka," I yelled as the condom fell off the shelf.

John caught it before it landed in one of the double sinks. "Hmm, I don't even remember buying this brand." He turned it over in his hand and squinted at it, perhaps looking for an expiration date.

"As long as it's not the one you carried around in your wallet all through high school, I think we're good." I leaned in for a long kiss and we started working our way back to John's bedroom.

"Hey, how did you know about my high school condom?" John asked later, after we'd finished making love. The late afternoon sun was peeking through the wooden slats of the blinds, and I felt like I could stay curled up here forever. Except that I had to pee and I was getting really hungry.

"Brothers," I said. "All three of mine had wallet condoms. Carol and Christine and I used to sneak into their bedroom after Sunday dinner while they were out in the driveway playing basketball and go through their wallets just to see if they'd used them over the weekend."

John laughed. He grabbed one of my feet and kissed a dog print-decaled toe. Then his eyes moved to the bedside clock. Horatio.

I'd forgotten to buy sandwiches for us at the restaurant. By the time we got John's car out of his garage, found a decent restaurant, drove around until we found a parking place within walking distance, went inside and ordered and ate, I didn't even have to suggest going back to the condo for a riveting game of pinball before we picked up Horatio. We were late already.

John decided it would be faster to drive to puppy play care. We battled traffic the whole way, and it turned out we probably could have walked the distance three times by the time we finally got there. Urban life was simply exhausting.

Of course, we couldn't find a parking spot near Happytails, so I waited in the car, double-parked with the motor running, while John ran in to pick up Horatio.

I rolled on some orange essence lip balm, checked my phone for messages just to kill some time. Not a one. Then I opened up my web browser and checked in on the private work chat the Gamiacs had set up for us. I'd scroll through the comments and formulate my next online assignment accordingly, using my extensive training and expertise to analyze their developmental progress and specific needs.

Wood u care 2 dine with me this evening RavenSureSong? ObsidianDream had posted moments before at 4:58 PM.

A post from RavenSureSong came in as I watched. *Id b dlited.*

I closed my eyes and took a moment to appreciate this beautiful milestone. Maybe I could have them all make timelines on the final day of the session. We could scroll through the chat archives and find the exact day and time of their breakthrough moments. I'd order a big roll of paper like the kind we used at Bayberry. Or maybe we could make the timelines digitally. The Gamiacs would know what computer program would work best.

When I opened my eyes, a new message had materialized. *Now pick restaurant and time 2 meet and make sure u give yourselves time 2 shower & change first.*

Posted by PrincessKeli at 5:03 PM.

My first thought was I couldn't believe she'd crashed our work chat. I mean, what part of *private* did she not understand? Then I switched into mentor mode. I was too young and vibrant to be a mother figure for her, so it would have to be more like an older sister figure. But, bottom line, what a great opportunity this was for Keli to learn from me. Who knew, if June got her own classroom one day, maybe Keli could even become my new assistant.

I logged in to the chat room. *Great job, everybody*, I posted. *Keep up the good work.*

John opened the back door on his side for Horatio. "Okay, buddy, hop right in. Guess who came to visit us? Sarah! And you know what that means. That means she's riding shotgun today!"

Why did people have to sound like such idiots when they talked to their dogs? Even the parents of pre-schoolers had more dignity, at least most of the time.

Horatio got in and immediately tried to jump the gear thingee between the two front seats of John's Acura.

John gave his leash a tug. "Block the opening with your arm so he can't get through, but casually, as if you're simply claiming your turf."

"Casually?" I said. "I only have one good arm left."

John shut the back door and jumped into the driver's seat. I fought the urge to cut and run before he started up the car.

Horatio sniffed the air, then let out a growl, low and mean, like he was gargling rocks.

John turned the key in the ignition. I moved my hand to get a better grip on the back of his seat.

Horatio lunged at my arm block and nipped me right above the elbow.

"Ouch," I yelled.

"Don't say *ouch*," John said. "And don't show any anxiety. Just grab the leash and make a correction. And keep your arm in block position."

I couldn't believe it. *Don't say ouch?* Talk about giving Horatio a free pass to behave like a canine barbarian.

"You're joking, right?" I finally said.

"No, I'm not joking. I've been knee deep in research all week."

I let out a puff of air. "How about if I just walk? I can meet you guys back at the condo." I crossed my fingers as I said the last part, since there was no way I was going back to John's condo if this was the kind of night I was in for.

As soon as I got safely out of the car, I'd call my brother Michael and see if I could still catch a ride home with him. Or if he'd already left, I'd jump on the train and make him pick me up at the Marshbury station. Assuming I could find the nearest subway and get to the train station from here.

Horatio must have seen me cross my fingers because he lunged and snapped again, his teeth grazing my flesh and coming together with an ugly snap. I hoped he'd chipped a fang.

John put the car into park and reached back and grabbed Horatio's leash. He gave it a quick yank and said, "Horatio, down." Calmly, as if we didn't have a four-legged psychopath in the backseat. Then he turned his Heath Bar eyes to me. "I know this is hard, Sarah, but you've got to trust me. It's important for us to get this right."

I sighed. By the time we got back to John's condo, my arm was shaking, but Horatio was still in the backseat.

"Round one goes to me, I'd say," I whispered to Horatio as John got out and opened the back door for him.

CHAPTER

Eighteen

John picked up Horatio so that I could walk into the condo first. I tried not to notice that he held him like a baby. I distracted myself by rummaging in the depths of my shoulder bag for the Dog Biscuit in a Bag.

Once I'd walked myself over the threshold, John carried Horatio over and put him down on the floor. He held on to Horatio's leash. I realized it was probably impractical for him to do this whenever I was in the condo, but perhaps we could discuss the possibility of installing brushed chrome hitches in every room so we could tie him up. That way Horatio could still hang out with us, but I'd be more likely to stay alive.

"Okay," John said. "First, I want you to claim Horatio's favorite toys."

"Excuse me?" I said.

"When you claim his toys you'll essentially be claiming a higher rung on our pack ladder."

I'd broken up enough knockdown drag-out preschooler fights over favorite toys to know that this was madness, pure and simple. I was glad I'd thought to shut my equipment bag in John's walk-in closet, because no matter what John said, reciprocity was off the table here. I had absolutely no intention of sharing my own favorite toys.

"How about we make that our back-up plan?" I took a step toward the kitchen. It was time for me to channel my inner Suzy Homemaker and bake up some canine confections.

John reached out and put a hand on my forearm. "Trust me."

I sighed. I squatted down and reached a tentative hand toward the toy basket.

Horatio snarled at me and leaped, heading straight for my carotid artery.

John yanked the leash. "Horatio, sit," he said calmly.

Horatio plopped his butt down on the hardwood floor and glared at me like I should offer to go get him a cushion.

"Okay," I said in the perkiest voice I could muster, "I think he's got the message now. I'll be in the kitchen if you need me. Ha, bet you never thought you'd hear those words come out of *my* mouth—"

"Horatio, down," John said.

Horatio slid his front paws forward until he was stretched out on the floor. He didn't fool me one bit. I could tell he was ready to pounce at any moment.

John turned his attention to me. "Now pick up one of his toys and rub it all over yourself."

"Eww." I said. "Like I want dog cooties."

He didn't even smile.

I reached into the basket and pulled out a Frisbee. It was glow-in-the-dark green and had actually been personalized with Horatio's name in big white block letters. And John wondered why he had territorial issues?

Horatio made the rock-gargling sound again. I put the Frisbee on my head and twirled around, then pumped it up and down like a top hat. The growl got deeper. I rubbed the Frisbee up one arm, across my shoulders, then down the other arm. Horatio's whole body vibrated. I put the Frisbee on the ground and sat on it. Horatio let out a painful whine.

"Good dog," I said with a smirk.

"Now lean over him to show your dominance."

I stood up and leaned over him. I might have enjoyed it more than I should have.

Horatio went limp, like a furry rag doll.

"There it is," John whispered. "He's submitting to you."

"Great," I said. I lowered my voice to a whisper and leaned a little closer. "I hope it was as good for you as it was for me, pup."

Horatio lunged for me. His teeth grazed my throat.

I screamed.

"Horatio, sit," John said calmly as he gave the leash a little love pull.

"That's it?" I said. "What happened to *Are you still alive, Sarah?*"

"Okay, now I want you to walk calmly into the kitchen, open the dishwasher, and take out his dish. We'll be right behind you."

This was getting really old, but I did it anyway, just to get it over with. No matter what John said, once I finished feeding Horatio, I was drawing the line. And Horatio could forget about any barefoot baking of Dog Biscuits in a Bag tonight, too. I was going to settle in on the couch with a glass of wine. John could order takeout for dinner. The one big perk about being in the city was that restaurants actually delivered.

I opened the dishwasher and took out Horatio's monogrammed stainless steel dog dish. It was freshly washed and sparkled not just with cleanliness, but with excess and indulgence. I had to admit it put my own dishes to shame.

Horatio gargled some more rocks.

"Okay," John said. "Now put the dish on the counter and open the refrigerator and take out a piece of that dark chocolate on the top shelf—"

"Isn't chocolate supposed to make dogs really sick?" As soon as I said it, I wondered if I should have kept my mouth shut. Not that I wished food poisoning even on Horatio, but a small stomachache might be character building. And give him some time to think about the kind of dog he wanted to be.

"There's a wedge of Stilton in the cheese drawer, too, if you'd rather."

I opened John's fridge. "Not to tell you how to run your dog, but have you ever heard of dog food?"

"It's chicken by-product-free, so it probably wouldn't hurt you, but I don't think we need to go *that* far."

I shut the refrigerator door. Then I closed my eyes.

One of my high school teachers used to say *dawn breaks over marble head* when the class finally got something. Because we were in Massachusetts, it was hard to tell whether he was saying marble head or referring to the town of *Marblehead* on the North Shore, so we were never completely sure whether or not we were being insulted.

This time I knew. "You want me to eat from his freakin' *dog dish*?"

"Just a few bites," John said.

"Just a few bites?" I screamed. I took a step back. "What kind of sicko are you?"

"It's clean," he said. "I ran it through the dishwasher. Twice."

"You planned this?"

"Of course I planned it. It's based on solid research. Eating from Horatio's food dish is the ultimate assertion of your superiority over him, the definitive claim on his turf."

I looked at John Anderson, the man I'd just slept with, the man I thought I might even love.

"*Asking* me to eat from his food dish," I said slowly and carefully, taking the time to enunciate each word, "is the definitive end to this relationship."

I held my head high as I marched out of the kitchen to pick up my toys and go home. When I passed through the living room on the way to the hallway, I noticed the Peace, Love and Pinball poster had been replaced with a framed sheet of paper covered in brightly colored smudges and paw prints. Horatio's puppy masterpiece—ha. My preschoolers could have done a better job with one hand tied behind their backs.

I locked myself in the master bedroom while I packed up my stuff.

John knocked on the door.

"Oh, go eat with your dog," I said.

"Sarah," he said.

"Leave me alone."

"Sarah," he said again. This time it sounded sad and wistful. Like punctuation at the end of a relationship.

People think it's the big things that cause break-ups. Cheating or sexual identity issues. Instability. In-compatibility. Politics or religion. But it can be smaller things, too. Things that you'd think would be totally resolvable, manageable, conquerable. Stupid little things.

Like Horatio.

I leaned my head against the door.

"This is ridiculous," John said.

"I agree," I said. "It's ridiculous and humiliating. And I can't handle it anymore."

I felt John lean his head against the other side of the door. We were, what, an inch or two apart? And light years away from each other.

"I think we need to walk through these next few moments very carefully," he said softly.

"And I think you need to take your dog for a walk so I can get out of here in one piece."

He didn't say anything.

"Just give me ten minutes," I said. This didn't have to be high drama. We weren't living together. I didn't even have a change of clothes in his closet. As soon as John left I'd call a cab to get me to the nearest train station, so I didn't have to take a rubber chicken on the subway. Then I'd call Michael and get him to pick me up at the Marshbury train station. Tomorrow I'd call John's boss, tell him something came up, suggest that Keli take over with the Gamiacs.

Happy ending all around. But my eyes teared up anyway.

It was John's turn to talk, but he still hadn't said anything. Even Horatio was quiet. Of course he was. He'd won.

We stood like this for a while, separated by a slab of white-painted hardwood, frozen like a bad game of statues. I was thinking about Kevin and the night he walked out for the last time. I wondered if John was thinking about his ex-wife. Maybe once you'd been through a divorce, it became the touchstone you always went back to when you were trying to gauge how bad something was.

John cleared his throat. "You know why you're doing this, don't you?"

Now it was my turn not to say anything. There was nothing to say.

"Your brother needs you, the distance we live from each other, all of it. Think about it. Horatio is just one more excuse to push me away."

CHAPTER

Nineteen

Michael opened the back of his 4Runner and helped me stow all my stuff inside. When I'd called his cell from the taxi, he'd still been at work, killing time before he drove to Logan to meet Annie and Lainie's flight from Savannah.

"*There's* my rubber chicken," he said with a grin. "I've been looking everywhere for that."

"Ha." I hauled my weary body over to the passenger door and climbed in.

"Thanks for giving me a ride," I said as we buckled our seatbelts. Michael had been waiting for me in front of his office building with his motor running when the cab driver dropped me off. Life didn't have to be complicated.

He put on his blinker to take a right on Congress Street. "Not a problem. As long as you don't mind hitting the airport before we head back to your place."

"Whatever," I said.

"Hey, you know that ice cream cake I put in your freezer? How long will it take to thaw?"

"You're asking *me*?"

"Never mind, I'll figure it out. Anyway, I stocked up on all of Annie and Lainie's favorite junk food, too. I figured I'd let them stay up late enough for a quick party. I even got balloons and party hats on my lunch break today. They'll probably think they're goofy as hell but I wanted to do it anyway. And I hope you don't mind, but I stole one of your poster boards last night after you were asleep to make a welcome home sign. I forgot to mention it this morning."

"You forgot to mention anything this morning. You were a total grouch, by the way."

"Sorry about that."

I sighed. "Yeah, well, I think I caught it from you, so don't expect too much from me tonight." I closed my eyes and tried to breathe my post-break-up headache away. The Dog Biscuit in a Bag I'd left on John's kitchen counter flashed before me.

"I'm working remote most of the week so I can be with the girls, and Dad says they can hang out with him if anything comes up."

"I'm pretty much open, too," I said.

Michael turned to look at me. "Are you okay?"

I shrugged. The night went from getting dark to dark as we drove into the Sumner Tunnel. As much as

I tried to tune it out, John's voice was playing over and over in my head, like a bad talk radio show. *Think about it. Horatio is just another excuse to push me away.*

Right. You ask me to eat out of your dog's dish, and I'm pushing *you* away?

I'd just finished peeling off my Ace bandage when we pulled into the central parking garage. I rolled up the bandage and tucked it into the glove compartment. It's not like I'd been faking it. Well, maybe a little. But now that Horatio was out of the picture, I didn't need it for even psychological reinforcement anymore.

"Which airline?" I asked as we pulled into a spot in the short-term section.

"US Airways." We pushed our doors open and climbed out of the 4Runner. Michael clicked the door locked and put the keys in his pocket. He'd shaved this morning and his haircut had softened enough that it no longer screamed New Haircut. He was wearing a nice pair of dress pants and a long-sleeved pale blue shirt with the cuffs rolled. Even if we weren't related, I'd think he was good looking. Once he got over Phoebe, someone would scoop him up in a heartbeat.

I winced as it hit me that Michael might find someone new before I did. Our relationship would flip-flop once again, and he'd be the one taking care of me.

The elevator was stark and cavernous, a big step down from the one at Necromaniac. We got out on

Level 4 and rode the moving walkway across the pedestrian bridge to Terminal B. Mayor Menino's recorded
mumble welcomed us to Boston, even though we'd been
here all along.

We stopped in front of the first Arrivals screen we
came to and looked up.

"On time?" I asked.

"Seems like," Michael said.

I scanned until I found *Savannah*. "Flight 2345.
8:21 PM. Wow, it's already landed. We'd better get to
baggage claim."

We rode yet another elevator down a level and found
the baggage carousel. Suitcases were already rolling
out of the chute. Passengers surged as it circled past.

I tried to pick out the girls in the swirl of people.
"So how is this going to work?" I whispered to Michael.
"Are we dropping Phoebe off or is she getting picked
up by . . .." An image of Uncle Pete popped into my
head and stopped me from finishing.

Instead of answering, Michael took out his cell
phone.

I yawned. It had been a long day, and I couldn't wait
to get home. With luck Annie and Lainie would sleep
in and I could wallow for a while tomorrow before I had
to fake the cheerful aunt. I'd been seesawing between
anger and sadness since I'd left John's condo, and now I
was just teetering in the middle, numb. What a stupid,
stupid end to a relationship. I hoped Horatio was happy
now.

Michael was intent on his phone, so I wandered off
to make a quick visit to the restroom. I carefully avoid-

ed looking at myself in the mirror while I washed my
hands, as if not seeing how bad I looked might keep me
from feeling even worse than I already felt.

The luggage carousel was still moving when I came
back out, but only one suitcase was riding around. It
was a leopard print thing made out of some kind of
hard material that made me think of a fiberglass boat.

I found Michael. "Do you think they missed their
flight?"

He shrugged. "Must have. The last one from Savannah gets in at 10:18. We might as well go grab something to eat to kill some time."

"Don't you think you should text Phoebe first to be
sure?"

"I already did." He flipped his phone from one hand
to the other and then back again.

"And?"

He shrugged again. "They're probably up in the
air."

"Good clam chowder," Michael said.

I nibbled a corner of my quesadilla and took a long
buttery sip of chardonnay. Michael was drinking water,
but he was driving. And he hadn't had my day.

We were seated at Legal C Bar, which we'd been
lucky enough to find on the pre-security side. It was
dark and cozy, with red shades on the wall sconces and
tables lit by candles tucked into amber glass holders. If
you had to kill a couple of hours at the airport, and you

had nothing better to do for the rest of your life anyway, you couldn't pick a better place.

Legal C Bar was owned by Legal Sea Foods, and it was supposed to only feature "C" foods, things like chowder, crab, calamari, classic Caesar and clams. It was a nice idea, though it didn't quite translate to the menu, which also included lobster, mussels, and my grilled shrimp quesadilla. These are the kinds of inconsistencies that drive preschool teachers crazy, though I had to admit the food made up for it.

Michael checked his phone again. I'd left mine buried at the bottom of my shoulder bag. If there were messages for me, I didn't want to know about them.

I sighed.

Michael sighed.

I took another bite of my quesadilla that didn't start with the letter C.

"God damn it, Phoebe," Michael yelled. "Pick up the phone."

His voice echoed in the almost empty baggage area. A uniformed woman pushing a trash barrel on wheels looked over at him. It was almost 11:30 PM and the baggage carousel for Flight 2661 was circling around, empty and purposeless.

I could relate.

I watched Michael hit Redial again. I realized I should tell him to knock it off, but the only thing I had the energy to do was yawn.

"Are you *sure* they were supposed to come home to-night?" I asked when I finished.

Michael just shrugged.

A thought worked its way through the fog sur-rounding my brain. I reached over and yanked his phone away.

"Michael, when was the last time you talked to Phoebe?"

He shook his head. He ran his hand through what was left of his hair. "When they landed."

"Wait. You talked to her when they landed? Where was I?"

Michael folded his hands together, almost like he was going to confession.

He sighed.

He rubbed his eyes with his fists.

"When they landed in Savannah," he said softly.

"*What*," I screamed. "We've been sitting here all freakin' night and you didn't even know whether they were actually getting in tonight or not?"

"That was the plan. Phoebe was going to text me the flight info."

"That was the plan *a week ago*. And you haven't heard from any of them since?"

He shrugged.

I woke up Michael's phone with my thumb and pressed Redial. It rang and went to voicemail.

From the depths of my shoulder bag, my own cell rang. I gave Michael's phone back to him and dug up mine.

I checked my Caller ID.

"What is your problem?" I yelled. "Why are you torturing my brother?"

"I can't take it anymore," Phoebe said quietly. "Tell him to leave me alone. He can have the house. He can have everything. The girls and I are moving in with my parents."

"*What?*" I said. "You can't do—"

"They can spend all their vacations with him. He can have them for every holiday." She let out a little sob. "Please, Sarah. He'll listen to you."

Twenty

Michael grabbed my phone. "What the hell is going on, Phoebe?" he yelled into it.

"Don't you dare hang up on me," he yelled a moment later.

He held the phone out to me. "She hung up."

I bit my tongue so I wouldn't say, *ya think?*

"What did she say to you?" he yelled at me. The woman with the trash barrel rolled by us again, looking like she might call security any minute. I smiled at her to show her we weren't crazy. Or at least not dangerous.

"Shh," I hissed at Michael. "She's pretty emotional right now, so I'm sure she didn't really mean it, but she's, um, thinking of staying in Savannah."

"She can't do that. It's my turn to have the girls." He paused. "How long?"

"Forever?"

Michael's face turned ugly. Then he ran.

"Michael," I yelled.

When I caught up to him, he was standing at the ticketing counter, but fortunately no one appeared to be working there at this hour. Or maybe they were sneaking in a nap out back. Just the thought of it made me yawn.

I reached for my brother's forearm. He shook me off and jogged over to one of the self-service kiosks. Given how long it took me to navigate those things, I figured I probably had enough time to call Carol to find out what to do.

I woke her from a sound sleep, but once she realized it was a true emergency, she clicked right into gear.

"No, no, no. Do not, under any circumstances, let him get on the next plane to Savannah."

"Any thoughts on exactly how I might manage to stop him?"

"Okay. Walk me over to Michael and hand him the phone."

"Oh, thank you," I said. "You're so much better at this stuff than I am."

"Hurry up, before he buys a ticket. You can kiss up to me some other time."

I'd been hiding just around the corner, so I made it over to Michael in three big steps.

I tapped him on the shoulder and handed him my phone. "Carol," I said. "It's an emergency."

I was dying to hear both sides of the conversation, but I didn't think it would go over very well if I asked Michael to put the call on speakerphone.

"I don't care what it costs to get on the next plane," Michael was saying. "Really? That much? Okay. Okay. I'll hang tight, but hurry."

I wandered around until I found a relatively comfortable faux leather chair across from a bench I could put my feet up on. There was a chair right next to it for Michael. In fact, most of the other chairs were empty, too, and the only restaurant that appeared to be still open was a tiny Dunkin' Donuts.

Michael ignored the chairs and paced. I followed him with my eyes until he dropped out of sight, then picked him up again when he'd finished circling the pre-security side of the terminal. Then I watched him until he disappeared again. And reappeared. Once he stopped and punched a wall. A man, stretched out on the floor nearby and using his backpack for a pillow, startled awake then closed his eyes again.

The ring of my cell phone woke me. I jerked back to consciousness, trying to locate Michael and make sure my shoulder bag hadn't been stolen at the same time.

I found my phone. "Yeah," I said. My voice sounded like I'd been out partying all night.

"Okay," Carol said. "I found a last minute vacation package."

"What?" I said.

"They buy out these blocks of airfares, and if they don't sell, they unload them dirt cheap at the last minute, so airfare and hotel combined are a fraction of what you'd pay for the airfare alone."

"Fascinating," I croaked. When I blinked, my eyelids felt like they were lined with sandpaper. I squinted to see if Dunkin' Donuts was still open. I was definitely going to need some serious caffeine if I had to drive Michael's 4Runner all the way back to my house at this hour.

"Mother Teresa," I said, as a new thought hit me. "Ohmigod, Michael didn't even go home after work. She hasn't eaten and she's probably peed all over my house—"

"Dad fed her and took her out last night."

"Oh, good. I'll take her out for a long walk when I get home. So, how is this going to work? I wait 'til Michael's on the plane and then drive his car home, right?"

"Where is his car parked?"

"In short term parking, on the second level. Row G. Or maybe it was J."

"Grab Michael and meet me there."

"When?"

"Now. I'm just pulling into central parking."

"Huh?" I said. "You're here? Why? And how'd you get here so fast?"

"Come on, Sarah, get with the program. It's almost 4 A.M."

❖

Mayor Menino welcomed us to Boston again as we rode the empty moving sidewalk back to central parking. The elevator opened right away and I pushed the button for the second floor. When Carol called, Michael had been dozing in the chair next to mine. When I shook him awake, he'd jumped to his feet, pretending he'd been awake all along.

I'd told him we had to meet Carol in the garage, and neither of us had said a word since then. We'd walked right past Dunkin' Donuts, the smell of brewing coffee whispering to me like a drug dealer, but I hadn't been able to function enough to decide whether or not we had time to stop and get some.

The elevator stopped with a bump. Michael rubbed an eye with one hand and reached to hold the door open for me with the other. "Hey, why is Carol here anyway? Couldn't she have just sent me everything in an email?"

I tried to get my fuzzy brain to put the pieces together. "Maybe to drive your car home?" I shivered in the damp, pre-dawn air.

Michael squinted. "Then who will drive *her* car home?"

I yawned. "Me?"

Michael yawned back. "Doesn't make any sense."

I yawned again. "Like anything does these days."

Carol was waiting for us next to Michael's 4Runner. She not only looked wide-awake, but my guess was that she had a clipboard in her minivan holding everything

Michael would need in the exact order that he'd need it. Carol was an event planner, a job that suited her extreme bossiness as well as her anal tendencies. Even though she was my sister and could drive me absolutely crazy, I'd hire her in a second. Not that there were any events in my foreseeable future.

"Hurry," she said. "We're going to have to move this shitbox to long term parking so it doesn't get towed."

"Huh?" I said.

"I don't get it," Michael said. "And don't call my car a shitbox."

Carol gave him her big sister glare. "When you wake me up at midnight, I can call anything of yours anything I want to."

"I didn't wake you up," Michael said. "Sarah did."

"Thanks," I said. "Throw *me* under the bus. I needed that right now."

"Shut up, you two." Carol held her hand out. "Give me the keys, Michael."

"What the hell is going on?" I said as I shoved my net equipment bag over and climbed into the backseat.

"Yeah," Michael said. "This better not be a trick."

"What kind of trick?" I said. I was so tired I had a crazy urge to put my Ace bandage back on again, as if it might somehow help me hold myself together.

Michael shrugged. "You know, like to try to keep me from going to Savannah."

I hadn't even thought of that. Probably because my brain hurt when I tried to think. Maybe Carol should just park Michael's car somewhere so we could all take a nap. Then once we were rested, we could get some breakfast and a cup of coffee or twelve. Things would start to make sense again, and before we knew it we might have an actual plan.

Carol drove up a level. I rolled down my window, hoping the dank morning chill might keep me awake. Short-term parking had been almost empty, but this end of the garage was more heavily populated. I kept an eye out for her red minivan so I could shout it out if I saw it first. It wouldn't be the world's biggest contribution, but it was all I could come up with in my current condition.

Carol screeched around a corner and pulled into an empty parking space.

My father was leaning back against his sea green Mini Cooper.

"Whoa, Nelly Belle," he said. "Drop the anchor on that boat before you take someone out. I'd like to live to see Savannah."

Twenty-one

"Dad?" I said after I'd clambered out of the backseat. "What are *you* doing here?"

He winked. "You don't think I'd let a perfectly good hotel room bed go to waste, do you now? It'll be a grand vacation. We'll have a boys' room and a girls' room, just like the good old days."

"Wait," I said. "I'm going? But I don't have any luggage." As if this was the only thing that was totally insane here.

My father opened the back of his Mini Cooper. The back seats were folded down and four almost identical black carry-on suitcases with rollers took up every square inch of space. "Tah-*dah*," he said as he gestured with both hands.

"I packed a suitcase for both of you," Carol said. "In my spare time."

"What about Mother Teresa?" Michael said.

"You're welcome." Carol reached in for a suitcase. "She's at my house. Dennis is going to work remote, and I bribed Siobhan to help out with the younger kids. Hurry, we're going to miss our flight."

Mayor Menino welcomed us to Boston yet again as we entered the pedestrian walkway.

Carol stopped. "What the hell did he just mumble?"

"Uh-uh-uh," our father said. "We'll have no making fun of His Honor the Mayor on my watch."

The rest of my family strode quickly along the moving walkway, but the combination of movement on top of movement plus exhaustion made me dizzy, so I jumped off and jogged along beside them.

When we got to security, Carol handed me an empty Zip-lock bag and I transferred my makeup and the rest of my potentially dangerous items into it. Then I chugged what was left in the water bottle I'd been carrying around for about a day now. Carol handed out our boarding passes and we breezed right through security, no big surprise since it was not quite 4:30 A.M.

Even Carol hadn't been able to get the four of us seats together. Or a nonstop flight. I spent the first half of our trip in a middle seat in the back of the plane, wedged between two strangers. Before I turned my phone off, I thought about sending a text to John, just in case. But what would I say? *Hope Horatio is happy now? Sorry we crashed and burned before I crashed and burned?* My sleep and caffeine-deprived brain couldn't come up with anything better, and what's the point of leaving an in-case-of-crash message if it's not going to be memorable, so I gave up.

We deplaned in Charlotte and rolled our bags to the next flight, following single file behind Carol, like a human twist on one of our favorite picture books growing up, *Make Way for Ducklings*. By popular request, our mother would read it to us practically every night. One or two of the younger kids would curl up in her lap on the sofa, while our dad and the rest of us would slide the coffee table out of the way and act out every scene. We'd fight over who got to be Kack, Lack, Mack, Nack, Ouack, Pack, Quack, and. . . .

I counted the ducks on my fingers as we merged with the throng of people already boarding the plane for Savannah. *Jack*. Jack was the name of the eighth duckling, the one I'd forgotten. I sighed.

I was wedged between two different people on the flight from Charlotte to Savannah. To make matters worse, apparently they weren't even going to serve us water since the flight was so short. The coffee I could have had on the first flight was just a fantasy now. My stomach growled at the thought of the over-salted pretzels I'd never taste. The guy to my right was hogging the entire armrest. I leaned in, hoping he'd take the hint. He didn't. Finally I just elbowed him out of the way. Sometimes you can't take it any more. *I hope John Anderson is happy now*, I thought randomly, as if it had been his elbow.

When we touched down at the Savannah/Hilton Head International Airport, it felt like I'd been struggling to stay awake for centuries.

I rolled my carry-on to the end of the jetway and found my family clumped together, waiting for me. "What time is it?" My voice came out as a rasp, like it was dying of caffeine withdrawal.

"Eight forty-eight A.M.," Carol said way too cheerily. There's nothing worse than being sleep-deprived in the company of someone who's a perkier version of Julie from *The Love Boat*.

I groaned. "How long till check-in?"

"Seven hours and twelve minutes." Maybe I wouldn't hire her for an event after all. "Can you believe this is the first time I've been away since Maeve was born? I've barely even gone to the bathroom by myself."

"We'll have no bathroom talk on this trip," my father said.

We rolled our suitcases behind Carol and I looked around for a place to nap. It was a cute little airport, charming and so beachy it even had a flip-flop store. The atrium was scattered with rocking chairs. They looked pretty damn comfortable from here. I pivoted to the left and started to roll my way toward one.

Michael grabbed my arm. "Come on, you don't have time to rock. We need to find a rental car."

"We just have to pick it up," Carol said. "It's already reserved. It's part of the package."

"You got the car thrown in, too?" I said.

Carol nodded. "I most certainly did. When you add it all up, it turned out to be cheaper to go than to stay home. At least that was the angle I pitched to Dennis."

Carol talked the guy behind the rental car desk into upgrading us from an economy car to a compact.

"We bought a vacation package for four," she said. "So it's your responsibility to make sure we have a car that will actually fit four people *and* their luggage without charging us one cent more. Otherwise, you'll be reading all about it on Trip Advisor." He gave in just to get rid of us.

"Not much of a bucket of bolts," our dad said when we finally set eyes on our no frills, white Ford Focus. "I was hoping for something more along the lines of the little deuce coupe your mother and I drove on our honeymoon. Salmon and white, brushed chrome fins. Holy mackerel, that car had some fins on it."

"Not now, Dad," Michael said. He grabbed the keys from Carol. He clicked the trunk open and we managed to cram our suitcases in. Michael and I climbed into the back seat, sitting sideways so our knees could fit.

Carol tapped *breakfast* into the GPS and before we knew it we were settled in at a table at Back in the Day Bakery on Bull Street in downtown Savannah.

"Wow," I said. "It's like we just time travelled back to the '50s." Our mid-century chairs circled a funky rustic table made out of reclaimed wood. Two old-fashioned bakery cases just across from us were filled

with every mouth-watering thing people used to be allowed to eat. I tried to guess the flavor of the
cupcakes: red velvet, milk chocolate, coconut something or other. . ..

A sign on one of the robin's egg blue distressed
walls said: *If you're afraid of butter, use cream—Julia
Child.* There was a huge chandelier-like mobile hanging over us made entirely out of marshmallows and
white kitchen string. Either that or I was so tired I was
hallucinating.

Carol decreed that it was too early for cupcakes, so
we ordered four large coffees and four savory ham and
cheese biscones, which turned out to be a Southern-
style fusion of biscuits and scones.

"I hope all y'all enjoy 'em all," a pretty blond waitress said as she put our plates down in front of us.

"All y'all?" I said after she'd walked away. "And
wasn't there another one in there, too? Can you actually have three *alls* in one sentence?"

Our father's eyes followed the departing waitress.
"You're darn tootin'," he said.

"Ohmigod," Carol said as she bit into her biscone.
"This is the most amazing thing I've ever tasted. Let's
just stay here the whole time and eat."

I pointed a finger casually over my head. "Does anyone else think those might be real marshmallows?"

My father winked at the waitress, who was now safely behind the bakery case.

"Dad," Carol hissed. "Knock it off. She looks about
twelve."

"Sorry about that, chief," he said. He took a sip of his coffee. "This décor is taking me back. For a second there, I might have imagined I was a young whipper-snapper again. 'Tis one of the true joys of getting older—you have a tendency to drift."

Michael pulled out his phone. "Shit, I'm supposed to be remote today."

"Ha," I said. "You couldn't get much more remote than this."

"Shh," he said. "I have to send a bunch of emails ASAP so it looks like I'm working."

Carol pulled out her phone, too. "I need to look busy, too. I've got three events next week."

I took another sip of my coffee. I should probably email John's boss to quit, just to make a clean break, but then again, I had almost a week before I had to show up at Necromaniac the next time. And even though Carol had found us an amazing deal, it probably wouldn't really turn out to be quite as cheap as staying home. Maybe I could post something to tide me over, and then I'd reassess after I'd slept on it.

I yawned and reached for my phone. I logged into our private work chat. Keli was living up to my confidence in her. She'd started several new threads and the Gamiacs had jumped right in. But it was important for me to add my expertise as long as I was officially involved. I was a teacher through and through, and a good teacher can always come up with an assignment, even on zero sleep. I thought for a moment.

*Let's talk about unrequited love, the one who broke
your heart. The one you haven't thought about in
years. Or minutes.*

I logged out again. My father opened his laptop. I
moved his plate and coffee mug out of the way to give
him some space.

"Why, thank you kindly, sweet Carol—"

I shook my head.

"ChristineSarah." He looked over his shoulder. "You
don't see any of that wire fire whosamajiggie around
here anywhere, do you?"

Michael looked up. "You mean Wi-Fi?"

"Doubtful," I said. "It doesn't look like the computer
was even invented yet around here."

"Of course they have Wi-Fi." Carol slid her chair
over so she could see the laptop screen. She ran her
finger along the mouse pad. "Look, it's right here.
Okay, all set, Dad." She slid her chair back and reached
for her biscone.

Our father looked over his shoulder again. "Where
do I plug her in?"

"It's Wi-Fi, Dad," Michael said. "The whole point is
that it doesn't need to be plugged in."

"I should have stuck with my Smith Corona." He ran
his hand through his mane of white hair, then pulled
one finger back and hit the mouse pad. "A gentleman's
messages are his alone. They're not intended for sharing with the whole wide wireless world."

I scooted my chair a little closer and squinted at his
laptop screen. "Ohmigod, Dad. You have a date."

Carol leaned over. "Savannah Sweetie?"

Our father grinned. "'Dear Billy Boy,'" he read. Maybe it was because I was so tired and we were in a bakery straight out of *Ozzie and Harriet,* but it was almost as if we were kids again and he was reading us a bedtime story.

He cleared his throat. "'Meet up with this Cray-Cray Lady tomorrow at high noon at the Crystal Street Beer Parlor for a Slow Ride. Your Sugar Butt.'"

"Whoa," I said. "I don't think we should let you go alone, Dad."

Twenty-two

Michael chugged the rest of his coffee and put his mug down with a thunk. "Okay," he said. "The three of you are going to have to lure Phoebe outside, and then I'll take it from there."

"We can't do that," I said. I turned to Carol. "Can we?"

Even Carol was starting to look a little bit weary around the edges. "Give me a minute to think this through."

She yawned.

The rest of us yawned, too. I put my forearms on the table to keep from falling into my empty biscone plate.

"I know," I said. "What if we just go to the hotel first? Maybe our rooms are ready and we can nap. It's almost eleven and check-in is at four, right? So that's

only . . .." I struggled to do the math but my poor dilap-
idated brain couldn't go there.

"Five hours," Carol said. "They'll never let us into
our rooms this early. That's how they get you. It's like
you have a zero percent interest credit card and then
you're one minute late on one payment, and they jack it
up to twenty-three percent."

"Oh, please," I said. "Can't we just take a little nap?"

"I wouldn't mind some shut-eye myself," our father
said. "I'd like to be well-rested for Sugar Butt."

Michael scratched his scalp with both hands, hard,
as if he were trying to dig a hole into his head. Then he
buried his face in his hands.

Carol and I looked at each other. She shrugged.

Michael lifted his head again. "Yeah, I'm too beat to
handle anything right now. Let's get some sleep somewhere and then we can figure out a plan. How long are
we here for anyway? Or do I already know that?"

"Three nights," Carol said.

"Three nights?" I said. *I can't stay here for three
nights,* I almost added. And then I remembered I could.
I had nowhere else to be and no one to notice I was
gone.

Going from the almost frosty air-conditioned com-
fort of Back in the Day Bakery to the heat and humidi-
ty of Savannah was a rude awakening, like stepping
into a sauna wearing yesterday's deodorant. We
bunched together on the sidewalk while Carol and I

rummaged for sunglasses. Our father put on his Coast Guard Auxiliary hat again. Michael just looked miserable.

We crossed the street and headed for our rental car. "So," I said. "Is the hotel right around here?"

"Not far," Carol said. "It's on Hilton Head."

"Hilton Head?" I said. "Isn't that in like a whole other state?"

"Hilton Head *Island*?" Michael said, as if there might be another Hilton Head that was closer. "Why the hell did you get us a room way out there?"

"It was part of the package," Carol said. "Relax, it's only an hour away. And I was saving this part as a surprise, but the place we're staying at is a waterfront resort."

I wiped a glob of sweat from my upper lip as I tried to imagine how a hotel room that cost less than staying home could possibly be waterfront.

Michael and I wedged our tired bodies into the backseat. Carol pulled up the GPS on her phone and started the car. My head bobbed back and forth as we took a couple of rights and then a left. We merged onto US 17 and a sign welcomed us to South Carolina.

When I woke up we were in paradise. We drove along a tropical road flanked with lush vegetation and past a guard gate, which appeared to be for decorative purposes only. Gorgeous walking trails snaked along beside us. I rolled down my window. It was still hot, but unless it was a mirage, the fronds of the palm trees were blowing in a gentle wind. I was pretty sure I could smell the ocean.

"Am I dreaming this?" I croaked.

We slowed to a stop to let a caravan of golf carts cross in front of us. The golfers waved. We waved back.

"I forgot how friendly Southerners are," Carol said. "It's so annoying."

"Unless you marry them," Michael said. "Then they stop being friendly real fast."

The long, winding road branched out in a series of forks, each marked by a carved wooden sign. One pointed to GOLF COURSE. Another to VILLAS. We turned left to follow the sign that said RESORT CHECK-IN.

The first glimpse of the resort blew me away. It was heavily landscaped and absolutely mammoth. A cara-mel-colored stucco building, maybe five stories high, appeared to stretch out forever in either direction. A welcome flag flew from a huge awning-covered portico.

Our dad put two fingers in his mouth and let out a long whistle. "Well, will you look at this. Fancy Schmancy."

"Okay," Carol said once we'd parked and wrenched our weary bones out of the rental car. "We're just go-ing to leave our bags at the front desk, find the nearest patch of sand with comfortable chaises and umbrellas, grab a towel, and nap until it's time to check in."

"It would have been a genius plan if we could find the lobby," I said a few minutes later. Two pelicans flew over our heads, which meant there had to be a beach around here somewhere.

We backtracked across the parking lot and switched directions again, only to dead-end at another roadblock

marked with black and yellow CAUTION tape. "Unbelievable," Michael said. "This whole place is a construction site."

"We're in," our father yelled. He held up a section
of some kind of temporary plastic fencing, bright orange with little square grid-like openings that reminded me of graph paper.

The lobby was closed for construction, too, so we
followed a long line of paper arrows until we came to a
card table in the hallway. Two men were painting the
ceiling with rollers attached to long poles as we approached. I put my hands over my head so I wouldn't
end up with white-speckled hair.

I turned my back on a bamboo-framed mirror hanging on the wall beside me so I wouldn't accidentally see
what I looked like. Carol had her hair pulled back in a
curly-messy ponytail and still looked relatively pre-
sentable. But our father's thick white hair was sticking
straight up in the back and one of his eyebrows looked
a little off-kilter. With his duffle bag slung over one
shoulder, he could have passed for a pirate. Michael's
button-down work shirt from yesterday was untucked
and had turned into a mass of wrinkles. He looked exhausted.

We piled our luggage together and Carol handed
over her credit card.

"Eureka!" Michael yelled when we finally made it to
the pool area.

Two gorgeous swimming pools stood before us. Off
to one side, a huge copper pelican stretched out in a
manmade lily pond next to a fountain, reading a copper

book. A sunken whirlpool, almost as big as one of the swimming pools, was tucked into a corner. I could feel the jets massaging the back of my neck already.

"Son of a witch with a capital B," Carol said. "We should have changed into our bathing suits."

"I thought about it," I said, "but it felt like way too much work. Maybe we can go in like this."

A chest-high white-painted metal fence surrounded the pool. We found the gate and Carol reached over and unlatched it from the inside. A young couple was sitting on the edge of one of the pools with their feet in the water. Other than that we had the place to ourselves. Except for the scaffolding that took over most of the pebbled concrete decking. And the big sign that read CONSTRUCTION ZONE KEEP OUT.

Michael walked over to a stone arch filled with rolled towels. He picked one up, shook the construction dust off it, and threw it on one of the lounge chairs. He slid the chair under one of the freestanding beach umbrellas. Then he climbed on, opened the towel and covered his face with it.

"Looks like a plan," I said. I picked out a lounge chair, climbed aboard, covered my face with a towel, started to get comfortable. "Is that smell me?"

"Siobhan and her friends call it smelling like ass," Carol said.

"I hope you show her the broad side of a bar of Irish Spring," our father said.

Carol laughed. "She'd haul me into court. You can't do that anymore, Dad."

"If you ask me," our dad said, "the whole world has gone to hell in a hand basket. And five will get you ten, Sugar Butt will agree with me on that."

I was pretty sure if I put one hand on the pool fence and followed it all the way around, I'd come to an opening that led to the beach. I bet the beach here was amazing. I couldn't wait to see it.

Just before I covered my face with the towel, a white stork flew overhead, the underside of its wings shaded black. Maybe it had just finished delivering a baby to someone.

Beside me, Michael let out a loud snore.

I woke up to the sound of laughing from the sky.

"What *is* that?" I said through my towel.

"God?" Carol said.

"Well, now, wouldn't that be a fine how-do-you-do," our father said. "I was hoping God would turn out to be the real deal. I'll bet your mother was relieved when she showed up at the pearly gates."

It was such human-sounding laughter that I couldn't help laughing along. Then everybody but Michael started to laugh, too.

"It's a laughing gull," Michael said.

"Is that related to a laughing cow?" I said.

"Shh," Carol said. "Don't wake me. I was having the best dream. I was on Hilton Head for three whole nights for practically no money and I had the whole bathroom all to myself."

"Forget about it," I said. "There's no way in hell I'm sharing Dad and Michael's bathroom."

I peeled the towel off my face and looked up. The sky was ocean blue and the clouds looked like puffy white sails. Seagulls in full squawky symphony dipped and soared above us. I tried to pick out the one that was laughing at us from the crowd.

"Phoebe and I came here once," Michael said. The towel muffled his voice like a confessional. "Not here-here, but Hilton Head. Her parents watched the girls for the night."

The gull laughed again.

"That," Michael said. "When a laughing gull does that, Phoebe told me it was good luck. It meant that we'd be laughing together for the rest of our lives."

"So much for seagull laughter as prophecy," Carol said.

There was a beat of silence and then we all burst out laughing, even Michael.

"Has anybody ever told you what a bitch you are," he said. He threw his towel at her and it landed right on top of the one that still covered her face.

"Language," our father said.

"Witch with a capital B," Carol said through two towels.

Twenty-three

"There must be a restaurant around here somewhere," I said. "Unless that's under construction, too."

Michael pushed himself up to a standing position and stretched. "I think that might be one over there. I'll go find out."

"I'm right behind you, Mikey boy," our father said.

"I'm going to see if that gate leads to the beach," I said. "I am dying to walk the beach."

"Wait," Carol said. "Let's see if they've brought our stuff up to our rooms. We can get cleaned up, check out the restaurant situation, then we can have a nice early bird dinner—"

"I like the sound of that," our dad said. "Especially if it comes with an early bird brewski or two."

"Agreed," Michael said. "I've got to send a few more emails to the office, too, once we get up to the room. So it doesn't look like I cut out early."

"I don't know," I said. "It sounds like an awful lot of work to me. How about you guys get us moved into our rooms. Just call my cell when you're done, and I'll meet you on the beach."

My phone rang. "That was quick," I said.

They were all looking at me so I had no choice but to dig my phone out of my shoulder bag.

I looked at the Caller ID. "Uh-oh. It's Christine. She's going to kill us for not bringing her. What should I do?"

"Lie," Carol said.

The truth about big families is that someone is always getting left out. If you took the time to make sure that didn't happen, to make sure all six Hurlihy siblings were invited to participate in each and every escapade, you'd never go anywhere. So hurt feelings were always on the horizon, and the larger group factioned and re-factioned into smaller cliques accordingly, based on who was pissed off at whom.

I pushed the Accept button. "Hey. What's up?"

"Where are you?" Christine said. "I just stopped by your house and nobody was there."

"Sorry I missed you," I said. "Listen, I'm in the middle of something right now, but I'll call you back later in the week, okay?"

I hit the End Call button. "How'd I do?" I asked.

Carol's phone rang. I reached over and grabbed it off the arm of her lounge chair. I looked at the display, not that I really needed to.

I handed Carol her phone. "Guess who?"

Carol took it from me and put it back down.

"You're not going to talk to her?"

"I'm on vacation," Carol said.

Around the corner from the pool we found a door that was propped open with a paint can. A sign taped to the wall just inside read PLEASE PARDON OUR APPEARANCE.

Michael peeled the sign off the wall and slapped it onto the back of my T-shirt.

Carol gave us her big sister glare. "Knock it off, you two. Don't you dare get us kicked out of here."

"I didn't do it," I said. "Michael did."

She yanked the sign off me and taped it back on the wall.

Our luggage was still piled next to the card table, but the good news was it was still there. And our rooms were ready.

Carol handed us each a plastic key card. A bellhop was just rolling an overloaded luggage carrier onto the elevator, so we piled on behind him. The woman who belonged to the luggage was tall and top heavy, and the man short and wiry.

"This room better be good," the man said. "The rest of the place looks like a dump."

"Shut up," the woman said.

"Don't tell me to shut up," the man said.

"What the hell was I thinking bringing you here with me," the woman said.

The bellhop stared straight ahead. Our father started to whistle "I'm in the Mood for Love." Carol gave him her knock it off look. He switched to "Love Potion No. 9."

We all got off at the fourth floor. My family and I stood to the side pretending to look for our keycards and let the lovebirds get ahead of us.

"Well, that sure made me homesick," Carol said once they were out of earshot. "I might have to break down and call Dennis."

I squinted at some rectangular plaques on the wall. "Okay, looks like our rooms are this way."

"Holy Toledo," our father said a few minutes later. "Is it just me, or is this the longest hallway you've ever walked? I don't mind telling you it's got me wishing for a skateboard."

"A wheelchair would work for me right about now," Michael said.

We kept walking. And walking. Finally the hallway opened up to a square vestibule with a big round table in the center.

"What is *this*?" Carol said. "There's no purpose to it. I hate things that don't have a purpose."

I squatted down and put my head on the table. "Maybe it's here so you can rest halfway to your room?"

"Come on," Michael said. "We don't have time to rest."

I pushed my aching body to a standing position. We crossed the vestibule and continued down the hallway. I wished I'd thought to bring a compass just to make sure we weren't going around in circles. Or possibly squares.

"Four-two-three-three," Carol chanted. "Four-two-three-four. Four-two-three-five."

Ahead of us, the bellhop was holding a door open for the couple from the elevator. We paused to give them a moment to disappear inside.

Carol's and my room turned out to be the very next one. "Four-two-three-eight," she said. "We made it."

"Look," Michael said. A sign just ahead said ELE-VATOR TO BEACH. "At least we can bypass the cross-country trek when we go out again."

"Perfect," Carol said. "Okay, our rooms are adjoining, so as soon as you're cleaned up, just knock on the door to let us know you're ready to go. Twenty minutes tops."

"Aye aye, sweetie," our dad said. "Anybody need a Slim Jim to tide them over? I brought plenty."

"It feels so good not to smell," I said as I finished towel drying my hair and rolled on some orange blossom stick perfume.

"Whoa," Carol said. "Enough with that stuff—you're going to start to attract fruit flies. Hurry up—I'm famished. I'm almost ready to take Dad up on that Slim Jim."

We heard a knock on the adjoining door. Carol walked over to let our dad and Michael in. Neither of them had taken the time to shave, but they were both wearing golf shirts and shorts and had slicked-back wet hair.

"I called the front desk," Michael said. "The kitchen is being renovated but they still have room service."

"If the kitchen is being renovated," Carol said, "where does the food come from?"

My exhausted brain would never have made that connection. "Good point," I said. "I think we should go out. I bet if we follow the beach we'll eventually come to a waterfront restaurant."

"To the beach elevator," our dad said. "I'll lead the way."

The beach elevator opened right away. Michael pushed a button that said BEACH LEVEL. As the elevator descended, somebody's stomach growled, possibly mine.

When we stepped off the elevator, a big black door with a sign that read BEACH was clearly visible at the end of the hallway.

"Allow me," our dad said. He turned the knob and held the door open. "Thanks, Dad," I said.

I took half a step and screamed. Michael yanked me back by my shoulders. In front of us was a sharp drop ending in a wasteland of concrete rubble. A single paltry strip of caution tape stood between me and sure death. Or at least some serious bruising.

"Yikes," I said. "I think you just saved my life."

Michael shrugged. "It was a lot less time-intensive than writing a speech for your memorial service."

"There has to be another way out," Carol said. We backtracked, found a stairwell, walked down two flights of stairs to a locked door. Turned around, walked back up the stairs, found the beach elevator that didn't lead to the beach. Pushed the button that said LOBBY. When the door opened, the former lobby was still a construction site.

Our dad held the elevator door open with one hand and ran his other hand through his still damp hair. "Perhaps we should go back to our rooms and see if we can get pizza delivered. Did anybody happen to notice what they had for beer in the minibar?"

"Think about it," Michael said. "If we can't get out, how is the pizza going to get in?"

Twenty-four

It's not easy to find a restaurant on Hilton Head Island, even with GPS on your phone, because everything is tastefully designed to disappear into the extreme landscaping.

"Let's just stop at the first place that looks promising," I said. "I don't want to drive around all night."

"I want a margarita," Carol said. "I haven't had a margarita since before my last pregnancy."

"Over there," Michael yelled. "It says Mexican Grill."

Once we finally found the restaurant tucked behind the shrubbery, we all ordered Gringo Burritos because we liked the name.

"And I'll have a margarita," Carol said.

"We don't serve alcohol," the woman behind the counter said. "But you can go next door and ask them to put your drink in a carry-out cup while you're waiting for your burritos."

Next door turned out to be a Thai restaurant at the far end of the same storefront row. "It's like a new fusion dining experience," I said as we carried our drinks back to the other restaurant. "Southern-slash-Mexican-slash-Thai."

Carol stopped for a sip. "Ohmigod. This is the best thing I've ever tasted."

We found an empty table off in the corner. I didn't even really like margaritas but I'd ordered one anyway, since it seemed easier than trying to figure out what I actually did want. Michael and our dad were drinking Dogfish Head beer straight from the bottles. When our burritos arrived, we chowed down in silence, watching the tourists in their golf shirts and shorts and flip-flops.

I wiggled my toes in my own flip-flops and took a long sip of margarita. Maybe it was what I'd wanted after all. "I have to walk the beach," I said. "Don't let me fall asleep again until I walk the beach."

Michael washed down a bite of burrito with a slug of beer. "And don't let me fall asleep until I get a plan. I need a plan. "

"Don't let me call home," Carol said. "The minute I call, they'll turn their brains off and I'll have to do all the thinking. They're fine. It hasn't even been twenty-four hours."

"I wonder what Sugar Butt is doing now," our father said.

At first I thought Kevin was yelling at me in a dream. I hadn't dreamed about my former husband in a long time, and it didn't seem to be a good sign that he was invading my sleep again. He sounded different now. He was louder and more aggressive. I was glad he hadn't been like that when we were still together. Back then, we usually just stopped speaking to each other when we were angry. Or we'd huff and puff and slam doors a little harder than was absolutely necessary. Actually, I'd huff and puff and slam, and he'd be so stiffly polite I wanted to kill him.

"I don't know what the hell I came here for anyway," he yelled.

"Unbelievable," Carol said.

"What are *you* doing here?" I said. The only thing worse than fighting with Kevin was having my family hear me fighting with Kevin.

Carol sat up in bed. "What do you mean, what am I doing here? What is that idiot doing in this hotel? He should be locked up somewhere."

"Huh?" I pushed my weary body into a sitting position.

"Don't you dare tell me to keep it down," the same voice yelled. "Just because you care what people think doesn't mean I give a shit."

"Don't tell me what I give a shit about," a woman's voice yelled.

"It must be that couple we saw checking in," I whispered, as if that wasn't completely obvious. "I didn't think they looked very happy."

"Don't you tell me shit about anything," the male voice yelled.

"Don't talk your shit to me," the female voice said.

"Shit," I said. "We're never going to get any sleep."

Carol was already calling the front desk.

"So," Carol said after she hung up. "What do you want to talk about while we wait for security to shut them up?"

"I don't know," I said. "What do *you* want to talk about?"

Carol yawned. "What's new with Jack?"

I yawned back. "His name is John. And we broke up."

"For real? Or just until you kiss and make up again?"

"For real."

"How come?"

"Don't tell anyone," I whispered. "But he wanted me to eat out of his dog's dish."

Carol started to laugh.

"It's not funny," I said.

She laughed harder.

"Fine. I'm officially not speaking to you."

"That's it," Carol said. "I can't take it anymore."

"That's it," the woman in the next room yelled. "I can't take it anymore."

"That would have been funny," I said, "if we'd slept for more than an hour and a half."

Carol turned on her bedside light and stomped across the room to the desk. She pulled a wad of tissue out of her telephone ear and picked up the phone. "It's me again. This is my third call, and if you can't get the people next door to shut up, I will expect a voucher for an all-inclusive vacation for four. And if my aging father has any adverse health repercussions from his extreme sleep-deprivation, I'll have to insist that you pay his medical bills as well, in accordance with the local noise ordinance."

I pushed myself up to a sitting position. "Wow, you're good. How did you know about the local noise ordinance?"

"I just made it up. Listen, help me drag this mattress into Dad and Michael's room. If I wanted to be sleep-deprived, I could have stayed home."

It's not as easy as you might think to drag a hefty hotel mattress off a bed. We'd only moved it a foot or two when Michael knocked twice and poked his head into our room. He was rubbing his eyes. Clumps of wadded toilet paper stuck out of each ear.

"Oh, no," I said. "You can hear them all the way over in your room?"

He pulled the paper out of his ears. "Who?"

"If I walk out that door, that's it," the man next door yelled. "You'll never see me again."

"Oh, walk," Carol said. "Please walk."

Michael shook his head. "I can't hear a damn thing in our room over Dad's snoring. I think we need to get him checked out for sleep apnea when we get home. Either that or buy him a muzzle."

"Go," the woman next door yelled. "But don't think for one goddamn minute you're taking the car. I'll throw the keys off the goddamn balcony before I let you take the goddamn car."

"Wow," Michael said. "Have you called security?"

"Now why didn't we think of that," Carol said.

We heard three loud knocks out in the hallway, followed by "Security."

"Not that we'll be here long enough to reap the benefits," Carol said, "but I hope some of the renovations around here involve sound-proofing."

"Hurry." I gave Carol's mattress a shove back toward its original position. "We've only got twenty minutes to sleep."

"Can you guys help me bring my mattress in here?" Michael said. "I can't take that snoring anymore."

Michael was all settled in and I was just dozing off when something hit the other side of the wall with a loud thump.

"What was *that*?" I said.

"It sounded like a shoe," Carol said.

"It might be a good sign," I said. "Maybe they're packing."

We heard another thump, this one wall-shaking.

"Yup," Michael said from his mattress on the floor. "There's the suitcase."

We started to laugh. And then we started to laugh louder, like three little kids in the dark, that full throttle kind of laughter that hurts your stomach and doesn't happen often enough once you're a grown-up.

"Stop it," Carol said. "After four pregnancies, I can only laugh a little or I pee my pants."

"Too much information," Michael said. We all started laughing harder.

"Shut the fuck up," the guy next door yelled.

"Ohmigod," I said. "Is he talking to us?"

"Don't tell them to shut the fuck up," the woman yelled. "You shut the fuck up."

"Language," Michael said.

"Shut the puck up with a capital F," I said.

"Eh," Carol said. "Doesn't have quite the right ring to it."

"It might if you're a hockey player," I said.

It wasn't really funny, but we started laughing again anyway, perhaps a little too loudly.

Another shoe hit the wall.

Carol sat up and turned her light on. I shaded my eyes while she walked across Michael's mattress and over to the phone. "It's me again. This is my fourth call and if you don't kick those people out of your hotel immediately, you're going to have to move my family and me to new rooms *and* give us a voucher for a return trip, complete with meals, should we ever be crazy enough to decide to come back. Okay. Okay. Thank you."

She slammed the phone down. "Done. Sarah, go leave a note on the other side of the door telling Dad not to wake us because we're sleeping in."

Michael sat up. "I can't sleep."

Carol sighed, long and loud. "Fine. How about this: Sarah and I will help you get a plan while we're waiting for the people next door to get kicked out, and then we can all sleep in."

"Yeah, okay," Michael said. "I was thinking that one of you could call Phoebe and tell her you just happen to be in Savannah and would love to meet her for lunch, and then I could be waiting—"

"Genius," I said. "That'll put her in a receptive mood."

Michael yawned. "Okay, hotshot. You come up with something better."

"Have flowers delivered to her," I said, "along with a beautiful note that says you're in Savannah and you'd like to meet her alone for lunch to try to get things right. Because whatever happens, for the rest of your lives you'll always be the parents of two beautiful girls that you both love very much, and you only want what's best for them."

"Whoa," Carol said. "Somebody write that down before we forget it."

"Thanks," I said.

"One question though." Carol yawned. "How can you come up with something like that when you always make such a mess of your own life?"

I threw one of my pillows at her.

"Guess what?" Carol said. "Sarah's boyfriend asked her to drink out of a dog dish."

"I hate you," I said.

"Grow up, you two," Michael said. He pushed himself off the mattress and grabbed a pad of hotel paper from the desk. "Assuming Phoebe goes for it, what do I say to her when she shows up?"

"I guess you wing it," I said.

CHAPTER

Twenty-five

Phoebe's parents lived on Jones Street, which every-body always said was the most beautiful street in the historic district of Savannah. Magnolias and enormous live oaks shaded streets and sidewalks still paved in brick in some parts, and tall elegant homes from the 1800s stood elbow-to-elbow in the steamy summer air.

A realtor might describe Phoebe's parent's place as a three-story plus garden level antebellum brick town-house complete with carriage house and oodles of charm. I wasn't quite sure what *antebellum* actually meant, beyond *old*, but it seemed to fit. An ornate black wrought iron railing followed two flights of stairs up to the freshly painted black front door, which was sur-rounded by a white portico. Some sort of serious-looking historical plaque adorned the brick to one side of the door.

I'd only been inside the house once, the weekend of Michael and Phoebe's wedding, at a party that took place the night before the wedding rehearsal. Most of that long weekend was a blur, but I could still remember walking through the front door and being blown away by a banister that was an exact replica of the one in our family house in Marshbury. The same softly curved solid mahogany in the same shape and proportions, even the same turned white spindles. But while our banister began in a wide center hallway and went up only one flight, this banister was pushed all the way over to one side of the narrow house and then soared up to an extra third floor.

It was like discovering our house had a taller, thinner long-lost relative, a Southern cousin. At the time we all thought it was a sign Michael and Phoebe were meant for each other.

All these years later, my family and I were parked in our Ford Focus just down the tree-lined street from the house. A white delivery van pulled up in front of the house. Michael leaned forward between the two front seats so he could get a better view.

"Right on time," Michael said. "Just like they promised."

It was Carol who'd remembered that Garden On the Square had done the flowers for their wedding. As an event planner, Carol collected cards wherever she went and added them to a database in case one of her clients ever wanted a destination event. She'd pulled the address up on her iPhone with uber efficiency.

We'd showered and changed this morning as soon as our alarms went off. After devouring coffee and egg sandwiches at a Hilton Head bagel place tucked behind some trees, we'd managed to find Abercorn Street. We'd just pulled into an empty parking spot in front of Garden On the Square when a pretty blond woman unlocked the front door.

The bell rang as we walked in. "How're y'all doin' this mornin'?" she said.

"A top o' the mornin' to you, darlin'," our father said as he tipped his Coast Guard Auxiliary cap.

Carol jumped in. "Hi there. Beautiful morning, isn't it? Okay, so is there any way you can look up my brother's wedding to see what kind of floral arrangements you did for it? He needs one delivered ASAP."

"I sure can." The woman smiled at Michael. "Almost forgot your anniversary, honey? Happens all the time."

"Something like that," Michael said.

Michael copied over his note on a thick white card in his best handwriting. He sealed the envelope and wrote Phoebe on it. A few minutes later, we were looking at a mason jar wrapped in lace holding a bouquet of blue hydrangeas, magnolia leaves, and Spanish moss.

"So sweet," Carol said. "I actually remember those from the wedding."

"Let's hope you're not the only one," Michael said.

I reached into a pocket on the inside of my shoulder bag and pulled out a seagull feather. I had no idea whether it came from a laughing gull or not, but when

I'd found it in the parking lot this morning on the way to the car, it felt like it might be a good luck charm.

I held it out to the woman. "Okay to add this?"

"Of course." She slid it into the bouquet at an artful angle.

Michael coughed and turned away.

"Okey-dokey," our father said. "Now that we've got that squared away, do you have anything I can look at in a wrist corsage for a certain cray-cray Southern Lady?"

"I sure do, honey," she said.

"By the way," I said. "You don't happen to know what cray-cray means, do you?"

She smiled. "I don't know what it means in your neck of the woods, but here in Savannah it means taking crazy to a whole 'nother level."

"Hurry up," I said as the door to the florist van opened in front of Phoebe's parents' house. "Let's go." This whole stalking thing was making me flash back to high school, when my friends and I would drive by the houses of all the boys we had crushes on, hoping for a glimpse of them. It was both thrilling and embarrassing back then, but by the time you got to be my age, the thrill had gone and all that was left was the embarrassment. I hoped I wouldn't be reduced to driving by John Anderson's condo a few months from now. I hoped I could just move on.

"Wait," Michael said. "I want to make sure Phoebe answers the door. If her parents recognize my handwriting on the card, they might not give the flowers to her."

Maybe we'd all time-traveled back to high school. "I thought Phoebe's parents liked you," I said.

"Do we still like Kevin?" he said.

"Good point," I said. "But then again, I don't think you ever liked Kevin."

"Only because he was an asshole," Michael said.

"Language," our father said. "Though, I might have to give you special dispensation on this one. Even on his best day, that husband of yours was a card-carrying cad."

"Gee, thanks," I said. "Funny how when I was married to him, none of you ever said things like that."

"We figured you already knew," Carol said. "Why rub it in, you know?"

"Oh, right," I said. "I forgot how much you guys hate to rub things in."

Michael dropped his head down. "She's opening the door. Come on, get me out of here. Fast."

Boston is a fantastic city, but the streets are a muddle of confusing twists and turns and changing street names. Savannah is laid out on a grid that actually makes sense. The GPS on Carol's phone sent us onto Montgomery Street, took us past the Savannah Civic Center, and circled us around a couple of charmingly landscaped squares complete with walkways and benches. We found the riverfront, putted along in traffic, then pulled into a garage just up a side street so we could kill some time walking around.

Carol and I wandered into a souvenir shop while Michael and our dad hung out on the sidewalk. "Do not let me buy anything that isn't for me," she said. She picked up a T-shirt in Maeve's size. Put it down again.

I found a Pinball Hero baseball hat. Picked it up, put it down, picked it up again.

"So," I said, as I put it down one more time. "How are we going to handle this thing with Dad?"

"Well, obviously," she said. "We're going with him."

We dropped Michael off a block or so from Reynolds Square so Phoebe wouldn't see that he'd brought his family for reinforcement. He'd asked her to meet him at The Olde Pink House, the restaurant she'd taken him to when he first visited Savannah. We were all sure he'd get extra points for remembering.

Michael reached for his door handle. "Do I look okay?"

"Smokin'," I said.

Our father turned around in his seat. "Like a stallion. Now march right in there and use your best apple butter on that baby cakes. It got her circled to you once, and mark my words, you'll be back in fat city before you know it."

"Thanks. I think." Michael managed a smile, but it didn't look very convincing.

"You look fine," Carol said. "Just remember, if Phoebe tries to start a fight, do not engage. Tell her she looks great, ask her how her parents are. Ask her if the girls are having a good visit."

"And whatever you do," I said. "Do not bring up Uncle Pete."

"Thanks," he said. "I needed that."

"Sorry," I said. "I just mean that you're there to talk about the girls and what's best for them. You need to stay focused on that and not on your personal relationship with Phoebe. At least for now."

I'd suffered through more than my share of agonizing conferences with parents whose marriages were in the middle of a break-up. One minute we'd be talking about their preschooler's verbal skills and the next they'd be using their own to throw daggers at each other.

"I know, I know," Michael said.

Our cramped economy car felt almost empty once he was gone. We sat there for a while, watching him walk down the street, getting smaller and smaller.

"He has a good swagger when he walks," Carol said. "Like I might be a nice guy, but don't mess with me."

"I'm proud to say I taught him that swagger," our dad said, "after two young hellions from his cub scout troop gave him a hard time. I had him going back and forth and back and forth in the basement rumpus room all one Sunday afternoon until he had it down cold. The likes of them never bothered him again, thank you very much."

"Good to know, Dad," Carol said. "I'll keep that in mind in case the boys need any swagger coaching. Wait, I'm not going to talk about my kids. They're fine."

"Ha," I said. "Remember when Michael used to call his favorite stuffed animal Winnie of Poo? And every time he said it we'd all crack up because it sounded like Winnie was made of poo."

"We were known for our sophisticated senses of humor," Carol said.

Our father let out a big laugh and hit the dashboard with his palm. "Your mother and I used to tell you kids you weren't allowed to have broccoli until you were twenty-one. You'd get down on your hands and knees at the dinner table and beg for the stuff."

"Nice, Dad," I said. "We couldn't have broccoli, but you'd give us sips of your beer."

Our father shook his head. "Only when your mother wasn't watching. Children sampling a wee bit of alcohol did not go over well with Marjorie Hurlihy, let me tell you. And here we were both brought up in households that believed Guinness was good for anything that ailed you, the next best thing to mother's milk."

"Remember," Carol said, "when Grandpa used to give us those disgusting orange marshmallow candies shaped like peanuts? He always had a bag hidden under his recliner when we came to visit?"

"Ha," I said, "Remember that time Michael, no, maybe it was Billy, went toddling into Grammy and Grandpa's kitchen screaming, 'Where's my penis?' and Dad pointed to his diaper, and said, 'Right here, big boy, right here.' And he kept saying it and getting madder and madder, and we finally figured out he meant *peanuts.*" I cracked up all over again, and Carol and our dad joined in.

"I'm pretty sure it was Billy." Carol wiped tears from her eyes. "Such a classy bunch."

"Speaking of which," I said. "We'd better get going. It's almost time for Dad's date with Sugar Butt."

Twenty-six

"Dad," I yelled as our father made a beeline for the Crystal Beer Parlor. "Wait for us."

"And tone down that swagger," Carol hissed. "You look like somebody crossed a penguin with an old John Wayne movie."

He turned around and waited for us to catch up to him. "Nothing wrong with the Duke."

"Don't worry," Carol said. "We're not going to hang around. All we want to do is check her out to make sure it's not some kind of scam."

"She's on the up and up, I can feel it right here." Our father put one hand over his heart. Then he held up his wrist corsage with his other hand. It was made out of yellow roses and peacock feathers and had twirls of purple ribbon dangling off the sides. "You don't think this is too extravagant for a first date, do you? I don't want her to think I'm made of money."

"It's perfect, Dad," I said. "Nice change of pace from your usual single yellow rose."

Carol grinned. "You mean like the single yellow rose he brought for *your* date?"

If I lived to be a thousand, my sisters and brothers would never let me forget that I'd once accidentally answered one of my own father's personal ads. As if it couldn't have happened to anyone.

My father being my father, the embarrassment was completely one-sided. "And what a lovely time we had, Sarry girl, now didn't we?" he said.

An older woman with an explosion of canary yellow hair was leaning up against the rough brick wall of the Crystal Beer Parlor under the shade of a crisp black window awning. She was wearing bike shorts and a stretchy lime green sleeveless shirt. The green of her wide-brimmed visor matched her shirt exactly and her black faux leather fanny pack was studded with round metal rivets, adding a touch of motorcycle edge to her bicycle look.

My father picked up the pace.

The woman slid her sunglasses up to the top of her visor. "Lord love a duck, you're handsome," she said.

"Billy Hurlihy," my father said as he extended the wrist corsage. "And you must be Sugar Butt."

Just as I was trying to decide whether to call her Sugar or Ms. Butt, she threw her head back and let out a great big laugh. Her yellow hair didn't move an inch.

"My special friends call me Sugar Butt," she said, "but my given name is Belva Rae O'Garrity."

"You'll always be Sugar Butt to me," our father said as he stepped forward. Sadly, she'd always be Sugar Butt to me, too. My father helped her into her wrist corsage, then introduced us. She wasn't our mother by a long shot, but she didn't seem all that dangerous either. Who knew, maybe she and our dad could work their way into a long distance casserole relationship.

Carol gave me *the look*. I took a step back. "Well," I said, " I guess we'd better get going so we're not late for, um, you know."

"You can't leave us before the Slow Ride," Sugar Butt said. "We'll do all the work, but you've got to at least come and watch."

"Excuse me?" Carol said.

Sugar Butt turned to our father. "Tell 'em it's okay, Daddy."

"Excuse me?" I said.

Sugar Butt pointed. An odd contraption filled with senior citizens was parked at the curb. It had a curved roof and a big sign on the front that said SAVANNAH SLOW RIDE.

"Jump on in," Sugar Butt said. "We've got two extra seats. Handley Crawford is resting up from having her face lifted and Jelly Roll Jenkins just up and died on us."

"That's encouraging," Carol said.

There was a good excuse to get out of this just on the tip of my tongue, but I couldn't come up with it fast enough.

"Welcome aboard," a bearded driver in shorts and a
T-shirt said as Sugar Butt herded us on. His seat faced
forward and he had a big steering wheel, which seemed
like moderately good signs. Sugar Butt took our father
by the hand and led him to one of the two empty seats
with pedals. I counted ten pedal seats in all—five on
each side facing each other across the length of the
trolley car-like vehicle. The center aisle was narrow
because a wooden wrap-around bar took up the rest of
the interior space, giving everybody including the driver a place to rest both their elbows and their drinks.

Carol and I found two empty seats just above the
back wheels. They were pedal-less. There was also a
vacant bench way at the back of the vehicle, maybe to
take a nap if you needed one.

A bald man wearing aviator glasses and a Hawaiian
shirt turned to us. "You're our back-up in case we lose
anybody."

I leaned forward. "What exactly do you mean by
lose?"

Everybody laughed. I hated being funny when I
didn't mean to be.

"Haven't lost one yet this week, honey," the driver
said.

I thought the pedals were some kind of touristy
gimmick, but they turned out to be the entire propul-
sion. Our dad got right into it, pedaling as hard as the
best of them. The thigh muscles on those senior legs
put mine to shame. Maybe I'd dust off my old bicycle
when I got home.

"You doing okay, Billy Boy?" Sugar Butt said a long time and maybe half a block later.

"Don't you worry about me, darlin'." He wiggled his eyebrows. "You know what they say about riding a bike."

Even without pedaling and with the roof for shade, it was so steamy hot I couldn't decide what I wanted more—a fan, a Popsicle, or another shower. The sundress Carol had packed for me stuck to my back like it had been slathered with preschool paste. I reached for my water bottle and took a long, warm sip.

Senior legs circling madly, our Slow Ride crawled along while our driver beeped and waved at people like he was running for mayor. Tourists chased after us with cameras and cell phones to take our picture. The driver pushed a button and suddenly The Everly Brothers were singing "All I Have To Do is Dream." Everybody joined in. My father made eyes at Sugar Butt as he sang.

Carol leaned over. "As soon as they stop for a Geritol break, I say we cut and run."

"Deal," I whispered.

We hummed along and smiled at everybody. Our Dad had somehow managed to acquire a beer in a plastic cup. He took a healthy sip and extended it to Sugar Butt. The peacock feathers in her wrist corsage fluttered as she reached for it.

"You don't drink from someone's else's cup," I whispered to Carol, "especially when you've just met. If she gives him mono, I will take her out."

"At least she didn't offer him a dog dish," Carol whispered. "You've got to give her that."

I glared at her. "I will never tell you *anything* again."

A woman in a big straw hat smiled over at us. "This is how we work up an appetite for our weekly lunch at The Crystal. Mr. Don is the yard bird master. Wait till you taste his fried chicken with succotash and smashed potatoes."

"And if you got a hollow leg," the Hawaiian shirt guy said, "you can start with the jawgia cracka nachos -- barbecued smoked pulled pork piled sky high on tortilla chips with cheddar cheese and diced onion, jalapenos, and chopped dill pickles."

"Love me some of that she crab stew and onion rings," somebody else said.

"Okay," Carol whispered. "Maybe we'll eat first, then we'll cut and run."

Doris Day started singing "Que Sera, Sera" as our driver pointed out Flannery O'Connor's childhood home.

"Ian and Trevor would love spitting over the edge of this thing," Carol said a while later. We were pulled over beneath a shady tree near Forsyth Park, waiting for the peddlers to get back from the public restrooms. "Even Siobhan would get a kick out of it, though Maeve would be a handful. Oh, God, I'm doing it again."

"That's okay," I said. "I don't mind."

Carol let out a puff of air. "It's not about you. God, I envy you your self-absorption."

"Thanks," I said. "And I envy you your tact."

"Do you know that I don't even remember how not to think about them anymore? Even when Dennis and I are out to dinner, we can't go more than three minutes without bringing up one of the kids. For more than a decade and a half it's been all about everybody but me, and even when they're not with me, I still can't get away from them."

I didn't say anything. I was stuck on the decade and a half part. I'd never really thought about it that way before, but for the last decade and a half I'd been almost married, then married, then almost divorced, then divorced and back to square one with nothing to show for it. Except for a house I wasn't all that crazy about in the first place and couldn't really afford on my own. I might as well have just skipped the whole thing. Why would I ever want to go through all that again?

Bathroom break over, our Slow Ride took off again, blasting "Sea of Love" as we crept along the street at the edge of the park under the shade of live oaks dripping with Spanish moss. At the far end of the park, tourists looked on as water sprayed from a majestic fountain. I wondered if I could get away with jumping the wrought iron fence and diving in to cool off.

"Hey, you two spring chickies in the cheat seats," Sugar Butt yelled back to us.

Carol gave a little wave. "Hey," she said.

I waved, too. "Hey."

"So, why don't Southern women do orgies?" Sugar Butt yelled.

"Holy shit," I whispered to Carol without moving my lips.

Carol faked a smile. "Gee, I don't know. Why?"

"Too many thank-you notes," Sugar Butt boomed.

Twenty-seven

"Irish road bowling?" Carol said. "What the hell is Irish road bowling?"

"'Twill be the high point of the day," our dad had said. "Like a trip back to the old sod."

Our father was born in Worcester, Massachusetts and had never actually been to Ireland, but we let him pretend that he had. We'd even talked about the whole family going over together one day, where I imagined we'd let him pretend to show us around his old stomping grounds.

After lunch at The Crystal, the Slow Ride gang had reconvened at O'Connell's Irish Pub and then carpooled over the bridge to Hutchinson Island. Carol and I followed along behind in our Ford Focus. Sugar Butt was driving a red Volkswagen Rabbit in front of us, and when she reached for her blinker, it made the ribbons of her wrist corsage dance.

"We'll just stay long enough to make sure he's safe," Carol said.

"Exactly," I said. "And then we'll cut and run. Maybe it'll be cool enough to walk the beach by then."

A long stretch of road was blocked off, and clumps of men and women appeared to be standing together in teams.

We pulled over to the side of the road and climbed out.

"Are those real cannonballs?" Carol said when we caught up to our dad and Sugar Butt.

I walked over and picked one up, just to make sure our father wouldn't get a hernia. Or worse.

"Twenty-eight ounces and seven inches in diameter," Sugar Butt said.

Our father winked. "I think you're underestimating me, darlin'."

"I think I'm going to be sick," I whispered to Carol without moving my lips.

"So how exactly does this work?" Carol asked a man with a shamrock on his visor.

He circled his cannonball backward with one arm as if he were a baseball player warming up for a pitch. "The course is a mile and a half long. The team that reaches the finish line with the fewest shots wins."

"What kind of shots?" I said. If this was some kind of a drinking game, I was packing up my father and taking him back to the hotel right now.

Sugar Butt laughed. "Don't worry, flufferpuff, that kind of shot comes later. Winning team buys the first round." She handed Carol a can of Deep Woods Off. "Just give yourselves a shot of this right now, then we'll put you girls on snake and gator watch."

"That last part's a joke, right?" I said.

"Faugh A Ballagh," somebody yelled.

"That means get out of the way," somebody else yelled.

If you didn't think about potential gators, it was a pretty interesting game to watch. A throwing mark called a butt, apparently no relation to Sugar, was drawn across the road in chalk. You had to step over the butt, or break butt, before releasing the bowl, which is what the cannonball was called. Wherever the cannonball stopped, they'd find the nearest point on the road and make a new butt mark for the next throw.

I wondered if I could come up with a version that either the Gamiacs or the Bayberry preschoolers could play, although we'd have to substitute something less lethal than cannonballs, and both groups would probably dissolve into laughter unless we changed the term *butt* to something not quite so giggle-worthy.

"Wow," Carol said. "Dad's still got a pretty decent arm on him."

We moved up the road behind the bowlers. I reached for the Deep Woods Off and sprayed another cloud around us.

"Faugh A Ballagh," somebody yelled.

"So," Carol said. "He really wanted you to eat out of a dog dish?"

"I don't want to talk about it."

"Dennis drank out of one of my high heels once. I think he saw it in a movie. It was kind of sexy, if you didn't factor in the cost of the shoes."

"It wasn't supposed to be sexy. He was trying to get his dog to submit to me."

"Whoa. That definitely crosses the line. No wonder you broke up with him."

I buried my head in my hands. "It wasn't like *that*."

"So then *why* is it you're not seeing each other anymore?"

I sighed. "All he thinks about is his dog. He even hung this stupid painting it did over his fireplace."

"You're jealous of his *dog*?"

"Of course not. Well, maybe a little."

"A man who loves his dog knows how to commit. So you might want to think twice before you screw this one up."

"I didn't screw it up. He did."

Carol swatted at a mosquito. "Come on, let's get out of here. I have no intention of spending the rest of my vacation scratching."

"Good idea," I said. "All this gator watching is making me paranoid anyway."

We took a few steps closer to the bowlers. "Give me a call when you need a ride, Dad," Carol yelled.

Our dad turned around and blew us a kiss.

Sugar Butt turned around, too. "Don't y'all worry about a thing," she yelled. "I'll drop Daddy off . . . one of these days."

Raucous senior laughter followed us back down the road.

"Jeesh," I said. "I hope she's not too much for him to handle."

"Don't worry about it," Carol said. "Even if she is, at least we'll know he died happy."

"I sure hope she can cook," I said. "I'm counting on those casseroles."

"Don't get your hopes up," Carol said. "Casseroles are too perishable to ship anyway, unless we can talk her into dry ice."

"Fine," I said. "Then she can visit, but just long enough to cook up a big batch. I think we need to seriously limit Dad's Sugar Butt time. I'm not sure she's a good influence on him."

"Agreed," Carol said. "As soon as he gets back to the resort, I'll help him fire up his laptop and we can look for someone closer to home and a little bit more buttoned down. I think he just needs some supervision while he's looking."

"Exactly," I said. "And speaking of supervision, it's not like I thought he'd really need it, but while he was in the shower this morning, I snuck a condom in his wallet, just to be on the safe side."

"I did, too," Carol said as she clicked the lock on the Ford Focus. "Oh, well, better safe than sorry. The STD rate for seniors isn't getting any lower. Damn Viagra."

Just as we were leaving Hutchinson Island, Michael called Carol's phone. We found him waiting for us down the street from The Olde Pink House, sipping from a bottle of water. He was sitting on a low wall

made of tabby, a mix of masonry and crushed oyster
shells that I couldn't get enough of. I wanted a house
made of tabby.

He gave a little wave when he spotted us inching toward him in the traffic.

"He looks sad," I said.

"But he's not pacing," Carol said. "That's a good
sign."

"How'd it go?" I said as soon as he jumped in the car.

"Okay," he said. "Where's Dad?"

"Sugar Butt said she'd drop him off later," I said.
"Way later."

"Uh-oh," Michael said. "Maybe it's a good thing I
put a condom in his wallet last night while he was snoring away."

We'd stopped for takeout on the way back to the resort so we didn't have to worry about going back out.
We were all too stuffed to eat again yet, so I put our
sandwiches in the tiny refrigerator in our room.

Michael handed us each a Sam Adams and put the
remaining three from the six-pack in the fridge in his
room. Housekeeping had dragged Michael's mattress
back to where it belonged, so Carol and I sat on one
queen size bed in our room and gave him the other.

"Okay, spill," Carol said. "I can't take it any longer.
What happened with Phoebe?"

Michael took a long slug of beer. "It went okay, I
guess."

Carol and I waited him out.

He took a smaller sip. "Sort of surreal, almost like we were on our first date or something. And we could finish our coffee and walk away and none of it would have ever happened—no marriage, no kids, no house, no dog. Just hit the undo button and be done with it."

He put his beer down on the bedside table, reached back with both hands, massaged his neck. "I mean, obviously, even if I could skip the whole thing, I wouldn't. Maybe I'm a little bit like that poor guy who lost both legs in the Boston Marathon bombing and kept trying to stand up anyway. I don't know if there's enough marriage left to hold us up anymore, but I can't seem to make myself stop trying."

I closed my eyes. I wondered what it would have been like if either Kevin or I had cared enough to keep trying to save our marriage. Whether or not it would have made a difference.

"How did you leave it?" Carol asked.

"Phoebe's going to let me see the girls tomorrow. I think she feels guilty she hasn't let them call me. She gave them some crap about my phone being broken. Anyway, it killed me, but I stayed calm and acted like it was no big deal. She's picking me up at nine. The girls want to play miniature golf."

"That's good," Carol said.

Michael shrugged. "We'll see."

I turned to look at him. "Does she know we're here?"

"I didn't mention it," Michael said.

"Smart move," Carol said.

We sat there for a while, sipping our beer. I was thinking about how relationships were so much damn work. That it was amazing anyone even bothered. It didn't seem like the most positive thing to add to the conversation, so I kept my mouth shut.

Carol picked up the remote and clicked through the channels.

"Stop," Michael yelled. "It's *Gilligan's Island.*"

"Cool," I said. "You know, being marooned in this hotel is a little bit like being shipwrecked on a desert island, isn't it?"

"Sure it is, sis." He made eye contact with Carol and they both pointed an index finger toward one ear and circled it, childhood code for crazy.

We sang along with the theme song the way we always did. "Kind of scary that we all remember every single word," I said.

"Not really," Carol said. "It just shows that our long-term memory is still intact."

The camera cut to the whole crew circled around a picnic table. "Why can't we find someone like Mrs. Howell for Dad?" I said.

"She's a little bit of a snob," Carol said.

"Yeah, but just think—white gloves and pearls instead of bike shorts and a fanny pack," I said. "The casseroles would have to be a step up."

"She's married," Michael said. "She'd only be thinking about Mr. Howell."

We watched as Ginger, MaryAnn and Mrs. Howell decided to hold a beauty pageant.

"Oh," I said. "I hate this episode. Beauty pageants are so offensive."

"I don't think that's the intention here," Carol said. "It was a different time back then. On another level—"

"I'm not sure *Gilligan's Island* has another level," I said.

Carol took a sip of her beer and kicked off her flip-flops. "Of course it does. Think about it. What kind of beauty is most important to you, and when you get right down to it, what do you want your life to be? Do you want to spend it with someone who's got breeding, poise and mature charm? Are conventional good looks the most important thing? Or being kind and easy-going?"

"Phoebe's all of them," Michael said. "Even when I hate her, she's all of them."

"Nobody's all of them," Carol said, "at least once the happy horseshit stage is over and everybody stops being on their best behavior."

"They should at least put the male castaways through a beauty contest, too," I said, "just to balance things." I took a long sip of beer. "I would so vote for the professor."

"The professor would never win," Michael said. "He's wearing white socks with his boat shoes."

"He actually reminds me a little bit of your Jack," Carol said.

"His name is John," I said. "And I don't want to talk about him."

There was a moment of silence.

"Woof," Carol said.

"Rrrrrruff," Michael said.

I shook my head. "Knock it off, you two. I said I don't want to talk about it."

"We're not talking about it," Carol said. "We're barking about it."

"Did he really ask you to eat out of a dog dish?" Michael asked. "I mean, if John Anderson is some kind of a sicko, I want to know about it."

"So you can beat him up?"

"Don't think I couldn't. He's not that big."

Carol wanted to take a long hot bath by herself without anyone bothering her, so we'd borrowed a flashlight at the front card table and managed to find our way to the resort golf course. I'd suggested it. Michael was nervous about tomorrow and I knew golf ball hunting always relaxed him.

"It's okay, Michael. He's not a sicko. And it doesn't even matter anymore. It's over."

Michael worked the beam of the flashlight back and forth across the golf course. "I just don't get why nothing ever lasts."

I looked up at the sky full of stars. "Maybe things will get better for us. Maybe Mercury's just been in retrograde."

"For what, our whole lives?"

I laughed and Michael joined me. He scooped up a golf ball from the base of a big clump of ornamental grass. I opened the plastic bag I'd brought so he could toss it in.

A sweet smell cut through the night. Orange trees? My perfume? Tucked against a palm tree I found two golf balls, nestled side by side. I gave them a little kick to separate them. They bounced against the tree trunk, then rolled into each other and stopped, a couple again.

Michael bent down and scooped them up, tossed them into the bag together.

"Holy shit," I said. "Was that an alligator that just ran by?"

We strained our eyes to see it, but it was long gone.

"Should we be afraid?" I whispered.

"Nah, I don't think so. Getting eaten by an alligator wouldn't even be the worst thing that's happened to us this year."

"Thanks for reminding me."

"I think it's pretty much what alligators do at night, hop from lagoon to lagoon."

"Maybe we should try it. Kind of like bar hopping, but without the hangover."

"It's a thought." Michael found another ball. He was really good at this, especially for someone who didn't golf. And didn't have any real use for golf balls.

I held the bag open. "Michael, if you were seeing someone and she didn't get along with Mother Teresa, what would you do?"

"Get another girlfriend?" Michael and the flashlight started moving in another direction.

"Great," I said. I jogged a few steps to catch up with him. If my brother and I were going to get eaten by an alligator, I wanted to go out together.

"I feel the same way about Mother Teresa as I do about Phoebe. Well, not exactly the same way, but you know what I mean. It's till death do you part."

Twenty-eight

I shook my head. "I can't believe Dad didn't even call to say he wasn't coming home, I mean here, last night."

"No kidding," Carol said. "He would have grounded us for a month if we'd pulled a stunt like that."

Michael rubbed his wet hair with a towel. "Hey, at least I got a decent night's sleep. All I can say is good luck to Sugar Butt with that snoring of his."

We'd stayed awake long enough to eat our sandwiches last night, flipped through some more old shows, turned in pathetically early. "Hey, Carol," I'd said right before we fell asleep.

"What? And hurry up, I'm almost asleep."

"Do you think it's really true that dogs and kids know who's a good person and who's only pretending to be?"

"Absolutely. Their bull crap detectors are extremely fine-tuned. Kids grow out of it once they get old enough to start lying to themselves, but dogs remain shrewd judges of character for their entire lives."

"So, if John Anderson's dog hates me, does that mean I'm not who I think I am?"

"Not necessarily. It could be that something's standing in the way and causing interference, and his dog can't get your true essence."

"Now *that* sounds like bull crap. What does it even mean?"

Carol's only answer was a snore. I tossed and turned, trying to think things through, then trying not to think, then just trying to get some sleep.

I finally drifted off, straight into a Technicolor dream. John and I were standing across from each other in a mansion dripping with spider webs. At first I thought we were in a room at Necromaniac, but then it morphed into the set of *The Addams Family*.

Not the movie from the '80s, but the original TV series I'd watched as a kid. John reached for my hand and kissed it. He wanted me to speak French to him. *Sarah est une jeune fille insouciante*, I said as I batted my eyes at him. How had I not realized that John was really Gomez before this? That Wednesday and Pugslie had been our children all along? I breathed a long, luxurious sigh of relief that the kid thing had already been resolved, and all that stress flew right out the window. I gazed at my Morticia-self in a dusty mirror. When I flipped my long straight black tresses, they rippled the full length of my back. I wasn't too sure about that

middle part in my hair, but other than that I looked
great. In my tight black sheath, you'd never even guess
that I'd gone through not one, but two, pregnancies.

"Bonus points," a familiar voice yelled. Out of nowhere, the floor tilted and all these annoying bells
started to ring. Soooooo loud. We'd been in the pinball
game all along. An enormous Keli with one *l* and an *i*
hovered over us, hands on the flipper buttons, aiming a
big orange ball right at me.

I choked on a scream and woke up. Somehow I'd
managed to slide off the bed and onto the questionable
hotel carpet. Carol was still snoring. It was close
enough to morning, so I tiptoed into the bathroom for a
long dream-purging shower. Then I took the rental car
to find coffee and breakfast for everyone.

I figured our dad had come back after I'd fallen
asleep, so I bought four of everything.

"Whatever," I said, once we all realized he wasn't
there. "Anybody want dibs on his egg sandwich?"

Michael held out his hand, so I tossed it over.

"You sure you don't want company today?" I asked
Carol.

"Nope, I want to spend the whole day wandering
around all by myself, without a care in the world and
without having to worry about anyone else. No offense."

"None taken," I said. "I love you, too."

"I can drop you off somewhere though."

"No, I'm fine. I think I'll just walk the beach and
hang around."

Carol crumpled the wrapper from her breakfast sandwich and reached for her coffee. "Just make sure you're both back in time for dinner. I made reservations at The Jazz Corner since it's our last night."

"What time do we have to leave for the airport tomorrow?" Michael asked.

"Our flight's at 9:17 A.M.," Carol said without even having to look it up. "We've got another stopover in Charlotte, so we'll arrive in Boston at 1:31. I wanted to make sure we'd get through Boston and be back in Marshbury before rush hour."

"Good thinking," Michael said.

"Okay, I'm out of here." I grabbed my father's coffee so it wouldn't go to waste. I walked all the way down the endless hallway again. I stepped off the elevator, smiled at the two women behind the card table in the makeshift lobby for the third time this morning, wove my way along the construction zone. It felt like I'd been walking for days.

I still couldn't wait to walk the beach.

Just past the PLEASE PARDON OUR MESS sign Michael had taped to my back, I found a stash of paint cans and used one to prop open a door to the pool deck.

"Good morning," I said to the copper pelican stretched out in the fountain reading his copper book. I walked around some scaffolding so I didn't have to risk bad luck by going under it. I worked my way to the gate at the far end of the pool deck.

I stopped for a sip of coffee and a breath of salt air, reached over the gate to unlock the latch. I followed a weathered gray boardwalk through another gate framed by a high curved arbor. A tall tassel of dune grass, summer green and rustling in the wind, greeted me from a softly mounded sand dune. I cut between two rambling lengths of storm fencing, some of the wooden slats snapped off like broken teeth, and kicked off my flip-flops. The warm powdery sand caressed my feet gently, so different from the coarse massage of the sand back in Marshbury.

The long stretch of beach was peppered with walkers and runners, but it was still early enough that most of the beach goers hadn't showed up yet to stake their claim.

I stepped over the high tide line down to the hard-packed sand. I waited for a couple on bicycles to pass, returned their smiles, then closed the distance to the ocean. When I stepped in up to my ankles, it felt like a warm bath to my rugged New England feet. I took another sip of coffee and watched a seabird I couldn't identify disappear behind a puff of cottony cloud.

A green Frisbee sailed by. I watched it soar like some kind of tropical bird, then drop into the curl of a wave.

A streak of chocolate brown dog caught me by surprise, splashing water all over me. Somehow the water didn't feel so warm when you weren't expecting it, and the cold shock made me scream.

"Easy, Coco," a man's voice yelled behind me. The dog had the Frisbee in its mouth already and was swimming it to shore with the precision of a lifeguard.

"Sorry about that," the man added in a softer voice. "She gets a little bit excited."

When I turned around, I had to admit I got a little bit excited, too. The guy before me was about my age, give or take, with windblown dark hair and ocean blue eyes framed with thick dark eyelashes. He was on the tall side and in good shape, but in an outdoorsy way, as if he parasailed rather than worked out at a gym. He flashed me a big white smile.

I was just launching into what I hoped would be a moderately flirtatious smile of my own when a swathe of wet fur hit me from behind, practically knocking me over. I took a big step forward to catch myself. The guy reached out and put his hands on my shoulders to steady me.

His dog circled around in front of me, dropped the Frisbee at my feet, and shook, long and hard.

"Coco," the guy yelled.

"It's okay." I pulled my wet T-shirt away from me so it didn't stick to all the wrong places. Coco sat down on the sand and offered a paw. "Aww," I said as we shook. When I started scratching its chest, it wagged its tail like a maniac and gave me a pleading *don't stop* look with its big brown eyes.

I stopped scratching so I could reach for the Frisbee. Coco nudged me with its nose. I went back to my scratching.

"Wow," the guy said. "She sure likes you. She doesn't act like that with just anyone."

"Really?" I said. I hoped it didn't come out sounding quite as needy to his ears as it did to mine.

He grinned. "Coco has a built-in bullshit detector. She's very picky."

I grinned back. "Smart dog. They're not always so discerning."

He bent over to pick up the Frisbee. His back muscles tensed under his thin gray T-shirt, and I resisted the urge to start panting myself.

He threw the Frisbee way out into the water. Coco flew after it, crossing the sand in three long leaps. With her head just visible over the water, she looked like a seal pup as she paddled away.

"So beautiful," I said. "What kind of dog is she?"

"A Labradoodle. Half Lab, half standard poodle. At least we're pretty sure. She's a shelter dog."

"I love shelter dogs," I said. "And Lab crosses are the best. We had a Lab/shepherd growing up, and also a Lab/Doberman." I started to mention that my assistant teacher had a Lab/shar pei, but I was stopped by an irrational and completely paranoid thought that he'd somehow know how pretty June was and ask me for her number. "I always wanted a chihuahua/dachshund," I said instead, "just so I could call it a chiweenie."

He laughed. Our eyes went to each other's ring fingers at the exact same moment. He stuck out his other hand. "Paul Ridgefield."

"Sarah Hurlihy."

"Hey," he said. "You don't want to go grab a cup of coffee, do you?"

I held up my coffee cup.

"You could dump it out and start all over again." He tilted his head and opened his eyes wide when he said it. In that instant I knew that he knew how good-looking he was, but it didn't make it any less true.

It would make a great story one day. That summer my family had dragged me to Hilton Head. I'd helped my brother reconnect with his ex-wife, chaperoned my father on a first date with a woman with canary yellow hair named Sugar Butt. Then, as was so often the case with my family, as soon as they were all squared away, they dumped me like a hot potato. So there I was, all alone, single again thanks in large part to a bully of a beast named Horatio, when a kinder, gentler dog showed up out of the blue to lead me to my future.

I could almost believe it. I could see myself standing here now. I could picture telling the story one day. But the space between the two was daunting, and I wasn't sure I was up for all that peddling.

Still, it wasn't like he was asking me for a date. It was only a cup of coffee. Plus, I was leaving tomorrow, so I'd be safely home before I knew it and anything that happened, on the off chance that anything actually happened, would be slow and gradual and long distance and not at all like jumping back into the dating fray, which I was really bad at and the thought of which made me want to go back to the hotel room and climb back into bed. Alone.

Perhaps I hesitated a moment, or twelve, too long. Perhaps Paul Ridgefield simply had a bad case of shiny object syndrome. In any case, Coco came charging out of the water at the exact same moment a bikini-clad woman was walking by. Coco cut her off at the pass and dropped the Frisbee at her feet. The woman smiled.

Coco shook. The woman screamed. Then she giggled, her still perky breasts jiggling adorably.

Paul Ridgefield turned away from me. "Coco," he yelled.

"It's okay," she said. She bent down to give Coco a pat. Coco sat and offered her paw. I watched Paul Ridgefield watching her breasts try to escape the inadequate fabric of her bikini top. It was as if I'd dropped off the face of the earth. It was as if I were invisible.

"Wow, she sure likes you," I whispered to myself as I walked away. "She doesn't act that way with just *anyone*." I grabbed the hem of my baggie T-shirt and twisted it until water dripped to the sand.

The sun was higher now. Even with a breeze off the water, I was starting to sweat. I walked the length of the beach, not really thinking, not really not thinking either. There were lots of kinds of men in the world. There were lots of kinds of dogs in the world. There were lots of men who acted like dogs in the world.

A dark-haired woman in shorts and a T-shirt carrying a bright pink leash strode quickly in my direction. "You haven't seen a big chocolate brown Labradoodle running around, have you? What part of no dogs on the beach between 10 A.M. and 5 P.M. does my idiot brother not understand? I don't care if it's my dog, he's going to pay that five hundred dollar fine if he gets caught."

"It's *your* dog?" I said.

"Yeah, we all rented a house for the week for a family reunion. Next time I'm staying home." She shook her head. "*Family*."

"Coco," she yelled as she ran off in the wrong direction.

"Wait," I yelled. The squawk of two gulls fighting over what looked like a piece of donut drowned me out.

I thought about chasing after her. Then I turned and jogged back in the direction I'd come from, my flip-flops in one hand, my empty coffee cup in the other. The sun was beating down on the back of my neck. My lips were parched and a trickle of sweat ran down my back. The coffee was going right through me and I needed to find a bathroom fast. But it felt good to run, good to break through the inertia.

Paul Ridgefield and his wannabe girlfriend were on their way up to the top of the beach, Coco dancing between them, leaping and lunging for the Frisbee Paul held high over his head. They stopped walking. The woman looked at her watch, then said something. Paul nodded.

"Hey, Paul," I yelled when I got close enough for them to hear me.

He turned around and gave me a vague smile.

"Your wife is looking for Coco," I said. "She said to tell you this time the no dogs on the beach fine is on you."

A look of horror came over the woman's face.

"Hey," he said. "I don't have a—"

"You're *married?*" the woman said. "And you just *hit* on me?"

"No," he said. "Really. Not married. No wife."

I smiled at him. "And you don't have a dog either."

It was an immature thing to do, but at the very least it made me feel better, and at best it might have saved another woman some aggravation. But what really bothered me as I walked back to my hotel room was how much of myself I saw in Dog Bait Boy. How much easier it was to fantasize about the next person instead of trying to make things work with the one you were with. How the grass was always greener around the relationship you weren't really having.

Twenty-nine

My cell phone had been languishing untouched in the bottom of my shoulder bag for so long that it was out of power. I rifled through my carry-on for my charger. I didn't doubt for a moment that Carol had remembered to pack it for me. I wondered what it would be like to go through your life so efficiently. I wondered how I'd be different if I'd gone through my own life without a big sister to pick up the pieces.

Carol had made both beds before she left. Of course she had. I sat down on the edge of my bed, trying not to mess up all her hard work. The absence of my family was almost a presence, a silent sound all its own. I got up again, opened the sliding door a crack, enough to let in some real noise but not enough to lose all the cool air.

I turned around again and yanked my pillow out from under the bedspread, quickly, like a magician pulling a tablecloth from under a full table setting. I flopped down on my back, kicked off my flip-flops, stared up at the ceiling.

When our mother was dying, when the cancer had metastasized and spread to her lungs and hospice had been called in and none of us, not even me, could pretend it wasn't happening, she spent time with each of us alone. It was winter and her soft Lanz of Salzburg flannel nightgown was covered with tiny blue spring flowers. It had ruffles of white eyelet around the neck, its bulk disguising her shrinking body, but not really.

I tried my hardest not to notice whether my visits came before or after Johnny's or Billy's or Carol's or Michael's or Christine's. When you're one of six children, particularly a middle child, you're almost never the first one to get anything, but you never stop wanting it, even as an adult.

I climbed into bed beside her, leaning up against the cherry headboard my parents had bought when they were first married. Every couple of minutes or so, sometimes more, sometimes less, she'd start to cough. Her cough was as sad and unrelenting as the march of death, and she'd wait it out with a brush of her hand in front of her face. Already I missed the belted dresses with full skirts she wore in our childhood, her red lipstick, the way she closed her eyes and tilted her face to the sun while she hung damp beach towels on the clothesline, the sophisticated crunch she made when she ate cornflakes—a sound I'd tried unsuccessfully my whole life to duplicate.

My marriage to Kevin was hanging by a thread at this point, and I was hoping I could hold it together long enough so that my mother wouldn't have to die worrying about me. My siblings and I had been taking turns spending the night, sleeping in our old rooms. Some nights I just stayed anyway, whether it was my turn or not.

I tried not to cry while we waited out another cough. I held my mother's glass for her while she sipped some water from a straw. I tried to fluff her pillow without hurting her. I rubbed lotion on her dry hands, massaged her fingers gently, twirled the diamond on her wedding ring back to center. I read her a chapter from one of her favorite books as a child, *The Outdoor Girls in a Winter Camp,* by the same author who wrote *The Bobbsey Twins.* I held the book carefully so she wouldn't notice the worn binding had started to crumble away.

I finished the chapter, closed the book, put it down carefully on the bedside table.

"My Sarah," she said.

I waited for her to tell me something that would get me through her death, maybe even through the death of my marriage, words that I could carry with me for the rest of my life. Something to guide me, help me figure out what I was doing wrong, why I just couldn't seem to get a handle on this life of mine, why the only place I seemed to have any success was in my classroom, and not always even there. Something. Anything.

Her eyes closed. She let out a watery breath that turned into a raspy snore.

I thought we'd talk more the next time, but that was the last time we were ever alone together. She died a few days later, at home, surrounded by all six kids and her husband, the loves of her life.

My Sarah. Maybe that had said it all. My mother had loved me. She'd had my back my whole life, and at the end of the day, at the end of a life, it was as simple as that.

I powered up my phone to check in on the assignment I'd left for the Gamiacs.

I found our private chat room, typed in SarahTeach and the password.

A red message popped up on the screen. *Password is incorrect. Please try again.*

I took my time, typed the password in again. And again. Got the same message. Clicked a link to send an email to myself to change the password.

This chat room is private. You must be a member to join in.

The Gamiacs had set up the chat room for me. I was its only administrator. Wait. No, I wasn't. Keli was an administrator, too.

I closed my eyes as dawn broke over marble head.

I typed in *PrincessKeli.* I thought for a moment, then flashed back to meeting her that first day. *It's my happy place,* she'd said as she held the door open with one hand. *I even use* elevator *as a password.*

I typed in her password, entered the chat room, found my assignment. *Let's talk about unrequited love, the one who broke your heart. The one you haven't thought about in years. Or minutes.*

I scrolled through the long thread of comments.

ObsidianDream: *Katie and I kissed few X when we were 6 or 7 but that was part of kissing tag so didn't really count. In 5th grade I developed serious feeling for her. Middle school asked her to dance and she said no but would I tell my friend to ask her.*

RavenSureSong: *I was crushing on this boy in middle school and one day we had to pick teams for dodge ball and I was new and was used to getting picked last so I was trying not to act like it bothered me and it was his turn to pick and he picked me. I was so happy I thought I would die that he even said my name and I didn't even care if it was a pity pick. And then two kids got hurt and someone from our team had to go over to the other team to even them out. His friend pointed right at me and told them to take the ugly girl and he laughed.*

ObscureEssence: *Nothing takes the taste out of peanut butter quite like unrequited love. Charlie Brown.*

DarkShadow: *There was this girl in college and we ate at the same table alot in the dining hall since some of our friends were friends and whatever. So one of my friends has a birthday and we all take him out to celebrate and she's there and we have a good talk. And then she went to the bathroom. We never spoke to each other again. Now I can look back and see that I needed to take it upon myself to make a more significant step.*

Clearly the Gamiacs were enjoying the angst of strolling down memory lane. Maybe talking about their awkward past would help them move beyond it. I wished self-awareness and confidence and joy and love and luck for each and every one of them. And for me, too.

I kept scrolling, giving each painful post the attention it deserved. Maybe at our next session we could print them all out and have a ceremonial burning in one of the funeral urns and talk about moving forward.

Finally I found it.

PrincessKeli: *Everybody always wants to date me but mostly they're dipshits. They shoot me a smile and think that's all it takes. But there's this one guy that's different. A little geeky but in a cute way. And he talks to me like I have a brain. One night a bunch of us went out for drinks and I asked him out. So we went out to dinner and instead of going onandonandON about himself like a dipshit, he actually asked about what I liked to do and what I thought about things. So by the end of the night I'm ready to have his baby, or at least jump his bones, and he drives me home, locks his car and walks me to my door. And then he thanks me for a friggin' lovely time and kisses me on the cheek and leaves. Seriously? So I bide my time and about a day or two later I catch him on the elevator at work which by the way you guys if you haven't stopped it between floors and kissed somebody there DO IT becuz it is like the sexiest place on the planet. So there we are on the elevator and I tell him I thought he could do better than that last kiss. And he got like all serious and said he's in love with someone else and even though they aren't actively together his heart is still engaged and he doesn't think it would be fair to me to lead me on. See, total non-dipshit right down to his toes. So of course I want him even more so I tell him I'll take my chances and kiss him anyway. Let's just say it didn't go over too well but every time I ride that elevator I think of him. BUT he's a love me, love my dog kind of guy so I'll win in the end. Dating tip of the day: Want to land a dog lover? Cover his girlfriend in the scent his dog hates most.*

I logged out and pulled up Google. I typed *What scent do dogs hate most?* I hit Enter.

Most but not all dogs hate the smell of citrus. Especially orange.

I was still staring at my orange blossom perfume when the door clicked open and Carol walked in.

I placed it on the nightstand next to my organic orange essence lip balm and sat up. "Ha," I said. "You caved."

Carol dumped two handfuls of shopping bags onto her bed. "I know, I know, I couldn't help myself. I tried to drive by the outlet stores, but it was like somebody had programmed our stupid rental car to turn in automatically."

"Right," I said. "Blame it on the Ford Focus."

She pulled a shoebox out of a plastic bag. "I even found Dennis's favorite running shoes. In his size *and* forty percent off."

"Great," I said. "I think that means this vacation just went from cheaper than staying home to actually putting money in the bank."

"And how about these?" She pulled a family's worth of white T-shirts out of another bag. I SHAMROCK SAVANNAH was embellished on the fronts in Kelly green letters.

"I'm feeling a Christmas card coming on," I said.

"Exactly," Carol said. "I'd never find anything identical for all six of us at that price, especially something that Siobhan might actually wear. I couldn't walk away."

I watched while she lined her purchases up on the bed: a seagull refrigerator magnet, a small stuffed pelican, fluorescent green sunglasses, a pair of feather earrings.

I slid off the bed and stretched. "So, I'm just wondering . . .."

She pulled a plastic dinosaur out of a bag and looked up. "What?"

"Did you buy anything for yourself?"

"Of course I did. A shamrock T-shirt. Obviously, I have to be in the picture."

"That's it?"

She put her hands on her hips. "Your point?"

I shrugged. "I thought I heard you say something about spending the entire day thinking only about yourself."

Carol contemplated her bed. It looked like a mini-Christmas had exploded all over it.

"Son of a witch with a capital B," I said for her.

"Exactly," she said. "I'm pathetic."

I nodded my agreement. What are sisters for if not to point out the things the rest of the world is too polite to mention.

She walked over and slammed the slider to the balcony shut. "So, *what*, do you live in a barn?"

"Ha," I said. "You sound like Grammy Hurlihy. *We can't keep heating the whole outdoors, kids.*"

Carol turned around to face me. "You know, I'm kind of done with this whole vacation."

"Turkeys are done," I said. "People are finished."

"If it ain't one thing, it's six," Carol said.

"Have fun and don't do anything stupid."

"Catholic girls don't wear patent leather shoes. Omigod, I just remembered one of the nuns telling us that if you're ever in the backseat of a car with a boy and tempted to go all the way, to think of Mary standing outside the car window crying. Or maybe it was Jesus."

"Ha," I said. "No wonder we turned out so well, with all that sage advice in our formative years."

Carol reached for one of her shopping bags. "Yeah, no kidding. Though I might have to try that car window line on Siobhan when I get home."

CHAPTER

Thirty

Somewhere in the chaos of the resort Carol had managed to get our boarding passes printed before we left
for dinner.

I held out my hand. "I can hang onto mine."

She ignored me, attached the sheets of computer
paper to her clipboard, threw the clipboard on top of
her suitcase. I could picture her handing them out to us
just before we went through security at the airport,
like cookies to three-year-olds.

I'd changed into nice jeans and the only decent top
Carol had packed for me. It was the outfit I would have
worn if Paul Ridgefield hadn't turned out to be a dog
owner impersonator-slash-womanizer. If we'd actually
had coffee that had actually led to a date. I was over

him, but a part of me still hoped I'd run into him tonight looking really, really good.

"I can't believe Dad and Michael are blowing us off
for dinner on our last night," Carol said. "They could
have at least called to say they weren't going to make it
back in time. We have *reservations*."

"So what," I said. "So our party of four turned into a
party of two. We'll just tell them the other two people
got sick, or our dates dumped us, and they'll give us a
smaller table. Whatever."

"It's so rude," Carol said. "This is what I hate about
big families. Everybody feels totally free to dump you
when they get a better offer. Because even if you stop
speaking to them, it doesn't really matter because there
are still plenty of siblings left to hang out with. There's
no scarcity."

Carol's phone rang. She scooped it out of her purse,
looked at it, put it back in her purse.

"Aren't you going to answer it?"

"It's Christine."

"That's so rude," I said.

My phone rang. I dove for it and answered on the
second ring. "Hello," I said. "I can't hear you. Hello?
Hello?" I threw my phone on my bed.

Carol rolled her eyes. "Yeah, I'm sure she fell for
that. We are so going to have to make this up to her
when we get home. Okay, where was I? Right, what
would it take to pick up the phone and say that you're
otherwise occupied for the evening?"

"When you're otherwise occupied, you don't always
think of it, because, well, you're otherwise occupied.

God, do you think Michael and Phoebe are actually getting along?"

"I don't want to talk about Michael *or* Dad," Carol said. "They don't deserve it."

The red walls of the restaurant enveloped us like a hug when we walked into The Jazz Corner. A group of musicians were playing the kind of swing music our dad would have loved.

I started to order an orange blossom martini then caught myself. Carol ordered a glass of Chilean chardonnay so I did, too.

"You're not going to pout all night, are you?" I asked as I dug into my citrus-less prosciutto-wrapped sea scallops with pear and apricot chutney.

"I will if I want to," she said.

"Fine," I said. "Be like that."

I tapped my feet to "Jump, Jive 'n' Wail" while we ate. The food was great but I had to admit I was over this impromptu vacation, too. I was even pretty sure I was ready to get on with my life.

The band announced a short break. Carol yawned. "Someday," she said, "I'm going to start a business."

"You already started a business," I said.

She reached for her wine. "Another business."

"Okay," I said. "I'll bite. What kind of business?"

She took a long sip. "I'm going to run an adventure camp for women who need to have some fun."

"But we're having fun," I said.

"*You* might be having fun," she said. "I spent the whole day wandering around by myself trying to have fun, and I couldn't freakin' remember how to."

"Language," I said.

"I said *freakin'*," Carol said.

"Relax," I said. "I'll help you run the camp if you want. I mean, I could use some more fun, too."

Carol shook her head. "Oh, please. Your whole life is fun."

"Right," I said. "It's a giggle a minute."

"Okay, I left messages for both of them," Carol said. "I can't believe they're still not answering their phones."

"Yeah," I said. "Who does that?"

Per Carol's instructions, I'd written Michael and our dad a note on a sheet of hotel paper so they'd know what time they needed to be packed and ready to leave for the airport. I chewed a piece of Trident spearmint gum until it was soft, then used it to attach the note to the bathroom mirror. The gum part was my idea.

I fell asleep while Carol was still flipping through channels on our shared TV. I woke up to the sound of her banging on the adjoining door.

"Hurry up in there," she yelled. "We need to leave for the airport in an hour."

Michael opened the door. He was wearing drawstring pants and no shirt and his hair was sticking up all over his head. "Where's Dad?"

"What do you mean, where's Dad?" Carol said. Instead of waiting for an answer, she pushed past him into the other room. I followed her.

"His bed is still made," I said.

"It was like that when I got in last night," Michael said.

"And you didn't tell us?" Carol yelled.

Michael shrugged. "I just figured he was spending another night with Sugar Butt and they'd meet us at the airport."

"Wait," I said. "Where's his duffel bag?" I pushed open the door to the bathroom. "His shaving kit is missing, too."

Michael reached down and opened the tiny refrigerator door. "Beer's gone."

"I'll kill him," Carol said. She turned and ran into the other room, grabbed her phone, hit a button.

"Dad," she yelled. "Pick up the phone. We're getting ready to leave for the airport so Sugar Butt needs to get *your* butt back here right now."

"Here, give me the phone," Michael said. "I've got it down to a science."

Michael hit redial a couple of times. Then I called our dad's phone from my phone. It rang three times then went to voicemail. Frank Sinatra crooned about his regrets being too few to mention. Then the music faded and my father's voice said, *What's tickin', chicken? Billy Boy's not home right now, so don't bother to beat your gums off time. Just plant your message and I'll dig it later.*

"Dad," I said when the beep finally stopped. "It's Sarah. Listen, you have to come home with us. You can catch up on your sleep, and then you can invite Sugar

Butt for a visit. We'll have a cookout. Okay, well, call me."

I hung up and looked at Carol and Michael. "Now what do we do?"

"Do either of you know if his phone is set up so we can track it with GPS?" Carol said.

"Remember?" Michael said. "We enabled it when we gave him the phone for Christmas."

"Do you know how it works?" I said as we followed Michael back to the other room.

He scooped up his phone from the nightstand between the two beds. "Yeah. Annie and Lainie have location tracking set up on their phones so Phoebe and I can keep an eye on them. I might have actually used it a few times to check up on Phoebe, too."

"Grab your stuff and make it snappy," Carol said. "We're going after him."

It was early enough that the tourist traffic hadn't completely clogged the roads yet, so we made good time getting off the island. We were all dying for coffee and breakfast, but in the end we chose our father over caffeine. We simply didn't have time for both if we were going to make our flight.

Michael sat in the co-pilot's seat, tracking the green GPS map on his cell phone. My growling stomach helped keep me awake in the backseat as we drove.

Carol shook her head. "Dad's Dad, but he still wouldn't do this to us. Would he?"

"Of course not," I said. "At least I don't think so."

"Hard to say," Michael said.

I managed to yawn and sigh at the same time. "I have this awful feeling that Sugar Butt is holding him against his will. You don't think she could manage to tie him up by herself, do you?"

"Sure I do," Carol said.

"Especially if there was some kind of a striptease involved," Michael said.

"Eww," I said. "It's way too early for that image."

"I can't shake the feeling," Carol said, "that we're going to knock on the door and she's going to pretend he's not there. And then she'll try to keep us from coming into the house. And she's got him tied up in her bedroom—"

"With a long yellow silk scarf," I said.

"Polyester," Carol said. "And blindfolded with a black sleep mask. Velveteen."

"He'd think he died and went to heaven," Michael said. "She wouldn't get carried away and hurt him, would she?"

"She might if he tries to get away," Carol said. "I just hope he has the good sense to just sit tight and trust that we'll come after him and not set her off."

We drove for a while in silence. I was lost in my lapsed Catholic version of a prayer, which always started with a mini-confession, followed by a longer apology for not checking in more often. *Just let him be safe, just let him be safe.*

"Okay, we're almost there," Michael said. "Get over to the left. It looks like the next turnoff."

Carol put on her blinker and we pulled off the main drag.

We drove slowly past an enormous brick sign with MOON CITY painted on it in big yellow block letters. Rows and rows of matching yellow flowers were spaced evenly in front of the sign. Ahead of us, down a palm tree-studded lane, a serious-looking guardhouse with an electric privacy gate blocked our way in.

"Are you sure this is it?" Carol said. "I thought Sugar Butt lived in Savannah."

"This is definitely it," Michael said. He turned his phone so Carol could see. "Look. It's right there—that little dot on the screen. Wow, there's like a million houses in this place. And three pools. Looks like a golf course, too."

"This feels so familiar," I said. "Wait, I know. Those people who were cooking chicken on their grill and an alligator tried to follow them into their house to get some?"

As soon as I said *alligator*, Carol clicked our car door locks.

"Remember," I said, "the picture was all over the Internet—it looked like the alligator was standing straight up, trying to ring their doorbell?"

"How the hell are we going to get past the security guard?" Michael said.

"Whatever I say," Carol said, "just back me up."

We crept our way to the guardhouse. Carol rolled down her window.

"Welcome to Moon City," the guard said.

"Hi there," Carol said. "We're here to rescue our father. He's getting older and he's not wrapped quite as tightly as he used to be. And well, we think he's being held against his will by one of your residents. And we'd just like a few moments to check in with him to make sure he's okay."

The guard yawned. "Name, please?"

"William. Well, actually, he prefers Billy. Billy Hurlihy."

The guard tilted his chin down and looked over his sunglasses at us. "I mean the Moon City resident's name."

"Oh, sorry. It's Sug . . . I mean, Bel—"

"Belva Rae Garrity," I yelled from the backseat.

The guard shook his head. "That Sugar Butt. At it again, is she?"

He pushed a button and the metal gate groaned open.

"Hurry," I yelled.

We took a right off Moon City Boulevard onto Moon City Lane, then a left onto Moon City Avenue and another left onto Moon City Trace. We passed a mammoth clubhouse, a dog park, a tai chi class in progress under a pergola. Seniors—on foot, riding bikes, driving golf carts—waved to us as we passed. If your father had to be kidnapped, it wasn't a bad place to end up.

"Right here," Michael said. "It's the next one on the left."

Carol pulled into the driveway of a house that looked pretty much like the other houses on the street. We flung our car doors open.

Michael made it to the door first and rang the door-bell. He banged on the door with his fist for backup.

"Dad," Carol yelled as we jogged up the front steps to join Michael.

I put two fingers in my mouth and let out a shrill, ear-piercing Hurlihy family whistle.

Thirty-one

Sugar Butt was wearing orangey-pink lipstick and a canary yellow visor that was an almost exact match for her hair. I had a vague sense of a knee-length sleeveless nightgown and terrycloth scuffs completing her outfit, but I kept my eyes averted.

"Where is he?" Carol shouted.

"Come on in and take a load off," Sugar Butt said. "And shut the door behind you. It's hot enough to fry an egg on a bald head already."

"Thanks, but we don't have time to take a load off," I said politely. My voice switched gears. "What have you done with our father?"

"Did I hear something about eggs?" our father said as he walked into the room. "I thought you were going to cook me pancakes, darlin'."

"Are you okay, Dad?" we all said at once.

"Peachy keen, kiddos, just peachy keen." He was wearing a bright yellow bathrobe that could only belong to Sugar Butt over his pajamas and carrying a cup of coffee.

We all kept talking at once.

Our father held up one hand. "Slow down now. Where's the fire?"

"Where's the fire?" I repeated. Carol checked her watch.

"Dad," Michael said. "Grab your stuff. We're going to miss our flight."

Our father put his arm around Sugar Butt. "Sorry, Mikey boy, but I'm staying right here. It's up to you to keep an eye on your sisters and make sure they get home safe and sound."

Being speechless was not something that happened often in the Hurlihy family, but Carol and Michael and I just stood there with our mouths open.

Our dad stepped away from Sugar Butt and put his coffee cup down on a little table. He opened his arms wide. "Come on now, give your daddy a big hug. I'll give you all a ring on the ting-a-ling right after Sunday dinner. You can just throw my mail and the newspaper on the kitchen table until I figure out what kind of thingamajigger I need to fill out to get my bills forwarded."

"You can't do this," I said.

My father ran a hand through his hair. "Don't make this harder than it has to be, Sarry girl. I'm a grown man. Love might not come a knockin' for me again in this lifetime."

"But you barely know her," I said. "You just met."

"'When You Are Old' by William Butler Yeats," our father said. He pressed one hand over his heart and began to recite:

> When you are old and grey and full of sleep
> And nodding by the fire, take down this book
> And slowly read, and dream of the soft look
> Your eyes had once, of their shadows deep;
> How many loved your moments of glad grace—

"Find his duffel bag," Carol cut in. "And his phone."

Michael took off down the hallway. "Got 'em," he yelled from another room.

Sugar Butt took a step toward our father. "Lord love a duck you're romantic, Billy Hurlihy. But the children are right. I'll be tore up to see you go but we've got too much horse sense not to give this some air to breathe. Now get your purdy little behind out of my robe and head on home."

My father cleared his throat and continued his Yeats recital:

> And loved your beauty with love false or true,
> But one man loved the pilgrim soul in you,
> And loved the sorrows of your changing face;

Sugar Butt leaned over and kissed him on the lips. "That dog won't hunt anymore, honeybun—we're going to have to save the sweet talkin' for another time. Now go change your clothes and skedaddle."

He stopped one more time on the way out the door. He reached for Sugar Butt's hand and brought it to his lips. "The pleasure was all mine, darlin'," he said.

Sugar Butt turned around and opened the door. "Call me."

As we drove past, the guard gave us a thumbs-up. We took a left on 278 West, merged onto 95 South.

Beside me in the backseat, my father closed his eyes and finished the poem softly:

> And bending down beside the glowing bars,
> Murmur, a little sadly, how Love fled
> And paced upon the mountains overhead
> And hid his face amid a crowd of stars.

"Sorry we had to rain on your parade, Dad," I said.

He sighed. "'Tis all for the best, Sarry girl, 'tis all for the best. I met a lovely filly on the wi fire this morning, and five will get you ten it wasn't going to fly so well with Sugar Butt."

Carol started to laugh first, then I did, then Michael. Our father joined in. As soon as we'd start to wind down, one of us would get us going again.

"Ohmigod," I said as I wiped a stream of tears from my cheeks. "I am in serious need of some caffeine. And a breakfast sandwich."

"I don't think that's going to happen till we get to Charlotte," Carol said. "We're just barely going to make the flight."

"It's a shame we had to leave before the pancakes," our Dad said. "Sugar Butt serves hers up with buttered honey syrup."

"Knock it off, Dad," Michael said. "All this food talk is killing me."

"She didn't happen to mention any casserole recipes, did she?" I asked.

"I thought Sugar Butt said she lived in Savannah, Dad," Carol said.

Our Dad leaned forward in his seat. "Her house got to be too much for her, so she downsized. Truth be told, I've dallied with a thought or two in that direction myself. There's a lot going on in those places for an old coot like me."

"You're not an old coot," Carol said. "You're an aging pain in the neck."

Our dad leaned back again. "Sugar Butt said I was distinguished."

"Better than extinguished, Dad," Michael said.

"Hmmm." Our father opened his eyes wide. "There's a wee chance I might have heard her wrong."

We laughed again, then yawned, one after another after another. I fought to keep my eyes open as the straight shot of highway began to rock me to sleep. We crossed from South Carolina into Georgia.

In the front seat, Michael cleared his throat. "Hey. Well. Thanks for coming with me and everything, you guys. I, um . . ."

I poked him in the back of the head. "You love us meeces to pieces?"

"Exactly," he said. "Thanks, Pixie."

"You're welcome, Dixie," I said.

"Okay, Mikey boy," Carol said. "It's payback time."

"Already?" Michael groaned. "Jeez, can't it at least wait until I have my coffee? And after I send a couple of emails so my boss knows I'm working?"

"Nope," Carol said. "Now. Call Christine and tell her it's all your fault we left her at home."

"Seriously?" Michael said. "Why should I take the fall?"

None of us said anything.

"Fine." Michael grabbed his phone from the dashboard, scrolled through his contacts, pushed Call. "Hey, Chris. It's Michael. Listen. I had an emergency and Sarah was with me, and Carol just happened to call. Anyway, I wanted to call you but Dad told me not to wake you up. Savannah. And Hilton Head. I know, I know. Next time I'll call you first. Promise. Yeah, yeah. I know, I know. Really? Oh, good. Thanks. Okay, I appreciate that. I'll pick her up this afternoon."

He threw his phone back on the dashboard. "Done. She's got Mother Teresa. Apparently Maeve tried to give her a haircut."

"I don't want to hear about it," Carol said. "I'm still on vacation."

"I told you not to wake Christine up?" our father said.

"It was just a figure of speech, Dad," Michael said. "I meant it metaphorically."

I poked Michael in the back of the head again.

"Knock it off," he said.

I yawned. "So, spill. How'd it go with Phoebe and the girls yesterday?"

Michael stretched both arms up over his head and echoed my yawn. "It went okay. Miniature golf, a movie, the beach, the whole nine yards. Phoebe's plan was to have me drop her back at her parents' house and let me use the car, but the girls and I convinced her to go with us. She didn't exactly come out and say it, but I got the feeling staying with her family is starting to get on her nerves."

"That's good," Carol said.

"We'll see," Michael said. "Anyway, we're going to talk on the phone this week." He turned around in his seat to look at me. "Oh, and Annie and Lainie said to tell you they have a new verse for their butterfly song and they're up to ten thousand likes on their Facebook page."

"Lovely," I said.

We got off the highway at Exit 104, followed the signs for the rental car returns, found our way to the return lot.

"Okay," Carol said as a guy finished checking our car in. "Grab your stuff and run."

The Savannah/Hilton Head International Airport was so small that we didn't even come close to missing our flight.

"The good new is," I said as Carol handed out boarding passes like cookies, "the trip home is always shorter."

"And Mumbles Menino welcomes us to Boston once again," Michael said as we dragged our suitcases along the moving staircase.

"Somebody needs to get that guy some elocution lessons," Carol said.

"His Honor the Mayor," our father said, "can speak any way he chooses. It's our civic duty to try to understand him."

We took the elevator to our floor, found our cars.

"Well," I said. "It's been real. Hey, what day is it anyway?"

"Friday," Carol said. "And yeah, we'll have to do it again soon."

"Hasta la vista, kiddos," our father said. "Thanks for buying lunch, Mikey boy."

"It was the least I could do," Michael said.

"That's for shit sure," I said.

"Language," our father said.

Carol and our dad piled into the Mini Cooper. Michael sent another quick email from his work account while I got our stuff settled into the back of his 4Runner.

We circled around the maze of the garage until we accidentally discovered the exit, headed south and paid the toll at the Ted Williams Tunnel, found 93 South.

We rode quietly, lost in our separate thoughts.

"So," I said, as Michael stayed left at the Braintree split. "What do you want to do for dinner? We can pick up something on the way to my place and nuke it when we're ready."

"I think Mother Teresa is on borrowed time at Christine's," he said. "I'd better head right over there and get her."

"Okay. I'll run to Stop & Shop while you pick up Her Poochness."

There was a beat of silence. "Thanks, but I think I'm just going to head home."

I felt oddly deserted and free all at the same time. "Seriously?"

"Yeah, I told Phoebe I was moving back in. You know, keep an eye on the house while she and the girls are gone. Maybe finish up some of the projects I was always meaning to get to."

"Does that mean she might really try to keep the girls in Savannah?"

"I don't think so, but who knows. We left it they'd all hang out in Savannah for as much of the summer as made sense, and I wouldn't bug her about it. And I'd take care of the house, and we'd kind of feel our way through this."

"Wow," I said. "That's frighteningly mature."

"I know. Who knew I could chill like that, right? Oh, hey, remember Uncle Pete?"

"Uh, yeah, vaguely."

"Turns out he's just this guy in Phoebe's yoga class. He broke up with his partner, who's a masseuse or something, and they're fighting over who gets to keep the apartment, and they also have to unload this timeshare they own together in Vegas."

"That sounds so familiar," I said.

"Anyway, they're just friends. I apologized for over-reacting."

"Impressive."

A sign for Exit 13 came into view. Michael put on his blinker, moved into the right lane.

I tried to keep my mouth shut as we pulled off the highway, but in the end I had to say it because he was my brother. "Just try not to forget that you and Phoebe have been here a few times, okay? I mean, you're miserable together and then you're miserable apart so you get back together. And then before you know it you're miserable again."

Michael didn't say anything, perhaps his subtle way of trying to get me to stop talking, too.

I took a deep breath. "I can't stop thinking about what you said. You know, about the guy from the Boston Marathon bombing? That even though his legs were gone, he kept trying to stand up? Well, it made me think of this interview I saw at the time. A doctor who was just back from Iraq. He finished running the marathon, and then he ran a couple more miles to the hospital and saved people all day. I'll never forget this thing he said to the reporter—that you always choose life over limb."

Michael cleared his throat. "Your point?"

"You might have to choose your life over your marriage, Michael."

We twisted and turned along the back roads to Marshbury. Unlike the sensible grid of Savannah or the manicured perfection of Hilton Head, they wiggled randomly hither and thither. We passed old homes and older homes, landscaped and not, an occasional cemetery or golf course popping up in the middle of nowhere, like a timeline of the last three centuries.

"I'm not there yet," Michael said. "I still think I can save them both."

CHAPTER

Thirty-two

"We'll just have to make our own sunshine," our mother used to say when we were stuck inside the house. She'd break out the Silly Putty and dig up the Sunday funnies, aka the comics, which she saved religiously for just this kind of dank, rainy day.

We'd gather around the pine trestle table in the kitchen. While our mother made blueberry muffins or banana pancakes, we'd spend the whole morning lost in our Silly Putty. We'd roll our shiny pinkish glob into a ball, then flatten it until it was shaped like a medallion. We'd press it down hard to capture a colored newsprint picture, admire our handiwork, fold it over and over until it disappeared, and then do it all over again.

All these years later, whenever I thought of Silly Putty, I could actually smell its sharp, distinctive scent, and it would bring me back to my childhood in a nano-second.

I scoured the shelves in the equipment closet in my former master bedroom-slash-office until I found a little wicker basket of red Silly Putty eggs. I'd bought them for my classroom, thinking the kids would be totally wowed. A couple of the more orally fixated kids tried to eat it, and one of the boys sat on a plastic egg to see if it would hatch, but other than that, it was mostly ignored.

I carried a Silly Putty egg out to my kitchen table and twisted it open. The newer Silly Putty seemed to break apart when you stretched it. I wondered if the ingredients had changed, or if the attention span needed to warm the putty with your hands and slowly stretch it into shape just wasn't a part of our repertoire anymore. And these days it was harder to find the kind of porous newsprint that let you lift the ink right off the page. It was harder to find newsprint at all.

I spent an entire hour completely in the moment with my Silly Putty, picking up random images from the pile of catalogs that had been waiting for me in the mailbox when I returned home.

Since Michael had dropped me off on Friday, I hadn't left the house or talked to a soul. When I realized I was hungry, I'd opened up a box of Annie's and made my famous Sarah's Winey Mac and Cheese, substituting chardonnay for the milk and serving it to myself in a wineglass.

I'd slept in on Saturday, then wandered around in my backyard, taking it in as if for the first time. The impatiens someone had planted before Kevin and I bought the house had reseeded again and were starting to bloom. The blueberry bushes that had also come with the house were heavy with perfectly ripened fruit. I picked some blueberries and popped them directly into my mouth. It wasn't exactly like living off the land on a deserted island, but it still gave me a little thrill. I went back inside for a bowl. I picked enough blueberries to sprinkle over my cornflakes for breakfast, plus extras, in case I decided to bake.

Saturday night I opened up a can of yellow fin tuna packed in olive oil for dinner. I drizzled it with lemon juice and ate it right out of the can.

I'd once read somewhere that solitude is the state of being alone without being lonely. When you grow up smack dab in the middle of six kids, you might be lonely sometimes, but you're almost never alone. Even as an adult, I couldn't remember the last time I'd disconnected from my family long enough to do nothing. And maybe even to feel something.

Lots of people do digital detoxes, turning off their computers and tablets and smartphones for a weekend or a week. But by Sunday I realized that I was also doing a family detox. Maybe I'd finally figured out my own existential questions: Who was I without my family? And what did I want my life to be?

I got up at the crack of dawn and drove to the beach to watch the sunrise, munching on another handful of blueberries I'd foraged off the land. The beach was practically deserted. I sipped my coffee, leaned back on my elbows. I kicked off my flip-flops and wiggled my toes in the coarse Marshbury sand.

As I watched the salmon and pink sun peek up over an endless blue ocean, it felt like I was making my own sunshine for the first time in years.

I could have called Michael to pick me up on the way to work on Monday, but I didn't. Of course, he could have called me, too. It was as if once he'd moved out, we'd cut the cord. Or maybe he was doing his own family detox.

I parked my car at the Marshbury station and found a seat way in the back of the train. It was a long ride, more crowded with each stop. I tried not to think about the packed subway ride that was waiting for me on the other end. No wonder people fantasized about living on deserted islands. But I was ready to come back to the world. I was ready to get on with my life.

John Anderson wasn't waiting in front of the Necrogamiac building with two cups of Starbucks coffee. Not that I expected him to be. I opened the door for myself, checked the sign next to the elevator, took the stairs up to the Human Resources department.

Keli was sitting at her desk, wearing a miniskirt, legs crossed in shiny hot pink skyscraper heels. One shoe was firmly planted on the floor, the other dangled precariously from one toe.

I cleared my throat. "May I talk to you for a moment, please?"

Keli jumped, her dangling shoe skittering across the floor. She got up, yanked down her miniskirt, did a high-low hobble until she caught up with her shoe.

"Hey," she said as she sat on the edge of her desk and wiggled her shoe back on. "What's up?"

"Now," I said. "Let's go."

I was ready to grab her if she decided to cut and run, but she followed me peacefully to the nearest restroom. I held the door for her, then shut it behind me. I crossed my arms over my chest.

"Knock-knock," I said. A good preschool teacher always has a knock-knock joke handy.

"Who's there?" Keli said in a singsong-y voice.

"Orange," I said.

If she didn't actually gulp, she wanted to. "Orange who?" she said softly.

"Orange you glad I'm onto you?" I said.

She wrinkled her nose adorably. "Are you okay, Sarah? You're acting really strange. And by the way, have you had any trouble logging into the Gamiacs' private chat room? It's been acting really wonky lately."

"Let's talk wonky," I said. "You put the moves on a certain someone. He tells you he's not interested. But instead of backing off, you decide you're going to try to sabotage his relationship with the person he is interested in. So you figure out his dog, like most dogs, hates the smell of oranges."

I hadn't had many Nancy Drew moments in my life, but I liked it. If I ever needed a break from teaching, maybe I could open up my own private investigation firm. I reached into my shoulder bag, pulled out the orange blossom perfume stick, the organic orange essence lip balm, the pure blood orange lotion, and placed them next to the sink, one by one.

Keli watched my every move. "It's just this thing I do," she said. "It's like I look around at everything I don't have yet and think: I want that and that. And that. And then I figure out how to get it all."

I stared at her.

She tilted her head and smiled. "I'm very resourceful. But don't worry. Once I have it I don't want it anymore anyway."

"And worst of all," I said, "you involved the Gamiacs. You took advantage of the trust I put in you. You changed the password."

She smiled harder. "No worries. I'll put it back right now."

"You can't put it back. You're no longer an administrator."

Her eyes darted toward the bathroom door, as if she might be contemplating a quick getaway in her pink skyscraper heels.

I wanted to grab her by a clump of perfectly foiled hair. Or even an earlobe. But I was a professional, so I merely gripped the back of her arm firmly and pushed the door open with my other hand.

I walked her to the elevator, pushed the button, waited for it to open.

"Sit," I said, as I gave her a little shove toward the tufted elevator bench.

Keli sat.

I leaned against the door to keep it open. I crossed my arms over my chest and gave her my best teacher glare, fine-tuned through years of practice.

"*What?*" she said.

"I want you to sit right here in this elevator, all morning if you have to, and I want you to think about the kind of person you want to be."

I reached into my bag again and pulled out the posts I'd printed. "And then, once you've finished your time-out, you're going to come with me and apologize to the Gamiacs. Then you're all going to read your posts out loud, discuss what you've learned since then. Then we're going to take them outside and burn them. And then we're all going to move forward."

I knocked on John's office door.

"Come in," he said in his professional voice.

I opened the door and leaned in. "Listen, I know this isn't the time or the place, and I know you've got work to do, and I have to get back to the Gamiacs, but I just have to say this. In a million years, I don't think I'd find someone I'd rather be with, and I know I'm the one who's been screwing things up. You're right, I keep looking for reasons that this can't work, stupid things like distance, and family, and Horatio, not that Horatio is stupid. By the way, do you happen to know if he hates the smell of oranges?"

John shrugged.

I took a deep breath. "I kind of just got back from a semi-deserted island, and the whole time I was there I kept trying not to think about you, but I couldn't. And it wasn't because I didn't want to be alone. It was because you would have made it better. You would have known that Irish road bowling didn't really originate in Ireland, but in Scotland, or Germany, or Poland, and you would have wanted to take a walk on the beach as soon as we got there, and mostly, you would have laughed in all the right places. I don't really get the whole pinball thing, but I know that second chances don't only happen in pinball, and, well, what I'm trying to say is that I'd really like to give it another shot."

He made an odd gesture with his eyes, as if something was stuck in one of his contacts.

"Are you okay?" I said.

He nodded.

"Um, in summation, I'd just like to say that I'm really sorry, not for all of it, of course, but for the parts that were my fault. So, if you can find it in your heart to hit the undo button on that last breakup . . .. Wait. Is something wrong?"

John pointed.

I turned my head. John's boss was sitting in a clear Lucite chair in the corner with his Nerf crossbow in his lap.

I resisted the urge to ask him to please shoot me now.

"Hey there," I said. "Happy Monday."

He nodded. "I've been hearing nice things about you. Keep up the good work."

I gave them both a little wave as I backed out of the doorway.

"Carry on," I said before I closed the door.

Thirty-three

I opened my door.

"Are you sure about this?" he asked once we'd finished kissing.

"Absolutely," I said. I hooked one arm around his waist as I leaned past him to get a glimpse of his car. Horatio's head was hanging out the window and the rest of him was desperately trying to follow. He was barking like a maniac.

"Okay," John said. "So, how're we going to work this? Do you want me to bring him inside for you?"

"No way," I said. "Thanks, but I want you to take a walk around the block. When you get back, jump in the car and disappear for at least an hour. Maybe longer. I'll call you when we've got things all worked out."

"How about if I kill some time, then head to the grocery store and pick up something for dinner? Maybe
bacon-wrapped scallops, grilled lobster tails, a nice
kale salad?"

"You know how to make all that?" I leaned in and
gave him another kiss. "I knew there was a reason I was
risking life and limb for you."

"Oh, and by the way, I squeezed an orange into a
glass and held it under Horatio's nose. He turned his
head away in disgust."

"I surmised as much," I said in my best Nancy Drew
voice. Someday I'd tell John about Keli's plot, but there
was no rush. We had plenty of time. And it's not like
Horatio had been all that crazy about me *before* I
reeked of orange anyway.

John put his hands on my shoulders. "Are you absolutely sure you want to do this?"

I nodded. "It's the only way. Don't worry, I've got
The Dog Whisperer on speed dial."

"Seriously?"

"Nope, but I watched three episodes of the show last
night. I'm good."

His Heath Bar eyes met mine. I gulped. He gave me
a final kiss, then turned and walked away.

Fortunately, in the short time he'd been parked in
my driveway, Horatio hadn't managed to swallow his
leash whole. Still, he'd channeled both his Yorkie fury
and his greyhound speed and was hurling himself in

the direction John had walked off in. As he hit the back window over and over again, the aftershocks made him look like a deranged bobble-head dog.

By my expert calculation, the biggest trick was going to be to grab the leash without losing an arm. When we were kids, Johnny, or maybe it was Billy, had this long-armed plastic robotic claw he would sneak to the Sunday dinner table so he could terrorize us. We'd be minding our own business, shoveling forkfuls of mashed potatoes into our mouths, when suddenly— *crunch*—the claw would clamp down on a knee or an ankle. It was exactly the kind of thing I needed right now. I'd just slide it through the open window from a safe distance, squeeze the handle to tighten the claw on leash. And we'd be good to go.

Alas, no such luck. Instead, I was wearing my thickest zip-up hoodie, partly for protection, and also because it had deep pockets that I'd filled with a cornucopia of doggie treats. I'd also dabbed a little bit of peanut butter on my ankles, just for good luck. And to counteract any residual citrus smell.

I took a deep breath. I lifted my head high, threw my shoulders back, and approached the vehicle.

Horatio leaped over the console between the front seats. He stuck his head through the open window on the passenger side again and tried to claw a bigger opening.

"Use your words, not your claws," I said.

He launched into a ferocious series of barks.

"There, there," I said. "Just let it all out."

I waited until he quieted down, possibly due to laryngitis. Then I lobbed a juicy treat through the window in his direction. He scrambled for it.

"Okay," I said once I had his attention again. "Let's establish the rules."

He appeared to still be with me, so I continued. "When you grow opposable thumbs, I'll let you be the boss. Until then, I'm in charge. Got it?"

Horatio gargled some rocks.

I waited him out.

"I know, I know," I said when he finally settled down. "The truth is sometimes hard to swallow."

He tilted his head at me. I threw him another treat.

He caught it while it was still airborne, gulped it down.

I put my hand in my treat pocket. Horatio opened and closed his mouth slowly as he began to salivate, both eyes glued to my pocket. I closed my own eyes and offered up a moment of thanks to Pavlov. The guy was a genius.

"When you're ready," I said, like millions of teachers had said before me and millions more would say after me, "we'll proceed."

Horatio put his butt down on the passenger seat.

I threw him another treat.

He caught it without moving, like a canine Venus flytrap. Then he held up one paw in my direction.

"Cute," I said. "I like it." I threw him another treat.

Even the most brilliant lesson can lose your students if it goes on too long, so I knew I had to move quickly. The handle of Horatio's leash dangled halfway to the floor, which in my professional assessment was still dangerously close to his teeth. I leaned casually into John's car, the fingers of one hand resting lightly on the door handle, wiggling the treats in my hoodie the way my father used to jingle the change in his pants pockets.

"What a good boy," I said. I threw another treat, this time the smelliest one I had, past Horatio and onto the driver's seat.

Horatio turned and dove for it. I swung the car door open, grabbed the leash with one hand, keeping my other hand in the treat pocket. Then I turned around fast, as if I didn't even notice I was holding the leash.

I took a step toward my house. Horatio jumped out of the car. I butt-bumped John's car door closed. I gave Horatio a chance to pee, then I led him down the street, carefully orchestrating our route so it wouldn't intersect with John's. I stayed in the lead and kept the leash relaxed, occasionally making a correction by pulling up on it and calmly saying, "Horatio, heel."

I'd read that a tired dog is a well-behaved dog, and I knew it was definitely true for toddlers, so we walked and walked until I was sure we'd accomplished the canine equivalent of a good climb on the jungle gym. Then we reversed direction without a hitch and walked back to my house.

I opened the front door and went in first. I made Horatio sit in the entryway. Then I gave him a treat, took off his leash. He headed right for the pile of dirty clothes on the floor of my laundry room. He dropped one shoulder and rolled over on his back on top of my underwear, paws in the air, as if he'd found a dead bird.

"Okay," I said, "so we've got a few details left to work out."

Horatio and I were curled up on the couch. He was watching an episode of *The Dog Whisperer* I'd seen before. He rolled over so his head was in my lap, fully exposing his tummy to me, which is like the doggie equivalent of sending flowers.

"Love you, too," I said. I gave him a gentle belly rub.

Then I went back to my laptop. I found Annie and Lainie's Facebook page. "Good job!" I posted. I uploaded a picture of a transparent glass wing butterfly from Panama. I knew my nieces would love it. And I didn't really care what anyone else thought.

When my phone rang, I thought it might be John.

"We need to spend the rest of those gift certificates," somebody else said. "Summer will be over before we know it."

It took me a second to place Lorna's voice, as if Bayberry Preschool existed in a completely different dimension. The reality that a new school year was fast approaching descended on me, filling me with equal parts dread and anticipation the way it always did, since the days I'd been a student myself.

"Okay," I said.

"How 'bout tonight?"

"Sorry," I said, "I've got company."

"Then next week. And just to give you a heads up, Gloria and I will expect a full report on that company."

I looked at my phone for a moment after we hung up. Then I called my sister Christine.

"What's wrong?" she said.

"Nothing. Hey, do you want to get together, maybe next week, or the week after, just the two of us? Before school starts up and I get crazy busy again."

"Did you ask Carol first?"

I laughed. "I didn't. I swear. Listen, text me some dates that work for you. I have to go now. I've got something baking in the oven."

"Ha-ha," Christine said. "That's really funny."

The blueberry applesauce peanut butter treats were perfectly done, solid throughout and lightly crisped. The parchment paper had been a great suggestion. They didn't stick at all when I lifted them up with a spatula. I arranged them on a pretty platter edged with hydrangeas. And then I called John.

"We're all set," I said. "You can come home now."

Horatio and I greeted him at the door. I leaned in for a kiss.

John kept one eye on Horatio as we kissed. Horatio wagged his tail. I took a step back and smiled.

"I'm almost afraid to say anything," he said. "Well, I guess I should get that seafood right into the fridge."

I reached for his grocery bags. "I'll do it. Why don't you guys have a moment alone." Horatio wagged his tail some more.

I took my time putting everything away. Then I picked up the platter.

"Appetizer?" I said as I walked back into the living room.

"Ooh, those look good." John reached for one and popped it into his mouth.

I watched him chew.

"Mmm," he said. "What's that I taste? Maybe blueberries?"

"Fresh from my garden," I said. I picked up another one and held it out to Horatio.

"Wait," John said. "I don't give him people food. It's not good for dogs."

I tossed it in Horatio's direction. He caught it while it was still in the air.

"It's not people food," I said.

John opened his Heath Bar eyes wide.

I smiled sweetly. "Don't worry. They're safe. No chicken by-products. Or at least not that many."

He scrunched his eyes shut and swallowed. "I guess I deserved that."

"Yeah, you did. And let's get one thing perfectly clear. Don't ever ask me to eat out of a dog dish again."

"Got it."

We looked at each other. "You know," I said, "I can't promise life will be easy if we try to make this work, but I think it will always be interesting."

Horatio wagged his tail. I threw him another treat.

HORATIO'S DROOLICIOUS BLUEBERRY APPLESAUCE PEANUT BUTTER TREATS

½ cup unsweetened applesauce
2 tsp. maple syrup
1/3 cup creamy peanut butter
1 egg
1½ cups old-fashioned oatmeal
½ cup blueberries
parchment paper

Preheat oven to 350. Line cookie sheet with parchment paper.

Process oats in blender until finely ground.

Mix wet ingredients in a bowl.

Add oatmeal and mix. Fold in blueberries.

Form dough into small round balls. Place on parchment paper and bake 20 minutes or until lightly crisped.

Let cool. Enjoy.

Refrigerate in sealed container for up to one week. Or freeze with your casseroles.

ACKNOWLEDGMENTS

Must Love Readers! Once again, my biggest slice of gratitude goes to you. Over and over again, via email and Facebook and Twitter, you asked for more from the *Must Love Dogs* characters, and I'm so glad I finally listened to you. I'm having a blast revisiting them and I hope you are, too.

A huge alphabetical thank-you to Lisa Bankoff, Ken Harvey, Beth Hoffman, and Jack Kramer for reading drafts of this manuscript and making spot-on and much-appreciated suggestions.

Thanks to Allison Winn Scotch and Karen McQuestion for camaraderie and generosity, and to Wendy Wax for being able to walk and share at the same time. Thanks to Pam Kramer for support and encouragement and all things dog. Thanks to the teachers on my Facebook and Twitter feeds for bringing that world back to me. Thanks to my Marshbury peeps and to my own big family for your support.

Thanks to the fabulous book clubs I've Skyped and emailed and chatted with for your enthusiasm and perspective, which always make me want to roll up my sleeves and get busy on my next book. Thanks to Marie Causey for sharing a story that triggered part of a scene.

Thanks to Jenny and Blake Long for Savannah insider guidance, to June Parsons and Dan Oja for sharing the Jesse Mount House with me, and to the fabulous Robin Gold and the rest of the Savannah Book Festival for putting me in the perfect place at the perfect time.

Forever thanks to Jake—first reader, best listener—and to Kaden and Garet for always being there. And thanks to Pebbles for shaking things up a bit by dropping by to give birth to four kittens under our front porch!

NEW LEASH ON LIFE
BOOK CLUB QUESTIONS

You can find discussion questions for all my novels at ClaireCook.com. I love chatting with book clubs, so if you'd like me to call or Skype in—or visit in person if I happen to be in your neck of the woods—just send an email via my website with information about your book club and some suggested dates, and I'll do my best to make one work.

1. Which Hurlihy family member is most like you? Which would you most like to hang out with?

2. Do you wish the Hurlihy family could adopt you? Or do they make you seriously grateful for your own family?

3. Reinvention is the overarching theme of Claire Cook's eleven novels. Which characters in this book do you think are trying to reinvent their lives in some way? How? Which ones do you think will be successful?

4. Sarah says about Keli, "She was every popular girl who had ever upstaged me, ignored me,

outshined me." Why do you think Keli triggers
these feelings in Sarah? Do you think most
people feel this way occasionally, or are they
able to leave the past completely behind?

5. John tells Sarah, "Horatio is just one more
excuse to push me away." True? Why or why
not? Do you think Horatio's jealous behavior is
common? Has this kind of thing ever happened
to you or anyone you know?

6. "Maybe once you'd been through a divorce, it
becomes the touchstone you always went back
to when you were trying to gauge how bad
something was." What other touchstones like
this can you think of?

7. "Maybe deep down inside we were all still in our
formative years. Maybe it was never to late for
any of us to change." Agree? Disagree?

8. About the Gamiacs, Sarah says to John, "It's so
not fair that childhood lasts longer these days."
Does childhood really last longer these days?
Does saying "these days" make you officially
old?

9. Sarah wonders "how anybody ever stayed with anybody and how they somehow, against all odds, managed to make it work." What do you think is the secret to making a long-term relationship work? Luck? Communication? Wine?

10. "What are sisters for if not to point out the things the rest of the world is too polite to mention." Do you think this is true? Is it also true about good friends? How are relationships with sisters and friends different? The same?

11. *Must Love Dogs: New Leash on Life* is the second book of the new *Must Love Dogs* series. What do you hope will happen in future books?

12. The original *Must Love Dogs* became a movie starring Diane Lane, John Cusack, Christopher Plummer, Stockard Channing, Elizabeth Perkins, Dermot Mulroney and more. Do you think Book 2, *Must Love Dogs: New Leash on Life* would make a good movie? Would you change the casting? Who do you think should play Sugar Butt?

(Copyright © 2002, 2013 by Claire Cook)

I decided to listen to my family and get back out there. "There's life after divorce, Sarah," my father proclaimed, not that he'd ever been divorced.

"The longer you wait, the harder it'll be" was my sister Carol's little gem, as if she had some way of knowing whether or not that was true.

After months of ignoring them, responding to a personal ad in the newspaper seemed the most detached way to give in. I wouldn't have to sit in a restaurant with a friend of a friend of one of my brothers, probably Michael's, but maybe Johnny's or Billy Jr.'s, pretending to enjoy a meal I was too nervous to taste. I

needn't endure even a phone conversation with someone my sister Christine had talked into calling me. My
prospect and I would quietly connect on paper or we
wouldn't.

*HONEST, HOPELESSLY ROMANTIC, old-
fashioned gentleman seeks lady friend who enjoys elegant dining, dancing and the slow bloom of affection.
WM, n/s, young 50s, widower, loves dogs, children and
long meandering bicycle rides.*

The ad jumped out at me the first time I looked.
There wasn't much competition. Rather than risk a
geographic jump to one of the Boston newspapers, I'd
decided it was safer and less of an effort to confine my
search to the single page of classifieds in the local
weekly. Seven towns halfway between Boston and Cape
Cod were clumped together in one edition. Four col-
umns of "Women Seeking Men." A quarter of a column
of "Men Seeking Women," two entries of "Women
Seeking Women," and what was left of that column was
"Men Seeking Men."

I certainly had no intention of adding to the dis-
heartening surplus of heterosexual women placing ads,
so I turned my attention to the second category. It was
comprised of more than its share of control freaks, like
this guy—*Seeking attractive woman between 5'4" and
5'6", 120-135 lbs., soft-spoken, no bad habits, financially secure, for possible relationship.* I could picture
this dreamboat making his potential relationships step

on the scale and show their bank statements before he penciled them in for a look-see.

And then *this* one. Quaint, charming, almost familiar somehow. When I got to *the slow bloom of affection*, it just did me in. Made me remember how lonely I was.

I circled the ad in red pen, then tore it out of the paper in a jagged rectangle. I carried it over to my computer and typed a response quickly, before I could change my mind:

Dear Sir:

You sound too good to be true, but perhaps we could have a cup of coffee together anyway—at a public place. I am a WF, divorced, young 40, who loves dogs and children, but doesn't happen to have either.

—Cautiously Optimistic

I mailed my letter to a Box 308P at the *County Connections* offices, which would, in turn, forward it. I enclosed a small check to secure my own box number for responses. Less than a week later I had my answer:

Dear Madam:

Might I have the privilege of buying you coffee at Morning Glories in Marshbury at 10 AM this coming Saturday? I'll be carrying a single yellow rose.

—Awaiting Your Response

The invitation was typed on thick ivory paper with an actual typewriter, the letters O and E forming solid dots of black ink, just like the old manual of my child-hood. I wrote back simply, *Time and place convenient. Looking forward to it.*

I didn't mention my almost-date to anyone, barely even allowed myself to think about its possibilities. There was simply no sense in getting my hopes up, no need to position myself for a fall.

I woke up a few times Friday night, but it wasn't too bad. It's not as if I stayed up all night tossing and turn-ing. And I tried on just a couple of different outfits on Saturday morning, finally settling on a yellow sweater and a long skirt with an old-fashioned floral print. I fluffed my hair, threw on some mascara and brushed my teeth a second time before heading out the door.

Morning Glories is just short of trendy, a delightful-ly overgrown hodgepodge of sun-streaked greenery, white lattice, and round button tables with mismatched iron chairs. The coffee is strong and the baked goods homemade and delicious. You could sit at a table for hours without getting dirty looks from the people who work there.

The long Saturday morning take-out line backed up to the door, and it took me a minute to maneuver my way over to the tables. I scanned quickly, my senses on overload, trying to pick out the rose draped across the table, to remember the opening line I had rehearsed on the drive over.

"Sarah, my darlin' girl. What a lovely surprise. Come here and give your dear old daddy a hug."

"Dad? What are you doing here?"

"Well, that's a fine how-do-you-do. And from one of my very favorite daughters at that."

"Where'd you get the rose, Dad?"

"Picked it this morning from your dear mother's rose garden. God rest her soul."

"Uh, who's it for?"

"A lady friend, honey. It's the natural course of this life that your dad would have lady friends now, Sarry. I feel your sainted mother whispering her approval to me every day."

"So, um, you're planning to meet this lady friend here, Dad?"

"That I am, God willing."

Somewhere in the dusty corners of my brain, synapses were connecting. "Oh my God. Dad. *I'm* your date. I answered your personal ad. I answered my own father's personal ad." I mean, of all the personal ads in all the world I had to pick this one?

My father looked at me blankly, then lifted his shaggy white eyebrows in surprise. His eyes moved skyward as he cocked his head to one side. He turned his palms up in resignation. "Well, now, there's one for the supermarket papers. Honey, it's okay, no need to turn white like you've seen a ghost. Here. This only proves I brought you up to know the diamond from the riffraff."

Faking a quick recovery is a Hurlihy family tradition, so I squelched the image of a single yellow rose in a hand other than my father's. I took a slow breath, assessing the damage to my heart. "Not only that, Dad, but maybe you and I can do a Jerry Springer show together. How 'bout 'Fathers Who Date Daughters'? I mean, this is big, Dad. The Oedipal implications alone—"

"Oedipal, smedipal. Don't be getting all college on me now, Sarry girl." My father peered out from under his eyebrows. "And lovely as you are, you're even lovelier when you're a smidgen less flip."

I swallowed back the tears that seemed to be my only choice besides flip, and sat down in the chair across from my father. Our waitress came by and I managed to order a coffee. "Wait a minute. You're not a young fifty, Dad. You're seventy-one. And when was the last time you rode a bike? You don't own a bike. And you hate dogs."

"Honey, don't be so literal. Think of it as poetry, as who I am in the bottom of my soul. And, Sarah, I'm glad you've started dating again. Kevin was not on his best day good enough for you, sweetie."

"I answered my own father's personal ad. That's not dating. That's sick."

My father watched as a pretty waitress leaned across the table next to ours. His eyes stayed on her as he patted my hand and said, "You'll do better next time, honey. Just keep up the hard work." I watched as my father raked a clump of thick white hair away from his watery brown eyes. The guy could find a lesson in . . . Jesus, a date with his *daughter.*

"Oh, Dad, I forgot all about you. You got the wrong date, too. You must be lonely without Mom, huh?"

The waitress stood up, caught my father's eye and smiled. She walked away, and he turned his gaze back to me. "I think about her every day, all day. And will for the rest of my natural life. But don't worry about me. I have a four o'clock."

"What do you mean, a four o'clock? Four o'clock Mass?"

"No, darlin'. A wee glass of wine at four o'clock with another lovely lady. Who couldn't possibly hold a candle to you, my sweet."

I supposed that having a date with a close blood relative was far less traumatic if it was only one of the day's two dates. I debated whether to file that tidbit away for future reference, or to plunge into deep and immediate denial that the incident had ever happened. I lifted my coffee mug to my lips. My father smiled encouragingly.

Perhaps the lack of control was in my wrist. Maybe I merely forgot to swallow. But as my father reached across the table with a pile of paper napkins to mop the burning coffee from my chin, I thought it even more likely that I had simply never learned to be a grown-up.

Keep reading! Download your copy of the original *Must Love Dogs* eBook or order the paperback wherever books are sold.

Be the first to find out when the next book of the new *Must Love Dogs* series comes out! Go to ClaireCook.com and sign up for Claire's newsletter to stay in the loop.

ABOUT CLAIRE

I wrote my first novel in my minivan at 45. At 50, I walked the red carpet at the Hollywood premiere of the adaptation of my second novel, *Must Love Dogs*, starring Diane Lane and John Cusack. If you have a buried dream, trust me, it is NEVER too late! And I guess it's no surprise that reinvention is the overarching theme of my novels *and* my life. I like to think the heroines in my (eleven and counting!) novels have helped lots of women find their own next chapters, and I also take great joy in sharing what I've learned so far on the Reinvention and Writing pages at ClaireCook.com.

My books have been called everything from romantic comedy to women's fiction to beach reads to chick lit. Honestly, it doesn't matter to me what you call them. I just hope you read and enjoy them!

I was born in Virginia, and lived for many years in Scituate, Massachusetts, a beach town between Boston and Cape Cod. My husband and I have recently moved to the suburbs of Atlanta to be closer to our two adult kids, who actually want us around again!

I have the world's most fabulous readers and I'm forever grateful to all of you for giving me the gift of this career. Midlife Rocks!

xxxxxClaire

HANG OUT WITH ME!
ClaireCook.com/newsletter
Facebook.com/ClaireCookauthorpage
Twitter.com/ClaireCookwrite
Pinterest.com/ClaireCookwrite

CPSIA information can be obtained at www.ICGtesting.com
Printed in the USA
LVOW13s1607290614

392202LV00006B/633/P